EOIN McNAMEE

THE NAVIGATOR

HarperCollins *Children's Books*

For Owen and Kathleen

First published in hardback in Great Britain by HarperCollins *Children's Books* 2006
First published in paperback in Great Britain by HarperCollins *Children's Books* 2006
HarperCollins *Children's Books* is a division of HarperCollins*Publishers* Ltd,
77-85 Fulham Palace Road, Hammersmith, London W6 8JB

The HarperCollins *Children's Books* website address is
www.harpercollinschildrensbooks.co.uk

1

Copyright © Eoin McNamee 2006

The author asserts the moral right to be identified as the author of this work.

ISBN 13: 978-0-00-720977-4
ISBN 10: 0-00-720977-0

Printed and bound in England by
Clays Ltd, St Ives plc

CHAPTER ONE

There was something different about the afternoon. It seemed dark although there wasn't much cloud. It seemed cold although the sun shone. And the alder trees along the river stirred and shivered although the wind did not seem to blow. Owen came over the three fields and crossed the river just below the Workhouse on an old beech tree that had fallen several years before, climbing from branch to branch with his eyes almost closed, trying not to look down, even though he knew the river was narrow and sluggish at that point, and that there were many trailing branches to cling on to if he fell. Only when he reached the other side did he dare to look down, and even then the black, unreflecting surface seemed to be beckoning to him so that he turned away with a shudder.

He had woken early that morning. It was Saturday and he had tried to get back to sleep, but that hadn't worked so he had

5

got up and got dressed. Before his mother could wake, Owen had slipped out of the house and down to Mary White's shop. Mary had run the shop for many years. It was small and packed with goods and very cosy, with good cooking smells coming from the kitchen behind. Mary, who was a shrewd but kindly woman, smiled at Owen when he came in. Before he had even asked, she handed him a packet of bacon, milk and half a dozen eggs. He had no money, but then he never had. Mary used to write down what he got in a little book, but now she didn't even bother with that. As always, she could see his embarrassment.

"Stop looking so worried," she said. "You'll pay it back some day. Besides, you have to be fed, for all our sakes."

She often said mysterious things like that, telling him that it was a pleasure and a privilege to look after him. Owen didn't know what she meant, for no one else seemed to think that way. Sometimes, when he walked through the little town at the bottom of the hill, you would think he had a bad smell the way people shied away from him and whispered behind their hands. It was the same in school. Sometimes, it seemed the only reason that anybody ever talked to him was in order to start a fight. He knew that he had no father, and that his clothes were older and more worn than the other boys and girls at the school, but something seemed to run deeper than that.

"It's not that they don't like you," Mary said, in her curious way. "They see something in you that both frightens them and attracts them as well. People don't like things that they don't understand."

When Owen got back to the house, he cooked the bacon and eggs and took them up to his mother. She woke and smiled sleepily at him, as if awakened from a pleasant dream, then looked around her and frowned, as if bad old memories had come flooding back. He handed her the tray and she took it without thanking him, a vague, worried look on her face. She was like that most of the time now.

Then there was the photograph. It had been taken shortly after Owen had been born. His father was holding him in the crook of one arm, his other arm around Owen's mother. He was dark-haired and strong and smiling. His mother was smiling as well. Even the baby was smiling. The sun shone on their faces and all was well with the world. After his father's death, Owen's mother had taken to carrying the photograph everywhere, looking at it so often that the edges had become frayed. As a reminder of happier times, he supposed. Then one day he noticed that she hadn't looked at it. "Where is it?" he had asked gently. "Where is the photograph?"

She looked up at him. "I lost it," she'd said, and her eyes were full of misery. "I put it down somewhere and I don't remember…"

He made a bacon sandwich for himself and took it to his room where he sat on his wooden chest to eat it. The lock on the trunk was missing and it had never been opened. There was a name on it, *J M Gobillard et Fils*. It sounded strange and exotic and always made him wish that he was somewhere exciting. Owen knew that his father had brought it back from somewhere, and had insisted on it being put in his room, but that was all he knew about it.

He looked around. The only things he really owned in the world were in that room. The old chest. A guitar with broken strings. A dartboard. A set of cards and a battered CD player. There was a replica Spitfire hanging on fishing line from the ceiling. There were a few books on a broken bookcase, a pile of old jigsaws and a Game Boy.

Owen stood up on the chest and scrambled through the window and on to the branch of a sycamore tree. He swung expertly to the ground from a low branch and set off across the fields.

Owen crossed the burying banks below the mass of the old Workhouse and climbed the sloping bank, passing through the long, tree-lined gully that split the slope. It wasn't that he was hiding from anyone. He just liked the idea of being able to move about the riverbank without anyone seeing him. So he found routes like the gully, or tunnels of hazel and rowan, or dips in the ground that rendered you suddenly invisible. The riverbank was ideal for this. There were ridges and trenches and deep depressions in the ground, as though the earth had been worked over again and again.

It took ten minutes to skirt the Workhouse. It was a tall, forbidding building of cut stone perched on an outcrop of rock which towered above the river. It had been derelict for many years and its roof had fallen in, but something about it made Owen shiver. He had asked many people about its history, but they seemed reluctant to talk. He had asked Mary White about it.

"I bet there are ghosts," he said. She leaned forward in the gloom of her small shop and met his gaze with eyes that seemed suddenly stern and blue in a wrinkled face.

"No ghosts," she had said, giving him a strange look. "No ghosts at the Workhouse. But there are other things. That place has been there longer than anyone thinks."

It took another ten minutes to reach the Den. Owen checked the entrance as he did every time. A whitethorn bush was bent across it, tied with fishing line. Behind that he had built up a barrier of dried ferns and pieces of bush. The barriers were intact. He moved them carefully aside and rearranged them behind him. He found himself in a clearing just big enough to stand in. The space was lit from above by the sunlight passing through a thick roof of ferns and grass so that it was flooded with greenish light. In front of him was an old wooden door he had pulled from the river after the Winter floods. He had attached it to the stone doorway of the Den with leather hinges, but it was still stiff and took all his strength to open.

Inside, things were as he had left them. The Den was roughly two metres square, a room dug into the hillside, its roof supported by old roots. The floor was earth and the walls were a mixture of stones and soil. Owen had found it two years ago while looking for hazelnuts. He had cleared it of fallen earth and old branches, and had put an old piece of perspex in a gap in the roof. The roof was under an outgrowth of brambles halfway up the steep part of the slope and the perspex window was invisible while still providing the same greenish light as the space in front of the door.

He had furnished the Den with a sleeping bag and an old sofa that had been dumped beside the river. There were candles for Winter evenings, and a wooden box where he kept food. The walls were decorated with objects he had found around the river and in Johnston's yard a quarter of a mile away across the fields. Johnston kept scrap cars and lorries and salvage from old trawlers from the harbour at the river mouth. Owen had often gone to Johnston's, climbing the fence and hunting through the scrap. That was until Johnston had caught him. He winced at the memory. Johnston had hit him hard on the side of the head then laughed at him as he ran away.

Before that, Johnston used to come to the house three or four times a year, selling second-hand furniture, but he hadn't been back since he'd caught Owen.

But that had been last year. Now Owen had a lorry wing mirror, a brass boat propeller, a car radio cassette and an old leather bus seat with the horsehair filling poking through. He had also found an old wooden dressing table painted pink. He looked at himself in the mirror as he passed. A thin face, his hair needing a cut. He had a wary look. His eyes a little older than they should be. He made a face at himself in the mirror and the eyes came alive then, youthful and dancing. He let the mask fall again and saw the same watchful face looking back.

He spent as much time as he could at the Den. Sometimes, he felt that people were watching him, whispering that he was the boy whose father had killed himself. Suicide, that was the word he heard. He could see it in people's eyes when he went into shops. A strange boy. One day he heard a woman whisper behind him. "Like father like son." "He'll go the same way," another voice said. Sometimes it was just easier to stay away from them.

Owen sat down heavily on the bus seat. He knew he was in trouble. He'd skipped school again that week and spent his day around the harbour where the river met the sea. He couldn't help it. He kept being drawn back. And yet when he got close to the edge of the dock, he could feel the terrible panic welling up in him. The coldness, the heavy salt greenishness of the water filling his mouth and his lungs, and then the terrible blackness below. Each time he would come to as if he'd been asleep, finding himself many metres from the edge of the dock, his limbs trembling and his mouth dry.

It had been like that for as long as Owen could remember.

He wanted to ask his mother if he'd always suffered from such fear, but she seemed so weighed down and lost in her own thoughts that she barely noticed him these days, and when he did ask a question she raised dull, lifeless eyes to him, staring at him as if she was struggling to remember who he was.

That was the worst thing of all, so he had stopped asking questions.

Owen emptied his bag. In the kitchen he had found some cheese and some chocolate biscuits. He took a magazine from the small pile that he kept in the Den. The cheese was a little stale and tasted odd with the chocolate biscuits, but he ate everything and washed it down with the milk. Outside, the wind sighed through the trees, but the Den was warm and dry. *These are the best times*, he thought to himself. No one knew where you were, but you were safe and warm in a secret place that no one else knew about but you.

He had found the Den a few years ago, when things were normal, or almost normal. Those were the days when he could talk to his mother. About most things, anyway. Except, of course, when he had tried to talk about his father. She would open her mouth as if to reply, but her eyes would cloud over and she'd turn away. But at least then they had been happy, living together in the small house. "Me and you, son," she would say. "That's how it is, me and you." And he had been glad to have her. In school he had always been a loner. Not that anyone actually bothered him much. They just seemed to think that it was better if he went his way and they went theirs. Fine with him.

But then his mother started to change. She said that something in the house was "weighing on her". That there was something in the air itself that left her unable to think straight. She started to forget things. Little things at first, then it seemed as if she forgot almost everything, wandering through the house, vague and forgetful.

Owen read on until the light changed, almost as if a rain cloud had arrived overhead, the light dark but silvery, so that he could still see the letters on the page. He listened for the sound of the rain falling, but there was nothing, not even the sound of the wind. In fact, a stillness seemed to have fallen outside, so complete that you couldn't hear the sound of birds or insects. Owen decided to investigate. He slipped on his jacket and heaved the old door open. He was careful to replace the branches that hid the door, even though he was aware of their loud rustling in the still air. He paused. There was a sense of expectancy. He began to climb towards the old swing, which was the highest point overlooking the river.

It took ten minutes to get up to the level of the swing tree. The air itself was dense and heavy, and Owen was breathing hard. He skirted the ridge until he got to the swing. It was a piece of ship's cable which had been hung from the branch of an ancient oak protruding over a sheer drop of fifty metres to the river. The rope part of the cable had almost rotted away to expose the woven steel core. No one knew who had climbed the branch to put the cable there, but Owen knew what it felt like to swing on it. It was both terrifying and exhilarating. You knew that if you lost your momentum or your grip there was nothing to save you from the long drop to the stones of the river far below. Local children had used it as a test of nerve for years. For Owen, it wasn't the bone-crunching impact of the stones that he feared, but the clammy touch of the water.

For some reason he couldn't explain he felt that there was someone watching. Almost without thinking, he crouched down behind a heap of old stones and peered out over the river. As he did so he saw a part of the bank below him start to move. At least he thought it was part of the bank, but as he looked closer he saw that it was in fact a man. He was wearing some kind of uniform, which might have been blue to begin with but was now faded to a greyish colour. There were no insignia on the uniform except for heavy epaulettes on the shoulders. The man's hair was close-cropped and steely grey. In one hand was a narrow, metallic tube, almost gun-shaped, and on his belt there were oddly shaped objects – thick glass bulbs with narrow, blunt, metal ends.

There was something else strange about him and it took Owen a little while to work it out. Then he realised what it was. Even though the man was obviously fully grown he was barely a metre and a half tall and just a little taller than Owen himself. The man was staring intently across the river. A small knot of hazel trees on the slope meant that Owen couldn't see what he was looking at, but a dip in the ground led towards the man's position and Owen crept along it.

As he got closer, he could see how tense the man was, how his left hand gripped the metal tube so that his knuckles were white. As Owen drew level with him, he could see that he was looking in the direction of Johnston's farm and scrapyard. Owen knew that Johnston's scrapyard had been getting bigger, but he hadn't looked at it for a long time and now he saw that it seemed to have expanded to cover field after field. At the fringes of the scrapyard he could see small black figures moving busily to and fro. And as he watched, a figure in white emerged from the fields of scrap and stood facing in the direction of the river. Owen heard a sudden intake of breath from the man in front of him.

"The Harsh!" he exclaimed then went silent as the cloaked figure raised his right hand in the air. Owen heard a voice that did not seem to be human, a cry that swelled and seemed to be both angry and triumphant, and full of youthful arrogance and ancient fury, a cry that seemed to flow like a raging river until Owen covered his ears and pressed his face to the ground.

And then, as suddenly as it had begun, the cry stopped. Owen looked up. The man in front of him had not moved. If the cry had shaken him, he did not show it. He seemed to be waiting for something. The wind had stopped and every branch and leaf was still. The birds and insects made no sound. Even the noise of the river faded away into silence. The man waited and Owen waited with him. The silence seemed to stretch on and on. Owen's muscles were taut and his hands were clenched into fists though he didn't know why. And then it came, soundlessly and all-enveloping. A kind of dark flash, covering the sky in an instant, sweeping across the land and plunging everything momentarily into total blackness like the blackness before the world began. And then, just as suddenly, it was gone and the trees and grasses seemed to sigh, the very stones of the land seemed to sigh, as if something precious had gone for ever.

"It has begun," the little man said softly to himself, his voice weary. And then there was another great cry, but this time filled with terrible triumph. Owen felt a chill run down his spine and he gasped. In a second, the man had turned and taken several swift steps towards him, brandishing the metal tube. But when Owen stood up, he stopped and rubbed his chin thoughtfully.

"So," he said, as if to himself, "it is to be you. I suppose it had to be."

Owen waited, suppressing the impulse to run. The man strode up to him and took him by the arm.

"We must hurry," he said. "We have a lot to do."

CHAPTER TWO

Owen didn't resist. He felt completely bewildered. When the man released his arm he followed. They were going in the direction of the old Workhouse, the small man moving with great speed through the tangles of willow and hazel scrub along the river. After a few minutes, Owen realised that they were following faint paths through the undergrowth, paths that he had never noticed before, but that seemed to be well-travelled. Every so often, the man would disappear from sight, but he never got too far ahead. Owen would round a bend to find him waiting.

"What's your name?" Owen said breathlessly as he hurried up to him for the third or fourth time.

"My name…" the man said, stroking his chin and leaning back against a tree as though the matter of his name was worth interrupting his headlong progress for, that it was something which merited sitting down and thinking about.

You either know your name or you don't, Owen thought impatiently. "My name's Owen," he blurted out, hoping to hurry the man along.

"I know your name," the man said in a tone which left Owen in no doubt that he was speaking the truth. "They call me the Sub-Commandant."

A sudden cold breeze made the trees around them rustle. Owen shivered. The man straightened up quickly.

"Let's go," he said urgently and started out again. Owen followed, almost running.

After ten minutes they were close to the Workhouse. To Owen's surprise the narrow paths had started to widen and there was fresh-cut foliage to either side of them. The grass had been stripped from the ground and he could see that the surface of the path underneath was cobbled. But that wasn't all. As they approached the Workhouse, he could hear the sounds of people at work, hammers tapping, wood being sawn, the rumble of masonry. When he rounded the corner he stopped and blinked and rubbed his eyes in amazement. The side of the hill leading to the Workhouse was swarming with people, many of them wearing the same uniform as the Sub-Commandant. And instead of there being a smooth stone face, archways were beginning to appear in the rock. Archways and windows, more and more of them. Men were unblocking entrances and passing the stones from them from hand to hand down the cliff. Other men were using the cut stones to construct a wall at the bottom of the hill. In the oak wood on the other side of the Workhouse, teams of women were working with saws at the trees.

Owen realised that he had stopped walking and the Sub-Commandant was now far ahead. He started to run after him, but stopped again when he saw the Workhouse. There were people in every window, smoke rising from its chimneys, and from the highest window a black banner with nothing on it stirred in the cold wind.

He realised that he could no longer see the Sub-Commandant, and that people were casting curious glances at him. He moved forward, calmly at first and then with increasing panic. On a small rise in the shadow of the Workhouse he saw a man who seemed to be directing the work. He was much taller than the others and was wearing a black suit. The suit was shabby and worn through to the lining, but his hair was cropped and steely grey, and his deep-set, penetrating eyes told you that this was no tramp. As Owen stared at him, he saw the Sub-Commandant emerge from the crowd at the base of the rise. Owen started towards them. As he did so, the tall man turned and saw the Sub-Commandant. The two men looked into each other's eyes for a long time, then the tall man strode forward and they embraced. Owen pushed through the people at the bottom of the rise. The tall man turned to look across the river, still holding the Sub-Commandant affectionately by the elbow.

"It has been a long sleep this time," he said.

"It has been a long watch, Chancellor," the Sub-Commandant replied.

"A long weary one, by your face," the tall man said, glancing at him shrewdly.

"I am tired, but there's no time for that. The Harsh have had a long time to prepare."

"I was worried about that," said the tall man. "We must be quick in our own preparations."

The tall man's eyes swept over the crowd until they reached Owen. It was almost a physical sensation; one that left him feeling uncomfortable, as if his most secret thoughts were suddenly visible. But just as suddenly the sensation stopped and the tall man's eyes were sad.

"I suppose it had to be," he said, sighing, "although I would have preferred somebody else."

"These decisions aren't in our hands," the Sub-Commandant said.

"I know, but I hope we do not have to pay a price for it."

Once again, Owen felt that searching gaze sweep over him.

Suddenly, a cry went up from the direction of the river. There was a flash of blue light and a sudden smell of burning in the air.

"It begins," the Sub-Commandant said quietly.

"A feint, I would say, nothing more. But we have to be ready. I'll talk to you later."

The tall man grasped the Sub-Commandant's shoulder and strode quickly off. Owen realised that he had moved up the hill as the two men spoke until he found himself standing beside the Sub-Commandant. Despite the man's small stature, Owen had the sensation of being sheltered and protected, more so as the man rested his hand on his shoulder.

"I have a lot to do," he murmured, then called, "Cati! Cati!"

A small figure detached itself from a group under the Workhouse walls and ran towards them. Despite the steepness of the slope, the figure came at full speed, taking great leaps and sliding dangerously on the scree. As the figure got closer Owen could see that it was a girl, her long black hair plaited at the back. She was wearing a uniform like the others, but it was covered in badges and brooches. Underneath a peaked cap, her hair was tied in brightly coloured braids. Her green eyes watched him warily.

"Cati," the Sub-Commandant said, "I want you to look after young Owen here."

"But I was going to go down to the forward posts, Father!" she exclaimed. "It looks like the Harsh are going to try to cross there!"

"There will be no crossing," the Sub-Commandant said

sternly. "At least not yet, but you must do what you are told, Cati. This is no time for disobedience, especially from you."

The girl bit her lip. There were tears in her eyes and two bright points of colour burned high up on her cheeks.

"Yes, Father," she said quietly. The Sub-Commandant turned to her and Owen could see his eyes soften. He put his hands on her shoulders and leaned his forehead against hers. Owen could not hear what he said, but the girl smiled and he could feel the current of warmth between them. The small man cupped the girl's face in his hands and kissed her forehead, and then he turned and was gone. The girl turned to Owen.

"Now, young Owen," she said, putting her hands on her hips, "I hope you're a bit tougher than you look. Come on!" Without looking to see if he was following, she turned and ran back towards the Workhouse, swarming up the slope with fierce agility. Not having a choice, Owen followed. Even so, he found it hard to keep up with her.

As he ran, the workers looked up at him curiously, men and women dressed in many different uniforms. Some of them were grey and worn like the Sub-Commandant's. Others were ornate and colourful. The faces that looked up at him were as varied. There were stern-looking people with straw-blond hair and hooked noses. There were smaller, dark men and women with a cheerful look in their eye who wore copper-coloured uniforms and looked as if they would be happier putting down their burdens and joining the two children. There were small, squat people, men with dark curly hair and beards, and others – so many that Owen's head hurt.

"Where did everyone come from?" he said, catching up with Cati. "What's happening? I mean…" He stopped. He didn't know which questions to ask first. He felt a sudden impulse to return to the Den, pull the bushes over the entrance and hide. It was all too strange that one minute the riverbank should be just as it always was, and an hour later it looked like a huge armed outpost preparing for war.

"The people have awoken from the Sleep. Or some of them have," Cati said as they passed a group of women who were looking around with dazed eyes, while others rubbed their hands and feet, softly calling their names.

"But where did you all come from? I mean you weren't here an hour ago."

"We were, you know. Two hours ago. Two years ago. Two hundred years ago. Asleep in the Starry."

"What's the Starry…?" Owen began. But he couldn't go on. There was too much to ask.

"Are you hungry?" Cati said. "Come on." She turned sharply left and plunged through an ornate doorway made of a brassy metal with strange shapes etched into it; what seemed like a spindly, elongated aircraft with people sitting on top, tiny men with tubes like the one the Sub-Commandant had

23

carried. There were tiny etched fires and people falling. Cati reached through the doorway and grabbed his shoulder. "Come on!"

Owen found himself on a wide stone stairway which spiralled downwards. Every few steps they met a man carrying a barrel or a box on his shoulder, or women walking with rolls of cloth and stores of one kind or another. They all smiled at Cati and she spoke to them by name. The stair seemed to go on for ever, until eventually it opened out into a broad corridor which appeared to be a main thoroughfare, for people of every kind were moving swiftly and purposefully through it. Owen felt dizzy. The corridor was lit with an eerie blue light, but he couldn't see where it was coming from.

Cati dived through a side door and Owen found they were now in a vast kitchen. It stretched off into the distance, a place full of the hubbub of cooking, with giant ovens lining one wall, roof beams groaning under the weight of sides of beef and men stirring great pots. People were baking, stewing, carving, spitting, and all the time shouting and cursing, their faces shining with the heat. To one side of the kitchen, Owen saw a giant trapdoor lying open and a team of coopers opening endless barrels that were being passed up from what must have been a huge cellar below. He saw round cheeses with oil dripping from them, herrings pickled in brine, sides of bacon. There were barrels of honey and of biscuits, and casks of wine carried shoulder high across the kitchen. As he watched, Cati darted across the top of the barrels with a piece of bread in each hand. Before the men could react, she had thrust the bread into the honey and skipped away laughing.

"Here," Cati said, thrusting one of the pieces of bread into his hand. The bread was warm and nutty, and the honey was rich and reminded him of hot Summer days spent running through heather moorlands.

"Hello, Contessa," he heard Cati say. Owen turned to see a woman standing beside the girl. She was tall and slender, and her ash-blonde hair hung to her waist. She was wearing a plain white dress which fell to her ankles. Her eyes were grey and ageless. Despite the heat of the kitchen, her brow was smooth and dry, and despite all the cooking and frying and battering, there wasn't a trace of a stain on her white dress.

"Hello, Wakeful," the woman said. Her voice was deep and low.

"Contessa is in charge of food and cooking and things," Cati said. "We have to live off supplies until we can plant and get hunting parties out."

"*Hunting* parties?" Owen said, thinking of the neat fields and little town with its harbour and housing estates. "There's nothing to hunt around here. I mean, it's the twenty-first century. You buy stuff in shops."

Cati and Contessa exchanged a look, then Cati reached out and touched Owen's sleeve. Almost casually, she pushed her finger against the cloth and it gave way, ripping silently.

Contessa and Cati exchanged a look. Owen stared, wondering why she had torn his sleeve, and how she had managed to do it so easily.

"I know it's all very strange," Contessa said gently, "but if you search in your heart, down deep, I think you'll find that in a way, it mightn't be so strange after all."

Before he could answer, Cati leapt to her feet. "Quick!" she shouted, spraying them both with crumbs. "They'll be raising the Nab. I nearly forgot. Come on!" Tugging at Owen's arm, she ran off.

"Go on," Contessa said. "It's worth seeing." Owen thought there was something he should say, but his mind was blank. With a quick smile he ran after Cati. Contessa watched him go, her face kind but grave.

"Like your father before you, you will be tested," she murmured. "Like your father." With these words, sorrow seemed to fill her face. With a sigh, she turned back to the bustle of the kitchen.

When Owen emerged on to the corridor, he saw that Cati was almost lost in the crowds ahead. He dashed after her, but the flaps of leather coming loose on his trainers made it hard to run. Cati dived through another doorway and Owen, following, found himself on yet another twisting staircase rising upwards.

"Hurry up!" Cati shouted back to him. He was panting for

breath when he emerged into daylight at the top. He stumbled on the top step and shot forward, landing flat on his face to find himself looking down the sheer wall of the Workhouse to the ground hundreds of metres below. A hand on his collar hauled Owen back. Cati was surprisingly strong and she practically lifted him to his feet before he pushed her hand away.

"I'm all right," he said, trying to sound gruff. "Leave me alone. I can look after myself." If she was offended by his tone, she didn't show it. She met his eyes for a few seconds and he felt that he was being judged by an older and wiser mind, but he thought he saw sympathy there as well. "What is so important anyway?"

She pointed behind him. Owen realised that they were standing on a flat platform in the middle of the Workhouse roof. The slates on the roof were buckled and covered in mildew, and the stonework was weathered and cracked. In the middle of the platform was a large round hole.

"It's a hole," he said. "I can see that."

"Listen," she said. At first, he could hear a faint rumbling deep in the hole. Then there were deep groaning and complaining noises, as if some very old machinery was grumbling into life. There was a boom which sounded a long way away and then the rumbling got louder and Owen started to feel tremors in the ground beneath his feet. As the rumbling grew, the whole building seemed to shake and pieces of crumbling stone began to fall from the parapet.

"What is it?" He looked at Cati, but her attention was on the vast gaping hole in front of them. More loud groanings and creakings and protesting sounded from the hole, followed by a long, ominous shriek.

"Stand back!" Cati shouted above the noise.

Just as he did, a vast cloud of steam burst upwards and then, with terrifying speed, what looked like the top of a lighthouse shot from the hole – a lighthouse which seemed to be perched on top of a column of brass, which was battered and scarred and scratched and dulled as though it was ancient. Owen realised that the thing was coming out of the hole section by section, like a telescope, the sections sliding over each other with deafening groans and shudders and bangs, the whole structure swaying from side to side so that he thought it would fall on top of them. Cati gripped his arm.

"Jump!" she yelled, propelling him forward. The stained brass wall reared up dizzily in front of him and he saw himself rebounding off it, being flung over the parapet.

"Grab hold!" Cati shouted, just as Owen was about to hit the wall. Terrified, he glanced down and saw a brass rail coming towards him at great speed. He grabbed it with both hands and Cati pushed him over it, until he landed on his back on a narrow walkway as the platform shot upwards, swaying and groaning sickeningly.

After what seemed like an eternity, the platform heaved and clanged to a halt. Owen raised himself cautiously on one elbow and looked through the railing. It was a long way down. The figures on the ground below them were tiny. He turned and looked up. The little turreted point that resembled the top of a lighthouse was maybe twenty metres above him. Despite the battered look of the rest of the structure, the glass gleamed softly as if it had just been polished.

"What is it?" he said, his voice sounding a bit more shaky than he would have liked.

"This is the Nab," Cati said.

"What's that up there?"

"That? That's the Skyward," she said, almost dreamily.

"What's it for?"

"For seeing, if it lets you. For seeing across time."

"You could have killed us," he said, "jumping like that."

"Don't be cross," she said. "I knew you wouldn't jump on your own." Owen opened his mouth then closed it again. There didn't seem to be anything to say. He looked around and saw that the platform they were on joined two sections of a winding staircase which led to the Skyward. He got to his feet, holding on to the rail. A sudden gust of wind caused the whole structure to sway gently. Owen took a firmer hold and looked out across the river.

Where Johnston's yard had been there were trenches and tall figures in white, although the pale mist that came and went made it difficult to get a proper look at them. But there was no mistaking the defences that had been thrown up on his own side of the river. Earthworks topped with wooden pallisades. Deep trenches. And down near the river, hidden by trees, the flicker of that blue flame. Further in the distance he saw the sun touch the horizon, an orange ball, smouldering and ominous. It reminded Owen that he should be home and his eyes turned to the house on the ridge at the other side of the river.

He blinked and looked again, thinking that he was looking in the wrong place, but he knew from the shape of the mountains in the distance that he was not. He was looking for his house. The long, low house with the slate roof and the overgrown garden that his mother once kept. The house at the end of the narrow road with several other houses on it. No matter how much he blinked he could not see them. The road, the other houses, his own house where his sad mother wandered the rooms at night – they were all gone, and in their place a wood of large pine trees grew along the ridge. As if they had always grown there.

"It's gone," Owen said, his voice trembling. "The house is gone, my mother…"

He felt Cati's arm around his shoulder.

"It's not gone," she said, "not the way you mean it. In fact, in a way it was never really there in the first place. Oh dear, that wasn't really the right thing to say…"

That was enough. Tearing himself away from her, Owen started to run, clattering down the metal stairs of the Nab, out on to the roof and then down the stone stairs inside the Workhouse. He could hear Cati calling behind him, but he didn't stop. Whatever was going on in this place, it was nothing to do with him. He was going to cross the river and get his mother. On he ran, through the busy main corridor now, elbowing people aside, shouting at them to get out of his way so that they turned to stare after him. The corridor cleared a little as he approached the kitchen, and he was running at full tilt, Cati's cries far behind, when the sole of his right trainer came off and caught under his foot. Arms flailing, he tried to stay upright, but it was no good. With a ripping sound, the sole of the left trainer came off and Owen went crashing to the ground, his head striking the stone floor with a crunch.

He lay there for a moment, sick and dizzy. He put his hand to his head, feeling a large bump starting to rise. He opened his eyes and saw a pair of elegant slippers. He looked up to see Contessa peering down at him with concern. Cati skidded to a halt beside them.

"I didn't tell him… I mean, I said it would be explained…" she stammered. Contessa held up a hand and Cati stopped talking. Owen sat up and Contessa knelt beside him.

"Our house," he said hopelessly, "my mother, they're gone…"

"I know," Contessa said gently. "I know. Here. Drink some

of this." She pulled a small bottle from under her robes and put it to his lips. The liquid tasted warm and nutty.

"I have to go," he said. "She might be frightened…" But as he spoke, everything seemed to become very far away, even his own voice. His eyelids felt heavier and heavier. He had to fight it. He had to go home. But it seemed that his brain refused to send the order to his legs to move. Instead, strong arms enveloped him and lifted him, and as they did so, he fell asleep.

CHAPTER THREE

Owen felt himself coming out of sleep as though he was swimming to the surface of a warm sea. He opened his eyes. It was dark, but it was a strangely familiar dark. Then he realised – he was in his Den. It all came flooding back to him – the Workhouse, Cati. Perhaps he had been asleep and dreamed the whole thing! He felt along the back wall for the store of candles he kept there and lit one. He pulled the sleeping bag around him and sat very still. That was it, he decided. It had all been a very real dream. He felt cold and he moved to pull his sleeve down over his forearm. As he did so, the seam disintegrated and the sleeve came away in his hand. He looked down on the floor and saw his trainers, both soles half torn away. It hadn't been a dream! He remembered sitting on the chest in his bedroom that morning and longing for something strange and exotic. Well, what had happened was certainly strange, but he wasn't so sure if he wanted it as much.

He tried to arrange what he knew in his head. The Sub-Commandant. Cati and Contessa. The Workhouse and the Nab. But it was no good. He couldn't make any sense of it. Owen jumped to his feet, and as he did so, he felt his clothes falling away. He looked down. His trousers were hanging in rags; his jacket and T-shirt seemed to have disintegrated.

Owen looked round the walls of the Den. The posters he had hung on the wall had faded, the images indistinct and the paper yellowed. The metal objects did not seem to have suffered as badly, although he noticed that the plastic on the cassette player had faded and warped. Only the brass boat propeller he had found in Johnston's yard seemed to be the same as ever. He tugged at the rotting fabric of his T-shirt in disgust. He couldn't go out without clothes. Then he noticed a neat pile of clothes in the doorway. Owen unfolded it. It seemed to be a uniform of the same faded fabric as the Sub-Commandant had been wearing. There was a pair of boots made of some material which seemed like leather but was not, and which fastened to the knee with brass clips. He imagined what would happen if any of the town children saw him in those clothes – how they would laugh – but a sudden draught on his bare skin made him shiver. He realised that he had no choice but to put on the clothes.

Five minutes later, Owen looked at himself in the mirror.

He seemed to look much older. The uniform was a good fit, although it was frayed here and there. He thought he looked like a soldier, somebody who had been in a long war far from home. He heard a noise behind him and he turned. Cati was standing in the doorway.

"It suits you," she said.

"This is my place. You have no right to come in here without asking," said Owen, suddenly defensive.

"I was only trying to help. You needed clothes."

"I don't need anything of yours!" he said angrily. "I just want to be left alone."

"Next time I *will* leave you alone," she snapped back. There were red spots high on her cheeks. "Next time I will leave you alone and you can go around in your bare skin."

They glared at each other for a minute. Then Owen saw a muscle twitch in Cati's face. He felt his own face begin to crease. A few seconds later they were helpless with laughter.

Owen laughed until his sides ached. He and Cati collapsed on the old bus seat, wiping their eyes. They sat for a moment in companionable silence, then Cati leapt to her feet without a word and went back outside. When she came back, she was carrying a basket. Delicious smells rose from it and Owen realised that he was ravenous.

"Contessa sent it," Cati said. She opened the basket and set out the contents neatly on the top of the dressing table. There was fresh, warm bread and sealed bowls of hot stew. There were roast potatoes, cheese sauce and all sorts of pickles which Owen didn't think that he would like and then discovered he did. They ate without talking, finishing up with two bowls of a delicious substance which was something like custard and something like cream. Owen lay back on the bus seat feeling that suddenly life did not look so bleak after all. But Cati leapt to her feet again.

"Come on," she said briskly. "We have to go to the Convoke."

"I'm too full for a Convoke now, whatever it is."

"I think you'd better come," Cati said, suddenly serious. "You need to know about your mother, apart from anything else."

His mother! Owen sprang to his feet and hurried after her. Outside, it was a cold, crisp night and he could see his breath hanging in the air. He hurried after Cati through the shadows of the trees.

"We've got time," she said. "There are two parts to this Convoke… and you're not allowed into the first part."

"Why not?"

She hesitated then spoke softly as if she was afraid that she might be overheard. "Well… it's actually about you."

"About me?"

"Yes. It's about whether you should be allowed to attend or not. And other things."

"Why wouldn't I be allowed to attend?"

"You'll find out."

Owen was puzzled. What was so special about him that they would waste time talking about whether or not he could attend the Convoke?

"Do you really want to hear the first bit?" Cati asked. "Really?"

"I suppose," he said. "if it's about me, maybe I'd better."

"There's a secret way into the chamber," she said. "I found it ages ago. Come on."

Cati turned on to a path which seemed to lead under the hill. Owen had noticed a gully there before, but it had been choked with trees and undergrowth. Now it had been cleared and the path was smooth underfoot. The path sloped downwards and high walls reared on either side, their ancient stones covered in moss and ferns and lichen.

"Where are we going?" Owen said, realising he was whispering.

"You'll see."

Cati moved swiftly on. It became darker and darker, but she did not falter and Owen began to wonder if she could see in the dark.

After what felt like a long time, Cati stopped so suddenly that Owen ran into her. As his eyes became accustomed to the dark, he saw that they were standing in front of a vast door made of brass and wood, so old and gnarled that it looked like stone. Again, it was decorated with spidery shapes that looked like a child's drawings of boats and planes. As Owen examined it, he realised that the drawings glowed faintly with a blue light he had seen everywhere that day.

Cati took a key from her pocket, a tiny key for a door so vast, but as she held it up he could see that it was ornately worked with complicated-looking teeth. She fitted it into a tiny aperture and turned it, once, twice, three times. There was a sound like heavy, oiled bolts being drawn and then the huge door swung silently open. Cati stepped inside and Owen followed. As they did so, the door closed soundlessly behind them. They were now standing in a narrow passage lit by faint blue light coming from the opening at one end. There was an odd smell, musty and old, but sweet as well.

Cati slowly stepped through the opening. Owen hesitated, then with a backwards glance at the closed door, stepped forward also.

He found himself in a vast chamber, stretching off as far as the eye could see. The ceiling, high above them, was speckled with points of blue light so that it seemed that they stood under a clear night sky. But that was not all. The chamber was filled with innumerable flat couches, each with a single sheet and a pillow. Most of the beds were empty, but as Owen's eyes got used to the dim light, he saw that some of them were still occupied. He looked for Cati, but realised that while he had been standing lost in awe she had moved quietly off. He watched as she moved slowly among the occupied beds which were scattered among the empty ones. The sleepers seemed to be of all ages, young and old, fair and dark. She stopped by one bed as Owen went towards her. He saw that the figure in the bed was a young man, a little older than him. He had curly dark hair and his breathing was deep and even. Cati reached out and touched his hair, smiling sadly.

"What is this place?" Owen asked.

"The Starry, where we sleep until we are called."

"Who are these people then?"

"Friends, most of them. When we get the call we are supposed to wake, but some do not wake and we do not know why."

Owen saw that the black-haired boy and two other children – girls with brown hair – were lying in a circle round a woman with work-worn hands and a pleasant face that seemed to be smiling even as she slept. Cati put her hand on the woman's shoulder and bent to kiss her. Owen wanted to ask who she was, but Cati seemed to be almost in a dream and he didn't want to disturb her. He noticed that each pillow had a small blue cornflower placed on it.

"It is our sign of remembering," Cati said. "A sign that we do not forget our friends."

The sweet, musty smell in the air seemed to be getting heavier. *If sleep had a smell, this is what it would smell like*, Owen thought to himself. His eyelids felt as if there were weights attached to them. The empty beds began to look very inviting.

Suddenly, he felt Cati shaking his shoulders. "The Convoke," she said urgently. "Come on. If you stay here, you'll sleep."

She led him towards a small doorway which opened on to another one of the winding staircases that were a feature of the Workhouse. The staircase was dark and apparently unused; cobwebs brushed their faces as they climbed, but there must have been a window to the outside world for Owen felt cold fresh air on his face, chasing away the sleep that had stolen over him in the Starry.

"What is the Starry for?" he said. "Why are they all sleeping? They look as if they've been asleep for years."

"They have," said Cati, sounding sad, "but that's another thing that needs to be explained." And she would say no more about it.

At the top of the staircase was another corridor, then another staircase, then they were under the Workhouse roof. Owen ducked his head to avoid the huge timber beams supporting the roof, half choking on the dust which rose in great clouds under his feet. Just as he was about to ask where they were, Cati turned and put her fingers to her lips. Following her, he got on to his hands and knees and crawled forward. He saw light coming through a gap in the stone wall in front of him. Cati disappeared into the light and he followed to find himself in a tiny wooden gallery suspended, it seemed, in mid air over great buttresses which went down and down until they reached the floor far below. Owen gasped and grabbed Cati's arm. She made a face at him to be quiet and pointed. Far below them, the Convoke had started.

It was a while before Owen's eyes adjusted to the light and he could make out the scene below. The first thing he noticed were the banners which hung from the ceiling, enormous cloth banners in faded colours which seemed hundreds of metres long. Then he saw that the banners framed a great hall of flagged floors and pillars and stone walls. Massive chains hanging from the roof held globes of blue light and in its glow he could see figures on the ground, some standing, others sitting on a raised dais, and many more standing in a circle around them. He could see that one of the standing figures was the Sub-Commandant and even from far above Owen could tell that the small man was pleading with the figures on the dais.

To the right of these figures was a fireplace where great logs burned, and in front of the fireplace a figure sprawled in a chair. It was too far away to see who it was and Owen was distracted just then as the Sub-Commandant began to speak. His voice was low and even, but there was an intensity to it and Owen guessed that there was some dispute going on.

"You are talking about history in this, Chancellor, but we

aren't certain about what took place," he said. Owen could just see Chancellor shake his head as if in sorrow.

"I think that you are the only one who doubts what happened, Sub-Commandant," Chancellor said. "We had the Mortmain and with it the security of the world, or at least as much as was in our power to guarantee. But the Mortmain is gone." His voice was mellow, but full of authority, a leader gently rebuking a much-loved but erring lieutenant. Even from his perch in the rooftop, Owen could feel that the crowd in the hall was swayed by him.

"We cannot judge the future by the past," the small man said. "There are many things that we don't know."

"I agree that there are many things we do not know," Chancellor said, "but we have to work with what small knowledge we have. I feel that the boy should not be admitted to our counsel."

The crowd began to murmur this time. Glancing sideways, Owen could see that Cati looked worried. Chancellor leaned back in his chair. He did not look triumphant, but weighed down by the gravity of the situation. Suddenly, Owen heard a woman's voice – a ringing voice with a tone of harsh amusement to it.

"The boy should be allowed in," the voice said.

"You have been listening to our arguments, Pieta?" Chancellor asked. The woman made a scornful sound.

"I have no need to listen to your talk, Chancellor," she said.

"I know what is right and so does the man who has watched for us these long years. The boy is allowed into the Convoke by right of who he is." Owen realised that the voice was coming from the chair by the fire.

"Would we leave him outside, parentless and confused?" the Sub-Commandant said softly.

"Is that your final position, Pieta?" Chancellor asked. His voice was low and there was a hint of anger in it. There was no reply from the chair, but Owen heard a bottle clinking against a glass and there seemed to be a kind of finality to the sound.

Chancellor sighed. "You have the right to ask much for your defence of us…"

"Yes. I have the right, Chancellor."

"I appreciate your reservations, Chancellor," Contessa interjected gently, "but I think justice demands that the boy be brought before us."

"You appeal to justice, Contessa, but are you certain that the boy does not appeal to another part of you?" This new speaker stood up. He was a long-haired man dressed in a uniform of sombre but rich red. As he spoke, he swept his hair back over his shoulder. A silence fell over the hall. Contessa did not reply, but Owen could feel a chill stealing over the hall.

"That settles it," the woman they called Pieta said. "Bring the damn boy and bring him now. If our resident peacock starts scheming about the thing, we'll never hear the end of it." The man in the coloured uniform glared at Pieta and made to speak again, but Chancellor held up his hand.

"Sub-Commandant." His tone was commanding.

"I sent Cati to get him," the Sub-Commandant said. "In case he was required," he added smoothly. Chancellor turned his gaze to the Sub-Commandant. Owen shivered. He could only imagine the scrutiny of those piercing eyes.

"While we are waiting," Contessa said, "we should discuss those who will not wake. The numbers have risen. We're desperately weak, Chancellor." Owen realised that she must have interrupted in order to break Chancellor's searching gaze at the Sub-Commandant. He felt Cati's elbow dig him in the side.

"Come on," she hissed. "Quick!"

Owen and Cati crawled back through the gap in the stone wall. They ran as fast as they could down the staircases, Owen's clothes covered in cobwebs and hands and elbows grazed from the rough stone walls as he tried to keep his balance. They practically fell out of the stairway into a brightly lit hall, dishevelled and filthy. A young man in the same richly coloured uniform as the long-haired man grabbed Owen under the arm and lifted him to his feet. His face seemed friendly but serious.

"Hurry," he hissed. "You do not keep the Convoke waiting."

The wooden door in front of them swung open and Owen was propelled into the hall.

Owen stopped dead. Every eye in the hall was fixed on him. He could see Chancellor standing on the dais. The young man gestured to him impatiently. Somehow, Owen managed to put one foot in front of the other, the crowd parting in for him as he did so. He felt his heart beat faster and faster, and as he approached the dais, his foot caught the hem of a woman's cloak. He would have fallen had not a hand reached out and grabbed his elbow. Owen turned and found himself looking into the eyes of a tall older man with a beard and a terrible scar which looked like a burn on one side of his face. The man grinned and winked at him, managing to look both villainous and friendly at the same time. The sight gave Owen heart. At least he wasn't without friends in the hall. He pulled himself upright and strode to the dais where the Sub-Commandant addressed him.

"You are welcome to the Convoke, young Owen. Have you anything to ask us?" But before Owen could open his mouth the man with the long hair broke in.

"He'll have time enough for questions. For the moment I want to ask him a few things about himself and how he got here."

For the next ten minutes Owen found himself answering questions about where he came from, his school, his friends, his age and how well he knew the area around the Workhouse. Such was the piercing quality of the man's eyes and his air of command that it was impossible not to reply.

Chancellor was particularly interested in Johnston's scrapyard. Contessa asked him about his home and about his mother, and listened sympathetically as he tried to make things with his mother sound better than they actually were, while feeling that he was letting her down with every word.

"Do you have any great fears, things that terrify you for no apparent reason?" Chancellor asked. His voice was casual, but Owen could feel that the whole Convoke was intent upon the answer. In his mind the image of a deep, still pool of black water formed, and he saw himself bending over it and realising that there was no reflection. He felt a single bead of sweat run down his spine and his voice dropped to a whisper.

"N-no," he stammered. Before he had time to wonder why he had lied, the man in the red uniform stood up.

"I've had enough of this. Where is the Mortmain? Tell us *that*, boy. Return it to its rightful owners!"

"Enough, Samual!" the Sub-Commandant said. He didn't speak loudly, but his voice cut through the tension in the room like a whiplash. The man in red sat down again, grumbling.

"That subject should not have been mentioned," the Sub-Commandant went on. "Let the boy ask his questions now."

Owen looked around. A thousand questions swirled in his mind. "Where am I?" he said and then, with his voice getting stronger, "Who are you? And what has happened to... to everything?"

"I will try to answer," Chancellor said, getting to his feet. "There are three parts to your question. As to where you are, you are in the Workhouse, the centre of the Resisters to the Harsh and the frost of eternal solitude that they wish to loose upon the earth. We are not the only Resisters. There are pockets elsewhere, perhaps even in other lands, but all hinges on us, on our strength and strategy." There was pride in his voice, even vanity, but sorrow as well.

"As to who we are," he went on, "we are the Wakeful. We sleep the centuries through until we are called. You could say we are the custodians of time. Like everything else, time has a fabric or structure. And sometimes that fabric is weakened or attacked and requires repair or defence. But we do not have much time to explain things, and others can tell you more of us. The most important of your questions is the last. What has happened?"

"I will answer that," the Sub-Commandant said, "since the boy and I both witnessed it, although he did not know it at the time."

"The floor is yours," Chancellor said stiffly.

Once more Owen could feel the people in the hall bend their attention to the slender figure, as if he was going to relate a terrible story that they had heard before but felt compelled to hear again.

"You may perhaps have learned that time is not a constant, that it is relative." Owen nodded, hoping that he looked clever. The words that the Sub-Commandant used were familiar from school, but to tell the truth he hadn't been listening when these things were talked about, and he hadn't understood what he had heard.

"What happened today is an extension of that. Do you remember when you saw that dark flash in the sky?" Owen nodded. "The process is complex and subtle, and many events took place both together and apart. But to put it in the simplest possible terms, a terrible thing has happened. A thing that our enemies have sought to achieve for many eras."

The Sub-Commandant paused. The whole hall seemed to hold its breath and Owen realised that although they knew in their hearts what had happened, it had yet to be confirmed to them. The Sub-Commandant's face was stern and grey and age showed in it, great age.

"They have started the Puissance," he said. "the Great Machine in the North turns again and time is flowing backwards."

CHAPTER FOUR

A shuddering sigh flowed through the hall. Owen stared blankly at the Sub-Commandant. How could time flow backwards? What sort of machine were they talking about? He didn't know how long he stood there until the Sub-Commandant stepped forward and gripped him by the shoulders.

"It's a lot for you to understand and I won't trouble you with any more tonight. You'll have questions and we'll answer them as best we can. But for now, I think it is best if you rest."

"Wait!" The man they called Samual rose to his feet. "I have a few more questions." He moved up close to Owen and walked round him, studying him, his eyes glittering with dislike. "What is your understanding of your father's death?" he barked.

Owen froze. It was something he tried not to think about. "There was an accident…" he stammered.

"Suicide," Samual said. "Wasn't that it?"

"No…" said Owen.

"Is there a point to all of this?" Contessa asked, her voice cold. She obviously didn't approve of Samual's questioning, but he ignored her.

"Have you ever heard of Gobillard et Fils?" he demanded sharply, his face almost pressed against Owen's now, his eyes eager.

Gobillard et Fils, Owen thought. That's what was written on the trunk in his bedroom! How did this man know about that? He could feel Chancellor and the others watching him intently.

"No…" he stammered, "no… I've never heard that name before…" The lie was out before Owen knew what he was saying. Why had he not admitted that he'd heard the name before? The blood rushed to his face. Would someone notice?

He was saved by the Sub-Commmandant. "The boy is not a prisoner to be interrogated, Samual. That is enough."

Samual looked for a moment as if he would defy the Sub-Commandant, then he thought better of it and turned away.

"You may go, Owen," the Sub-Commandant said gently.

Owen's mouth was dry and his head was spinning, but he knew that there was one question he must ask before he was made to leave the hall. He turned towards the

Sub-Commandant and his voice was no more than a whisper.

"Please," he said, "what has happened to all the people?" There was a long silence then Contessa spoke.

"You are thinking about your mother, of course. I will explain it as we understand it. In turning back time, the Harsh intend to go back to a time before people. The minute they started the reversal, the people disappeared as if they had never been. So nothing has happened to them, but they have never *been*. Except for us, stranded on an island in time – as you now are."

"If we stop the Harsh you'll get your mother back!" It was Cati's voice. She had somehow evaded the watchers on the door. "You'll get her back and it'll all be the same again!"

Contessa gave Cati a stern look, but Owen thought he could see the ghost of a smile hovering around her lips. "That is true. We have stopped them before."

"But this time is different," Chancellor said. "The Harsh are stronger than ever and we are weaker. I cannot see how we can overcome them."

"We are the Resisters," the Sub-Commandant said softly, "and it is our duty to resist, come what may."

Chancellor looked as if he was about to say something more, but in the end he only shook his head and sighed.

"Cati," Contessa said, "you should not be here, but as you are I would like you to take Owen out of the Convoke. We have many other issues to discuss."

Cati took Owen gently by the arm and the crowd parted again for them as they walked towards the door. Owen wanted to ask more questions. What was the Starry? And what had the Mortmain – whatever it was – to do with him? And why were the Resisters so interested in him anyway?

Owen glanced towards the armchair beside the fire. To his surprise, the owner of that harsh voice was much younger than she sounded. Pieta was slim with blonde hair and a girlish face. She was asleep, snoring gently, and wearing a faded uniform similar to his own, but attached to her belt was an object unlike anything he had ever seen before. It looked like a long, coiled whip, but this whip was made of light – a blue light shot through with pulses of energy so that it seemed a living thing. Beside the woman was an empty bottle and a glass. As Owen stared, she opened one eye and looked directly at him. Her eye was bloodshot and bleary, but Owen felt instantly that she knew everything there was to know about him.

Pieta's lips curved in a brief smile, weary and sarcastic, then her eyes closed again and Owen felt Cati haul him towards the door, which opened for them as they reached it and closed gently but firmly behind them.

Owen felt numb. He had never thought about time before, or the fact that it might possible for it to go backwards. "What did Contessa mean by an island in time?"

"That's where the Workhouse is – on an island in time,"

Cati said. "Time is like a river flowing around us, but the Workhouse never really changes. And we don't change either."

"You mean you don't get older or anything?"

"'Course we get older," Cati said with a heavy sigh, as though she was explaining to an idiot. "It's just that we grow old at the same rate as normal people, no matter what time does. You look like you need air."

"I need…" Owen began. But what did he need? A way to understand all of this? Sleep to still his racing mind? A place to hide until it all went away and things returned to as they were before? He was tired, his eyes felt grainy and his limbs fatigued, but an idea was beginning to take shape.

Outside, a mild, damp wind was blowing drizzle in from the direction of the town and you could smell the sea on it.

"Do you want to talk?" Cati sounded anxious.

"No," he said. "No thanks, I'm really tired. I need to sleep, I think."

"You can sleep here. Contessa will find you a bed."

"No!" said Owen, more sharply that he intended. "I want to go back to the Den."

"I understand," she said. "I'll walk there with you."

"I want to be on my own," he said stiffly.

Cati watched as Owen turned abruptly away and walked towards the path to the Den. He felt bad. He didn't want to offend her, but there was something he had to do. As soon as he had rounded the first corner in the path, he dived off it into the trees.

Owen climbed steadily for ten minutes. He knew the landscape well, but it was dark and the rain made it murky, and there seemed to be trees where no tree had grown before. By the time he reached the swing tree, his hands were scratched from brambles and there was a welt on his cheek where a branch had whipped across it. He got down on his belly and crawled to the edge of the drop. He looked across the river, but it was shrouded in gloom. Down below, could just make out what seemed to be trenches and defensive positions which had been dug the whole length of the river.

As Owen looked closer, he saw that they were hastily dug in parts and in other places there were none. He studied the defensive line and saw that it was at its weakest under the shadow of the trees, in the very place where he had crossed that morning. Silently, Owen slipped over the edge and began to slither down the slope, any noise that he made smothered by the insistent drizzle.

At the bottom of the slope he made his way quietly through the trees. Almost too late Owen realised that there was now a path running along the edge of the river. He shot out of the trees into the middle of the path and as he did so he heard a man clearing his throat. Quickly, he dived into the grass at the verge and held his breath. Two men rounded the corner. Both were bearded and carrying the same strange weapon as the Sub-Commandant. They looked alert, nervous even, and their eyes kept straying to the river side of the path – which was just as well, as Owen was barely hidden by the sparse grass at the edge of the trees. They walked past him as he held his breath and pressed his face into the wet foliage. Within seconds, they had rounded the next corner and were gone.

Owen stood up, shaking. He took a deep breath. He had avoided the patrol through luck and he realised that it might not be long before another one came along. He darted to the other side of the path and plunged through the undergrowth towards the river.

It was dark on the riverbank; only the sound of the water told him where it was. He felt his way along the bank until he found the old tree trunk that he had climbed across that morning. Suddenly, he felt sick and dizzy at the thought of crossing the black water. He grabbed the tree trunk firmly. If he didn't start across now, his courage would fail him completely.

Breathing hard, Owen swung himself on to the log. It was wet and slick to the touch. Inching forward, he glanced down and saw the water glinting beneath. He shut his eyes and moved again. The sound of the water grew louder and louder. He opened his eyes. With a start, he realised that he was halfway across.

Owen fixed his eyes on the far bank. He had started on his

hands and knees, but now he found himself on his belly, slithering along the wet trunk. It was when he was three quarters of the way across that he felt it – a slight flexing of the tree trunk, barely noticeable, as if there were now some extra weight bowing the wood. He risked a glance back over his shoulder. There was something on the trunk behind him; something small and fast-moving. Panting, Owen tried to move faster, scrambling for grip. He looked behind again. It was halfway across now and gaining fast. He gulped for air and it sounded like a sob. Then he got to his feet and tried to jump the last couple of metres. Just as he jumped, Owen was hit hard and fast from behind. He felt himself gripped and turned in the air, and as he hit the muddy bank with an impact which drove the air from his lungs, a small powerful hand grabbed him first by the hair, then covered his mouth and his nose so that he couldn't draw the shuddering breath that his aching lungs needed.

"Stupid boy!" Cati hissed furiously. "Where do you think you're going?"

It was several minutes before Owen could get enough air to enable him to talk. Cati crouched beside him, staring intently into the dark.

"We have to get away from here," she whispered urgently.

"I'm not going back," he said. "I'm going home."

"It's not *there* any more! You'll be caught or killed looking for something that's gone. *Listen* to me."

"That's the problem," said Owen. "I've been listening to everyone about time turning back and people sleeping for years and great engines and people disappearing. But I have to *see*. I have to see that my house is gone. I have to see that... that..." He gulped and turned his head away, hoping that she wouldn't see the tears in his eyes. Stumbling to his feet, he wiped his eyes with the sleeve of his jacket.

"I have to *see*," he repeated.

Cati gave him a long, level look, then seemed to come to a decision. "All right, but I better come with you."

"You can't," he said. "I'm going on my own."

"Don't be silly. You made enough noise going through the trees to wake the whole Starry, and you left a trail a blind man could see. If I come with you, at least we have a chance of getting back. Not much of a chance, mind you." Cati seemed almost cheerful about the prospect.

"Come on then," she said. "Might as well get it over with." And set off at a crouch, moving fast and silent. Owen had no choice but to follow her along the riverbank.

A few minutes later he thought he had lost her, then almost tripped over her. Cati was squatting on the ground.

"Careful," she hissed. "Get down here." She had a twig in her hand. "Look."

Owen squinted in the darkness. He could just about see the two parallel lines she had drawn in the earth.

"This line is the river," she said, "and this one is the Harsh. We're in between, here. And the place where your house used to be is here, just in front of their lines. We can get to it, if we're really quiet and really lucky. But you have to do what I tell you, all right?"

Owen nodded dumbly. He hadn't really thought through what he had set out to do, and now he was feeling foolish and headstrong. Cati had called him a stupid boy and he was starting to feel like one.

"Let's go!" Cati said. He followed her, moving slowly now. They turned left and started to climb the hill towards the Harsh lines. There was more cover than he had expected. Where once there had been open fields there were now deep thickets of spruce and copses of oak and ash trees. Progress was slow. Cati whispered that there might be patrols about, and more than once she glared at him as he stood on a dry twig or tripped over a low branch. He did not recognise anything in the place where he had once known every tree and ditch, although sometimes he stumbled over something that might have been the crumbling foundation of an old field wall.

After what seemed like hours, Cati turned to him and held her finger to her lips. They stepped into a clearing – a patch of low scrub. With a start, Owen looked around him. There was no real way of telling, but his heart said there could be no doubt; he was standing in the place where his house had been.

Was that flat piece of ground with saplings growing in it the place where the road had been? And was that young sycamore the same gnarled tree that had stood outside his bedroom window? Owen moved forward carefully until his foot struck something. Pushing back the vegetation he found the remains of a wall. He moved along the wall until he reached a corner and then another corner. It was the right size and shape as his own house. In fact, he was standing underneath the window to his own room, if it had been there. The room with the model hanging from the ceiling, and the guitar, and the battered trunk he had stood on to climb out of the window.

"I don't understand," he whispered. "If time is going backwards, how come the sycamore tree is getting younger, but the house is getting older? Surely the house would turn back into bricks and stuff."

"Living things get younger as time goes backwards," Cati said, "but things built by man just decay. It has always been like that."

Owen began to notice that the grass and weeds were criss-crossed with scorch marks, and that the leaves of low-hanging trees were blackened and dead. Cati reached up and broke off a leaf which crumbled in her hand.

"The Harsh have been here," she whispered fearfully, "searching for something by the look of it. We have to go."

But Owen wasn't ready. He moved his foot and something

clanked against it. He put his hand down into the undergrowth and groped around until his hand closed on an object. He held it up. It was the hand mirror that his mother used when she brushed her hair. The brass back was tarnished and the glass was spotted and milky in places, but it was the same mirror, and as he looked at it, he could picture his mother brushing her hair, her lips pursed, whistling tunelessly to herself. The glass was becoming yet more faded, until he realised that his eyes had misted over.

Cati said something, but he didn't hear her. And he was only barely aware of the cold that started to steal over him. It wasn't until he heard a faint crackling that Owen glanced up at a small twig which hung in front of him. As he looked, it seemed that hoar frost crept up the leaf from the tip, then to another leaf and then another, until the stem itself froze and cracked with a gentle snapping sound as the sap expanded.

Owen looked around. The crackling sound was caused by dozens of leaves and twigs snapping in the same way. He turned to Cati, but she was staring off into the trees and her face was a mask of fear. He followed her terrified gaze. Far off, but moving inexorably closer, were two figures, both white, both faceless, and seeming to glide without effort between the trees. Cati's voice when it came was no more than a whimper.

"The Harsh," she said. "They're here."

CHAPTER FIVE

The cold seared Owens lungs. Somehow he knew that the Harsh were talking to each other in mournful voices full of desolate words that were just out of earshot. The pitch of the voices rose to make a noise like the howling of wolves being carried away on an icy wind and Owen wondered if they had been spotted.

"Come on," he said to Cati in an urgent whisper. "Run!" But it was no good. She seemed to be paralysed with terror. "Please, Cati," he said. "I think they've seen us."

"No," she moaned, "they don't see well. They can smell us though. They can smell the warmth."

Owen grabbed Cati by the arm and hauled her to her feet. She stumbled after him. The Harsh were moving sideways, slipping through the trees. They were going to cut Owen and Cati off from the river. Cati wasn't resisting him, but she wasn't helping either. Owen thought he could hear the voices again and he felt a chilly dread steal over him, a sense that things were lost and that there was no point in running. He realised that this must come from the Harsh and was why Cati was paralysed with terror.

"Come *on*, Cati," he urged. "You've got to fight it." Owen started to run, dragging her behind him. He could no longer see the two Harsh, but when he stopped for a moment he could hear the gentle crackle of frost attacking twigs and leaves to his right. It was only minutes to the river, but the trees and undergrowth made progress slow. Several times Cati fell and would have lain there if Owen hadn't forced her to her feet again, and all the time he felt the cold dread stealing over him, weighing down his limbs so that it was an effort to lift his feet.

Suddenly, Owen and Cati broke free into a clearing which seemed to lead down to the river. Owen turned. Less than fifty metres away he saw the two Harsh and stopped. The force of their presence dragged at him. Cati sank to her knees as Owen turned towards them. The Harsh made no effort to move nearer. Icy vapour from the frozen ground at their feet curled round them so that they seemed to float in the air. Owen's gaze was drawn to the places where their faces should have been; the blank, white spaces. But there seemed to be a mouth to whisper cruel and seductive words, and eyes which bored into him and demanded surrender.

In the distance, Owen heard a shout and knew that the

defenders on the other side of the river had seen them. There was a crash and a burst of blue flame close to the river and then another one, but the Harsh did not stir. With one last desperate effort, Owen tore his gaze away. He reached down and caught Cati under the arms. Half dragging, half carrying her, he stumbled down the slope towards the river. Though he dared not look around, he knew that the Harsh had not moved. There was another burst of blue flame and Owen heard men's voices shouting encouragement to them. Even Cati seemed to hear and forced herself to run towards the river. They were just short of the water now and Owen realised they had to cover more ground upstream to reach the log crossing. He risked a glance backwards – the Harsh had still not moved. They were almost clear.

Suddenly, he felt Cati slow and stop and sink to the ground once again with a moan. Two more Harsh stood less than a hundred metres ahead, blocking off all access to the bridge and approaching slowly.

Owen looked round wildly. They couldn't go back, they couldn't go forward, and they couldn't stay where they were. There was only one way out. He went towards the low, ruined river wall and peered over it. The water below was black and deep, but at least it would carry them away from the Harsh. He dragged Cati towards the wall.

The Harsh seemed to realise what he was doing and started to move faster. Owen lifted Cati on to the wall and looked down again. He felt sick. He knew that if he dropped Cati into the water, she would not be able to look after herself. She was too lost in fear. He heard a shout from the trees across the way. The bearded man from the Convoke was sitting astride the branch of a tree, shouting, and Owen knew he was telling them to jump into the water. But even summoning up all his strength, even feeling the frost stealing through his jacket and into his flesh, even with his new friend whimpering in his arms, Owen could not do it. And somehow from the knowledge that he could not do it, he drew some strength. He reached to the ground and found a large branch. Turning his back on the river, and pushing Cati behind him, he stood to face the Harsh.

Owen could feel the cold attention of the Harsh on him. And he heard a cold voice inside his head say a single word. *Mortmain.* Then, as he turned, one of the creatures opened the white maw where its mouth should have been and Owen was hit by a frozen blast of what felt like the coldest sleet he had ever experienced; sleet like frozen knives, cutting through his clothes with a noise like the howling of a terrible wind. Cati cried out. He flung the branch towards the Harsh and saw it turn in the air, freeze and splinter into a thousand pieces, and then he was driven away from the river.

Somehow, Owen managed to turn his back to the blast and wrap his arms around Cati's cold shoulders as the blast grew fiercer. He gasped for air, but it seemed too cold to breathe. He knew then that all was lost. And he felt deep calm settle over him. Then the blast stopped.

Owen lay on the ground panting for breath. It was seconds before he could turn his head to see what had happened. The Harsh were still in the same place, but standing in front of them was Pieta. She was about fifteen metres away and she carried the whip of light casually at her side. The Harsh towered over her, so that she looked small and frail, but Owen could see that she was smiling a bleak, dangerous smile. The hand at her side moved quickly. Faster than the eye could follow, the whip of light swung back behind her. Owen gasped as it uncoiled, loop after loop, making a sizzling, whistling noise as it opened out, a living thing of deadly power.

He saw Pieta adjust her stance and with unbelievable power and speed the whip flew forwards. She laughed as fifty metres of writhing energy whistled towards the Harsh, hissing as it cleaved the frozen air. The end of the whip stopped just short of the two creatures and, as the whip cracked, Owen had to cover his ears to protect them from the deafening sound which was followed by a flash of brilliant blue light that illuminated the whole riverbank. There was a smell like iron filings which stung his tongue and the back of his throat.

When Owen looked again he saw that the Harsh were floating slowly backwards, their intense white forms somehow dimmed. He scrambled to his feet. Cati's eyes were closed. She was breathing, but there was a coat of hoar frost in her hair and round her mouth. The whip cracked again. This time the Harsh dimmed and retreated. Owen saw that the way to the tree trunk across the river was clear. He lifted Cati and half ran, half staggered towards the riverbank. He had to run between Pieta and the Harsh, and for a moment he thought he heard their cold whispering, then the whip cracked once more, going over his head this time, the force of its uncoiling making him stagger.

He reached the bank. The bearded man was now astride the log and he reached out for Cati. Owen dropped the unconscious girl into the outstretched arms and, with an agility which belied his size, the man scrambled back across the tree trunk. Owen looked down at the water, shivering uncontrollably. He knew that he could not balance on the log.

Suddenly he was hit hard in the back. It was Pieta.

"Get across now," she hissed angrily. Looking back, he saw that the two groups of Harsh now stood together. This was too much even for Pieta. Owen felt the cold begin to stream towards them again and he scrambled on to the trunk, Pieta pushing him from behind. Owen threw himself forward and fell. He got up again, but this time he slipped. First his foot and then his hand and then his whole body was plunging towards the dark water. He screamed as his foot hit the water then felt Pieta grab one outflung hand. Effortlessly, she swung him back on to the log and pushed him forwards. Gasping and half blind from cold and terror, he fell off the end of the tree trunk and landed heavily on the ground.

Owen kept his eyes closed, allowing the fear to subside. His heart was beating wildly. When he finally opened his eyes he saw the Sub-Commandant, Chancellor and Contessa. There were others standing behind, but it was the still form of Cati that brought him to his feet.

"She will recover," Contessa said. "They attempted to freeze her, but they did not succeed."

"No thanks to him!" the long-haired man said angrily, stepping forward. "He took Cati across the river to deliver her into the hands of the Harsh."

"He tried to shield her from them, Samual," Pieta said, her voice ringing across the space between them. "She would now be frozen for ever if it was not for him."

"It's a trick," Samual said. "He's trying to fool you!"

"That is enough, Samual," Contessa said, and a dangerous light burned in her eyes. "The young man has just escaped with his life. Now is not the time."

"I saw what happened," Samual said slowly and deliberately. "I saw what happened when his foot touched the water! He couldn't hide the agony on his face."

No one said anything. None of them would look at Owen except the Sub-Commandant, who fixed him with a level, grey-eyed stare which revealed nothing.

Cati stirred. Her eyes seemed dulled and milky, and when she spoke her voice was weak and her breath hung in the air in frozen clouds, the way warm breath does in cold air.

"I... I... could not move. I was so scared. I followed him... I followed him to his mother's house. He carried me. He saved me."

Her head slumped back again. Contessa looked grimly satisfied, as if any question about Owen had been decisively answered. The Sub-Commandant swept Cati up into his arms and walked away swiftly. He did not look back.

"I must make up my mind about this," Chancellor said heavily. "I will sleep on it."

Samual looked as if he would say something more, but instead turned on his heel and stalked off into the darkness.

"Owen needs rest," Contessa said. "This has been the longest day of his young existence, Chancellor. He has been bereft and thrown into another world. His life has hung by a thread this past hour."

"All I did was look for my mother," Owen said, trying to keep his voice steady. "There's nothing wrong with that, is there?"

"No, Owen," Chancellor said, "but do you understand that we are all in great danger? None of us can do what we want, even if your mission is as important as looking for your mother. Do you understand?"

Owen nodded slowly. The cold breath of the Harsh was

still fresh in his head. He knew that this wasn't a dream. He shivered. No one had ever wanted to kill him before.

"He will want to go back to his Den," Contessa said, "but I don't think he should be on his own. He has enemies that he does not yet know about."

"I'll go with him," the bearded man said. "On my way back I can deal with the sentries that allowed the boy and the girl to walk right through the lines." He grasped Owen's hand. "My name is Rutgar, I am the Sergeant here, head of the military, such as it is. Come with me."

Owen felt Chancellor's eyes on him as Rutgar steered him towards the path away from the river. The journey back to the Den seemed endless, but each time he stumbled Rutgar caught his elbow. He was too tired to talk, but Rutgar seemed to understand this, although he muttered to himself under his breath as he walked, about the sentries who had allowed Owen and Cati to slip through their lines.

Rutgar knew exactly where the Den was. "There's not one stone of this riverbank I don't know," he said. "Do you think that this is the first time I've had to defend it? Go on and sleep. You'll be looked after tonight."

"I don't want to be watched," Owen said faintly. Rutgar studied him for a minute.

"All right then," he said. "My men will watch the paths around your Den – and they'd better watch them properly this time, to make sure nothing gets in and you don't get out again." He sounded angry, but as he spoke he clapped Owen on the back.

"Go in and get to sleep. You'll need your energy." Owen nodded quickly and ducked into the Den. Rutgar looked after him thoughtfully for a minute, then turned away.

In the Den, Owen collapsed on the old sofa. He pulled the sleeping bag over him and kept his clothes on. There was a cold feeling lurking in his bones, but before he could think about the Harsh and their icy terror, tiredness overcame him and he slipped into a deep, dreamless sleep.

Down at the river all was quiet. A sentry called out and another answered in the dark. They did not want to be caught out again. One of the sentries appeared at the end of the fallen log, examined it and walked on. All was still. Then a shape detached itself from the shadows underneath the trees on the Workhouse side of the river. Keeping low to the ground, the shape moved towards the trunk, looking at first like an animal and then like a human figure hunched under a cloak. It clambered on to the end of the log and then, moving in a fluid and seamless way, it crossed the river, slipped off the end of the log and disappeared into the field beyond. As it did so, a fine lace of ice formed along the edge of the river where the water met the bank. And as the figure disappeared with no more than a rustle into the darkness, there was a whispering noise as the ice melted and dissolved back into the black water.

CHAPTER SIX

Owen woke early the next morning and ran straight to the Workhouse without even a drink of water. He ran up the stairs and into the main hallway. Even though people were busy, moving with purpose, he saw more than one curious glance cast in his direction. He found the stairway that led to the kitchen and plunged downwards. When the stair opened out into the kitchen he found it calmer than the previous day. The great ovens were glowing and many huge pots were simmering on them. He saw Contessa and he half walked, half ran over to her. She turned to him. Her face was grave, but she spoke before he did.

"Cati will recover, Owen. I think you saved her. But only just. I had to put her back to sleep in the Starry. She was frozen to the very core of her being. I am suprised that you were not. Perhaps you have a special resistance."

"I was cold," he said. "Freezing."

"The cold they emit is not just physical, Owen. It freezes the very quick of you. Your soul. You're very strong."

"Strong," said a voice. "You'd be good and strong maybe. But maybe they had fair cause not to freeze you. Them ones could have had cause to spare you."

Owen turned to see a tall, thin youth with a solemn face. His trousers were torn and on top he wore something that might have been a shirt at some time, but now was so ripped and dirty that it could have been anything, and was certainly no protection against the cold morning air. When Owen looked down he saw that the boy's feet were bare.

"Wesley," Contessa said sharply, "I won't have malicious gossip repeated in my kitchen."

"It's what people do say," Wesley said, but he grinned in a mischievous way and stuck out his hand. Owen took it and Wesley shook his hand vigorously.

"Wesley," he said. "I do be one of the Raggies. I brung fish for the lady Contessa."

Owen looked down for the first time. There were perhaps twenty boxes of fish on the ground around them, bringing with them a smell of the sea.

"I have an idea," Contessa said. "There are those who wish to ask you about last night, and their thoughts are not kindly for the moment. You would be better out of the way. Would you take him to the Hollow with you, Wesley?"

73

"I will, lady."

"I want to see Cati," Owen said.

"She is asleep," Contessa said, suddenly seeming taller, her eyes glittering with a dangerous light. "Are you not listening?"

"Come on," Wesley said cheerfully, pulling at Owen's sleeve, "before the lady do devour the two of us." Contessa didn't say anything and her eyes were like stone, but as they walked away with a chirpy "Cheerio, lady!" from Wesley, Owen thought he saw the ghost of a smile tugging at the corner of her mouth.

Wesley walked quickly, even in his bare feet, and Owen had trouble keeping up. They left the Workhouse and Wesley started on a path which followed the river down to the sea, curving towards the town and the harbour. At first, Owen fired questions at Wesley, but the boy only turned and grinned at him and pressed on even harder. They came to the place where a new concrete bridge had crossed the road between the town and his house, but there was no bridge and no road. Owen climbed up the riverbank. Despite everything he had been told, he still expected to see the familiar streets of the town.

The town was there, but with a sinking feeling Owen realised that it looked as if it had been abandoned for a hundred years. The houses and shops were roofless and windows gaped blank and sightless. The main street was a strip of matted grass and small trees, and ivy and other creepers wrapped themselves round broken telegraph poles.

Where new buildings had once stood there was bare ground or the protruding foundations of older buildings. The rusty skeleton of what had once been a bus sat at right angles in the middle of the street. A gust of wind stirred the heads of the grasses and the trees, and blew through the bare roofs of the houses with a melancholy whistling sound.

Owen slipped back down the side of the bridge. The town was starting to crumble back into time, taking with it the memory of the people who had once walked its streets. He remembered what Cati had said about living things growing young, but the things made by man decaying as time reeled backwards.

"Never pay no mind," Wesley said gently. "That's just the way it is now. All them things can be put right, if we put old Ma Time back the way she should be, running like a big clock going forward. You just stick with us. We'll put all yon people back in their minutes and hours, and Ma Time, she'll put us boys back to sleep again. Come on," he said, lifting Owen to his feet, "let's get on down to the harbour."

This time Wesley walked alongside Owen. The water in the river got deeper as they approached the harbour and Owen found himself veering away from it, which Wesley noticed.

"That's what I heard," he said, with something like satisfaction, "that you can't abide the water."

"Who told you that?" demanded Owen.

"They was all talking about it," Wesley said, "that the new

boy, Time's recruit, did fear the water."

"I don't like it too much," Owen said.

Wesley rounded on him sharply, his face close to Owen's, his voice suddenly low and urgent.

"Do not be saying that to anyone. No one. Do you not know? I reckon not. The Harsh can neither touch nor cross any water – not fresh nor salt – and the touch of it revolts them unless they can first make ice of it. If any see you afeared of water, they will think you Harsh or a creature of the Harsh."

Owen remembered how the long-haired man, Samual, had reacted when he had seen Owen's foot touch the water. "I think they know already," he said slowly.

"Then it will be hard on you," Wesley said. "it will be fierce hard."

"You don't think I'm one of the Harsh, do you?" Owen said. His voice trembled slightly, but Wesley just threw his head back and laughed.

"Harsh. You? No, I don't think you're Harsh. I think you're like one of us, the Raggies. You been abandoned and the world treats you bad, and even though you ain't as thin as Raggies, I do know a hunger when I see it."

* * *

Owen didn't expect the harbour to look the same and he wasn't disappointed. The metal cranes were twisted and rusted. Most of the sheds had gone and the fish-processing factory was a roofless shell. The boats were still tied up, but it was a ghost fleet. The metal-hulled boats lay half sunk in oily water. The wooden boats had fared better and some of them still floated, but the paint had long faded from them, and their metal fittings had all gone.

"It's like they've been abandoned for twenty years," Owen said.

"Longer than that," said Wesley. "Ma Time, she goes back more fast than she goes forward."

Thinking about time made Owen's head hurt. He looked back the way they had come. He could see the slateless roofs of the town, then a white mist where the Harsh camp was, and beyond that, the mountains that hemmed the town into this little corner of land, their tops white with snow. He realised that Wesley was making for the area of rundown warehouses that was always referred to as the Hollow. As they got closer, going out on to what Owen knew as the South Pier, but which now seemed to be a causeway over dry land, he saw that the buildings had not changed at all. There were five or six stone-built warehouses with empty windows in the front of them. Owen thought he could see rags or cloths in each window. As he looked, many of the rags started to stir, and then he realised that each one was a child or young person dressed the same way as Wesley. A shout went up from them and Owen thought that there was dismay in the sound. As they closed in rapidly, he saw that they were looking out to sea. Wesley said something under his breath and climbed the parapet of the South Pier. Owen followed.

At the top, Wesley stood staring out to sea, his hand shading his eyes. About half a mile from shore Owen could see a boat, but it was not like any he had ever seen before. It was an elongated shape, copper-coloured, but with high sides that curved in at the top, and a single tall mast with what looked like a small crow's nest at the masthead, topped with one of the blank black flags he had seen at the Workhouse. In each side of the boat there were five round holes, and in each hole there was a long, spindly, coppery stick, too long and thin and delicate, it seemed, to be an oar. But as Owen watched, the sticks started to beat violently and the whole craft was suddenly lifted on them and propelled at speed across the top of the water. Owen thought it looked like the insects you saw on ponds, the ones that walked on the surface of the water. The craft splashed back into the water, the sticks beating slowly this time, then it rose and shot forward again.

"Look!" Wesley shouted. Owen followed his outstretched arm. High in the sky above the strange boat, Owen saw three shapes. At first he thought that they were birds then he realised they were much bigger. One of them detached itself from the others and dived towards the boat, swooping down in great circles, and Owen saw it was an aircraft of sorts, with two impossibly long and delicate wings that beat slowly. The body of the aircraft was like a very fine cage with a long fin at the back, and at the centre sat the figure of a man, crouched over a set of controls and staring down at the boat through huge oval goggles.

As the craft wheeled over the boat, the vast feathery wings glittered with a metallic sheen. Then a blaze of blue light shot from the body of the flying craft and struck the water beside the boat. There was an immense sizzle, and the boat disappeared momentarily in a cloud of steam and spray. When it reappeared Owen saw ragged children clambering frantically over the superstructure of the vessel. Baskets of fish were being passed up at great speed from the depths of the hold and flung over the side. Another of the flying craft swooped on the boat, closer this time. Owen felt sure that the flash of light would hit it, but at the last moment, the beating oars raised the hull from the water and flung the boat forward with such violence that it swerved to one side, almost out of control. Once again it emerged from a cloud of steam and spray, but this time there was a long burned streak down its side, and one of the oars hung broken and useless. When it made to move forward again, it began to slew to that side.

"They're dead, dead to the world," Wesley said softly. "They cannot make it ashore." His face was white with fear.

But then a strange thing happened. Owen became aware of a great shrieking. The water around the delicate vessel was covered with the fish that had been thrown overboard and seabirds were converging on the unexpected meal, thousands of them it seemed – herring gulls, black-headed gulls, black cormorants. Within a minute there were so many gulls that Owen could barely see the boat. The spindly aircraft were buffeted in the air by the beating wings of so many birds, and then they too became invisible. More and more gulls blanketed the ocean. Owen could not see the boat, but it seemed that it was still under attack. There were flashes of blue from within the swirling flock and there were dead seabirds among the thousands that squabbled for the floating fish.

Minutes passed and then a great cheer went up from the anxious children onshore. On the very edge of the flock of seabirds, the prow and then the rest of the boat emerged. There were children standing on its deck, some of them sitting along its rail. Many of them were very young, pale and frightened, but the tall, freckled girl at the tiller looked defiant.

The oars beating slowly, the boat swung in against the quay and the girl leapt lightly on to it. Wesley went over to her. Owen followed, hanging back a little. He could see the long scar running down the side of the boat.

"They near got us," the freckled girl said.

"Birds saved your hide," said Wesley.

"That was a good idea, throwing out the fish," Owen said. The girl looked at him curiously.

"That him?" she said to Wesley. Wesley nodded. The girl stuck out a hand. Her eyes were a curious greenish colour and she was wearing oily overalls. "Silkie's my name, and I only threw out the fish for to save weight. I never thought about the birds."

"Is she broke?" Wesley said, looking anxiously at the boat.

"She's all right," Silkie said. "She has a bit of a burn on her, but she'll sail again. The little ones is scared though. Them Planemen was never that brave before; they come pretty close."

"I do think the Harsh is stronger this time and they do push Johnston harder."

"Johnston?" Owen said. "The man who has the scrapyard? I was playing there once and he chased me with dogs."

"It's a good thing he chased you with nothing worse," Wesley said. "Johnston is a terrible cruel man."

"A man though," Owen said. "Not one of the… the Harsh?"

"No," said Silkie. "You know the way that the Sub-Commandant is the Watcher, staying awake through the years until the Harsh return and it is time to wake the others to fight?"

"I think so," Owen said.

"Well, Johnston is a Watcher too, except that he watches for the Harsh and makes sure that all is ready for their return."

"His own men sleep in their Starry and he wakes them for

the Harsh," Wesley said, "The Planemen you seen attacking – they're his men."

"I'm starving," Silkie said.

"You're always starving," said Wesley with a grin, "but you do deserve something to eat for the fright you got from them Planemen. Come on."

Wesley led them into the nearest of the buildings. The ground floor was completely open with a big hearth at one end where a fire of driftwood crackled, a sweet smell of burning wood drifting through the room. A long table with benches on either side stood in the middle. There were children everywhere, all of them dressed poorly. Some of the smaller ones walked straight up to Owen and stared at him with large solemn eyes. The older ones climbed quickly up and down the ladder which led upstairs, or perched in the high windowsills.

Despite all the young people milling about, Owen realised that there was a sense of order. The table was being set with flat wooden plates and food was being carried in. Within minutes all the Raggies had seated themselves round the table and the older ones were serving food. Owen was put at the top of the table, beside Wesley and Silkie. Every plate was full, but no one moved to touch it. It wasn't until Wesley pulled his plate towards him that the children grabbed their own and began to eat hungrily. Owen realised that he too was starving. There was fish and fried potatoes. He tried them and thought they tasted like fish and chips. The noise in the room died to a murmur as everyone concentrated on the food in front of them, eating rapidly with both hands.

Within minutes, every plate was empty. While the younger children carried out the crude wooden plates, Wesley, Silkie and Owen moved over to sit on the rough stone of the fireplace. As they did so, others sat on the floor in front of them or gathered on the ladders and windowsills. The sun shone through the windows and dust motes floated in the beams. Owen felt warm and full and surprisingly contented. He realised that the children were watching Wesley expectantly.

"We near lost Boat today," said Wesley. "Planemen near got her." No one in the crowd spoke but Owen could feel the wave of dismay and concern that ran through them, almost like a shiver.

"Silkie done well and brung her home," Wesley said. Once again Owen could feel the emotion of the silent children, but this time there was relief and gratitude to Silkie. She smiled and went pink with pride under her freckles. Owen realised that the children could make their feelings be known to each other, but without saying anything, almost like a crowd at a football match.

"I think we need to arm Boat," Wesley went on, "for if she is sunk, we are all sunk."

This time the feelings of the children were confused. Some seemed angry, others resigned, others seemed to feel a deep,

deep sadness. Wesley held up his hand.

"I know that it is against us and the Code of Boat to use weapons, but we done so before and now we need it more than ever. All our crew could've died out there today. This is what I thinks. I thinks we give magno bows to Uel and Mervyn, and them two boys go out every time with Boat. We can trust them, though it is a hard enough ask for them two boys."

Children moved away from two tall, solemn boys standing in their midst. Owen felt that the crowd was questioning them with love and concern, asking them if they wanted to do this thing. "Brothers," Silkie whispered in his ear. "There used to be three, but one of them got killed in fighting with Johnston. They don't like fighting. That's why Wesley is asking them. He knows they'll only fire if they have to."

The two brothers looked at each other before nodding slowly. Owen could feel the relief and approval in the room. The children round the two boys touched them on the shoulders, took their hands, and they smiled shyly back. Wesley removed a wooden box from an alcove in the fireplace. He unlocked the ancient lock on it with a key that hung from a chain round his neck. Owen saw that the box was full of small bows, like crossbows. Wesley removed two and carefully locked the box again. He brought it back to the alcove then returned with a smaller box which he unlocked with the same key. As he did so, Owen examined the crossbows. They looked very old and deadly, made of age-darkened wood with a brass-coloured metal spring, the wood engraved here and there with silver writing too small to read. Wesley had meanwhile removed handfuls of crossbow bolts from the other box. The bolts were brass arrows, about the length of Owen's forearm, and instead of a point, they had a small glass vial filled with a tiny amount of the blue substance that Owen had seen everywhere in the Workhouse. Owen decided that he would ask about it later.

Wesley called Uel and Mervyn forward and gave them each a bow and a handful of bolts. The boys seemed reluctant to touch them, but when Wesley told them to make sure that the crossbows were working properly, they handled them in a way that left no doubt that they knew what they were doing.

The children started to drift away. Wesley said he was going outside to look at the damage to Boat. Silkie asked Owen if he would like to look around. He followed her up one ladder and then another, leading from room to room, most of them taken up with sleeping quarters. There were wooden beds and coverings stitched together from strange, rough materials that Owen did not recognise, with drawings of stars and crescent moons on them. The rooms shared by younger children had bright drawings on the walls and wooden toys which looked as if they had been made by the older ones. There were horses and doll's houses and many different versions of Boat in many sizes. Looking at Boat made Owen think of the question he had.

"You know the blue stuff you see everywhere," he said. "What is it?"

"Oh, you mean magno," replied Silkie. "I can't tell you just what it is for I don't know, but I can show you what it does."

She reached into her pocket and took out a small brass box. Inside was a little piece of the blue material held by two sturdy brass bolts. Silkie pointed it towards a lump of iron in the corner which looked as if it came from a ship and would take four men to lift. She gripped the box tightly. Owen saw the metal begin to rock backwards and forwards, then start to slide towards them, slowly at first, then faster and faster, and at the same time Silkie was drawn across the floor, her shoes slipping on it, almost out of control until it seemed that she must collide with the heavy metal. Quickly, she slipped the lid back on the box and the lump of iron stopped abruptly in the middle of the floor.

"It's a magnet!" Owen said excitedly. "You do everything with magnetism!"

"I don't know,' Silkie said, frowning. "All I know is that it is magno. It does lights. It makes Boat work."

At the top of the first building they crossed a makeshift ramp which led to the next building, Owen trying not to look down. Silkie opened a door at the far end and they stepped off the ramp. It was dark and it took Owen's eyes a little time to get used to it. After a while he saw that they were standing in a room which resembled the Starry at the Workhouse, where he had seen all the beds and the people still sleeping. This room was much smaller, but there was the same pale gleam, as if of stars, from the ceiling. The beds were smaller because these were for children and young people, but, as in the Starry, some of them were still occupied, and on each pillow there rested a blue cornflower. Sign of remembering, Cati had said. In the corner two girls were sleeping. They looked like sisters. Silkie stopped by one bed. A small boy slept in it. He had the same sharp, freckled face as Silkie. She brushed his hair back from his face with a sad smile.

"My brother," she said. "He never was good at getting up in the morning." Owen could see that she was trying to make a joke of it, but there were tears in her eyes. "Come on out of here," she said gruffly.

As he hurried towards the door, Owen stumbled slightly and his hand brushed against the forehead of a small girl. He realised that he had not expected the skin to feel warm. He looked down at her. The little face looked pinched and careworn. He wondered what she was dreaming about, or if she dreamed about anything.

"Come on," Silkie said shortly, and he hurried after her.

Silkie brought him up to the roof of the building. Far below they could see that Wesley and others were busy repairing the broken oar on Boat, if oar it was, thought Owen, remembering the way the craft had almost flown across the water. The wind was cold, blowing hard from the north, but they sat in the lee of the parapet where the sun had warmed the stone.

"Where do you come from?" Owen asked.

"Me?"

"No. I mean the Raggies. Where are all the adults?"

"The story we tell is this. That there was a man called Smith who was put in charge of all these children. And each child was given a gold coin for their future. But Smith was a bad man. He wanted the money for himself. He abandoned the children and took their money, leaving us on this shore for ever."

She spoke in a sing-song voice so that Owen thought that this was the explanation that was given to the younger children by the olders ones. He felt sorry for them, losing their parents, being all alone in the world. Then he realised that he too was alone.

They sat on the roof until it started to rain. The rain was icy, blown in by a north wind which had suddenly sprung up. Looking down on the causeway, Owen saw that the waves were now pounding against it. Peering through the spray, he saw a small figure darting across the causeway. It was Cati. They went down and found her in the kitchen, dripping wet.

"You shouldn't be here," said Owen. "You're supposed to be sleeping, Contessa said—"

"Contessa's great," Cati interrupted, "but she's a bit of a mother hen. I was bored to the back teeth."

"She said you were frozen," Owen said slowly. For the first time the hint of a shadow crossed his friend's face.

"I was... I think," she said slowly, then more brightly, "but I'm going to freeze now for definite if you keep me standing out here!" Owen jumped out of the way as she darted into the big room and went to the fire. She stood warming her hands, steam beginning to rise from her clothes.

"They're looking everywhere for you, by the way," she said. "Far as I can see, you're in big trouble." She seemed to relish this idea.

"Why?" he said. "It was Contessa who told me to come here."

"That explains it," she said. "Samual's the one who is stirring up all the trouble. Keeps saying you're one of the Harsh. Got some people believing him too."

"Why do people keep saying that?" Owen said. "You don't think I'm one of the Harsh, do you?"

"Me? No. You've got a face for a start; a fairly ugly one it has to be said, but a face all the same. I never saw one of the Harsh with a face before."

"That's a relief at least," Owen said sarcastically.

"You see," Cati continued, ignoring him, "Contessa hates Samual so she's not going to tell him where you are."

"How did *you* know where I was?"

"I heard Contessa telling my father. They thought I was still asleep. Besides, I more or less knew you'd find a bunch of scruffs like yourself."

"What am I going to do?"

'Not to worry. You've got Contessa on your side, and my father. And Pieta likes you for some strange reason. Pieta doesn't like many people. It doesn't help that there hasn't been any sign of the Harsh all day. They're up to something. We'll have a talk with my father when we get back tonight."

"You'll be going nowhere tonight," Wesley said, coming in. He seemed completely unaware that he was soaked through and that his hands and feet were blue with cold. "Look."

They went to the door. The causeway was now almost completely under water, wave upon wave crashing in great foaming bursts over the rock.

"High tide and the storm," Wesley said. "You'd best stay here tonight."

"Contessa…" Cati began, alarmed, then stopped and shrugged. "I've only known you for two days" she said to Owen, "and you've already got me into more trouble than in the whole of the rest of my life." She turned to Wesley. "What time's dinner? I'm starving."

Dinner consisted of lobster and the same kind of potatoes Owen had eaten that afternoon. Once again, the children waited for Wesley to begin. After the meal was over, they gathered round the fireplace, the little children playing games, the older ones talking together. It was cosy in the big room with strong wooden shutters closed against the howling wind, the firelight casting flickering shadows on the walls. Wesley started to tell Cati about the attack on Boat. Owen left them and slipped over beside Silkie who was braiding a piece of rope with strands of what looked like dried seaweed.

"Tell me more about… what did you call it? Magno?"

"Why do you ask me?" Silkie said. "There are others who can tell you more."

"Who?"

"Dr Diamond could tell you."

"Who is he?"

"Dr Diamond works the Skyward. He knows about things."

"What things?"

"Just things. The proper places for things and what happens to things and where magno comes from and where time goes to." It sounded as if Silkie was reciting something she had been taught.

"So he makes magno?"

"Nobody makes magno," Silkie said slowly and

patiently, as if she had taken an idiot in hand through the kindness of her heart. Owen thought that when he got back to the Workhouse he would keep his eyes peeled for this Dr Diamond.

After an hour or so, Wesley stood up and clapped his hands. The younger children formed into groups, with an older child at their head.

"He puts everyone to bed," Cati whispered. "We'd better follow."

Wesley said goodnight to each of the Raggies by name, ruffling the hair of the youngest. As they moved off, Owen could hear the low murmur of the oldest child's voice as she began to tell a story.

The whole process took more than an hour, by which time some of the younger children seemed to be asleep on their feet, and Owen was beginning to feel his own eyelids grow heavy. He had started to wonder whether his encounter with the Harsh had drained more enegy out of him that he had thought. At last they reached an empty room and Wesley ushered them in.

"Sleep well," he said solemnly. "May old Ma Time bear thee gently till morning."

"Night," Cati said, stifling a yawn.

"Goodnight," Owen said. Wesley grinned at him and patted his arm.

A tiny piece of magno in a glass case on the wall cast a dim light over the room. There were two beds in it. Cati jumped straight into one.

"I can hardly see I'm so tired," she said, yawning again. Owen climbed into the other bed and he slipped his clothes off under the blankets. The mattress was a little hard and the bedding a little scratchy, but he was too tired to care. Besides, the room was warm and the thick walls and shutters closed out the howl of the wind and the noise of the raging sea. He lay still for a moment. Cati's breathing was slow and even.

"Cati?"

"What?" she said sleepily.

"Time is going backwards, isn't that right?"

"Yes."

"Well... how do we make it go again?"

"The Puissance," she replied.

"The what?"

"The Puissance. The Great Machine in the North makes the Puissance and the Puissance makes time go back. It has to be stopped."

Owen waited for a moment, listening to the distant howl of the wind.

"How do we do that?" he asked eventually, but Cati's only answer was a gentle snore. Owen put his head down on the rough pillow. Images from his old life came into his head. His school. His old bedroom. The guitar that he had been so fond of. But everything seemed such a long time ago and strangely seemed almost *dusty* in his mind. He remembered the old photograph his mother had carried around. He'd been a member of a family then, a happy, smiling family. If only things could be like that again, just once. But the photograph was lost. Things could never be the same. A wave of tiredness rushed over him and soon he too was asleep.

The wind could not be heard in the Starry far above their heads. The breasts of the children rose and fell imperceptibly, lost in the sleep of centuries. It was warm, for the temperature in the Starry did not change. It was quiet, because the sounds of the outside world did not penetrate the thick stone walls. And still they slept, dreaming who knew what dreams. They slept, except for one child. The little girl whose head had been touched by Owen. Her eyes were open, gleaming gently in the darkness.

CHAPTER SEVEN

Owen was woken by a hand on his shoulder, shaking him insistently. It was Wesley.

"Message from the Sub-Commandant," Wesley said urgently. "Owen's got to go to Dr Diamond. Samual's asking you be arrested."

"What will Dr Diamond do?" Owen said, sitting up and trying to put his trousers on under the sheet, aware that Cati was watching him with an amused expression.

"The people trust Dr Diamond," she said. "If he says you are who you say you are, then Samual won't dare go against him. Hurry up!"

When they got downstairs, Owen noticed a small figure standing stock still by the fireplace, half obscured by Wesley. He moved to the side to see better.

"Is that...?" he said.

"The girl from the Starry," Wesley said. "She must have wakened some time last night. She was standing there when we came down this morning. Haven't been able to get a word out of her. I'm not sure, but I have a notion that this is the first waking she's had for many a year."

The little girl stood perfectly still. Her feet were bare and the dress she wore was threadbare. Her pinched little features were solemn and unmoving.

"She looks like she needs somebody to pick her up and hug her," Cati whispered. Owen knew what she meant, yet neither of them made a move towards her.

"There is a fierce need there," said Wesley, frowning, "but I cannot work out what it is." He did notice, however, that as they moved about getting ready to leave, the little girl's eyes followed Owen everywhere. And when they crossed the causeway, Owen turned to see her standing at the window, her large eyes, so dark they seemed almost bruised, still followed him.

When they got to the Workhouse there was tension in the air, groups of men hurrying towards the river looking grim. Pieta was walking up from the river with the magno whip coiled at her waist. When she saw them she gave Cati a sardonic wink and blew a kiss in Owen's direction. He felt his face turning red and Pieta laughed as she strode past him.

"I don't know why she has to be so unkind," Cati muttered.

"I think she's just sad inside about something," Owen said.

"Since when did you become the big expert on women?" Cati said, a little crossly. "Come on. I have to see Contessa."

Before Owen could answer, she was off racing through the big doors. He ran after her. They crashed through the kitchen door together, then tumbled on to the floor, laughing. When they looked up they saw Contessa standing over them, watching with a calm, measured look which made both feel mildly embarrassed. They picked themselves up from the floor, brushing off their clothes.

"I'm glad to see that you're both alive and obviously none the worse for your experiences the other night." She took Cati's face in her hands and looked long and hard into the girl's eyes. Then she took a small metal rod from her pocket. "Open your mouth."

Contessa slipped the rod under Cati's tongue and waited for a moment before taking it out and looking at it. Owen could see fine markings on it and realised that it was a thermometer. Contessa seemed to look at it for a long time.

"Your temperature is now a little lower than other people's, Cati. It will stay that way for the rest of your life. You can't be assailed by the Harsh like that without consequences."

"Does it matter?" Owen asked, suddenly anxious for his friend.

"Physically, not really. But in the mind... the soul, I suppose, who knows? You can expect dreams of terrible cold, feelings of emptiness..." Contessa's voice trailed away. She shook her head and wrapped her arms around her shoulders as if she suddenly felt cold.

"You are to see Dr Diamond," she said to Owen. "Perhaps you had better go straightaway. Morning is a good time to see him. Sometimes, later on, his head gets… congested." Cati giggled.

"Go on," Contessa said kindly, "I don't think you have anything to worry about."

"Where are we going?" Owen asked when they got out of the kitchen.

"To the Nab," Cati said. "Dr Diamond works in the Skyward. You'll like him. He's very intelligent. Although sometimes things get a bit confused."

"Confused in what way?" asked Owen suspiciously.

"You'll see," Cati said with a grin, skipping ahead of him before he could ask any more questions.

It was a long climb to the Skyward, not helped by the way the Nab groaned and swayed alarmingly every time there was a gust of wind. Once they got halfway up, Owen could see the other side of the river. Or rather he couldn't see it: the whole area was shrouded in a cold, white mist. He could also see how the Workhouse defences had been strengthened. More trenches had been dug right up to the river, and all approaches from the river to the Workhouse seemed to have been sealed.

They eventually reached the top of the Nab. It couldn't

come soon enough for Owen, who was starting to feel seasick from the swaying of the slender tower. They stepped on to the broad platform on which the Skyward stood. The glass walls gleamed softly. Peering through the glass, Owen could make out instrument cases, strange, spindly machines, all shape and manner of objects, and in the middle of the room a long spike pointing down with what appeared to be a clock hanging from it.

"Are we going in?" he said.

"We have to wait until the doors are lined up," said Cati.

Owen suddenly noticed that the contents of the Skyward were in a different position from the last time he had looked. Then he realised that although the outside glass wall had not moved, the interior was slowly revolving. There was a door in the outer wall and one in the inner wall which was turning so that the two doors would be lined up.

"You have to move quickly," Cati said. She grasped the door handle which was shaped like a long, thin hand with narrow, brass fingers. "Ready?" There was a loud click as the two doors lined up, Cati swung the outer door open and hauled Owen through behind her. They fell on their knees inside and the doors clicked shut behind them. Owen picked himself up. He was getting used to being thrown around by Cati.

He looked about him. He could see delicate instruments in cloth-lined cases. Copper piping flowed round the room in complicated and delicate patterns, but much of the machinery seemed to have been scavenged and put to some other purpose. Liquid flowed through a glass pipe into an old vacuum cleaner which turned itself on with a self-important cough every few minutes and spewed warm, green-coloured liquid into a glass jar. Tiny plants grew under controlled conditions on an old record turntable that was revolving very slowly. A set of heavy levers coming out of the floor looked as if they belonged in a railway signalman's hut. A chair which looked like an old aeroplane seat was bolted to the floor in the middle of them. Two chrome hubcaps set on spindles whirled on some unknown business.

As Owen stared, he noticed a man standing in front of what appeared to be an ordinary domestic fridge, except that it was producing extraordinarily cold conditions. The man was of average height with long black hair fastened at the back. He was wearing blue overalls like a garage mechanic. The overalls were tied in the middle with a leather tool belt, except the tools in this one were of all sorts of shapes and sizes and mostly looked as if they had just been invented. The man was wearing huge leather gauntlets and holding a long-stemmed red rose in his right hand. Cautiously, he extended the hand into the interior of the fridge from which cold vapours wreathed to the ceiling. There was a vicious crackling hiss and he jumped backwards, slamming the fridge door. He looked down at the flower, which had been turned into an ice rose, cold and glassy. The man smelled it then yelled "Ouch!" as it touched his nose. He began to rub the place vigorously as if there was a danger of frostbite.

Cati cleared her throat. The man whirled round. He had strange, sloping green eyes, which were watering profusely. He stared at Cati then broke into a smile, still rubbing at his nose.

"Hello, Dr Diamond," she said.

"Again you see to good it's Cati, hello," Dr Diamond said.

Owen stared. What had the man just said?

"This is my friend Owen," Cati said.

"You about me telling been they've. You meet to pleased I'm, yes Oh."

"What's he saying?" Owen whispered furiously.

"Excuse me, Dr Diamond," Cati said kindly, "I think you're talking backwards again."

"I am? I mean, am I? Yes, of course you're right, Cati. I'm thinking in backtime."

"It's the time going backwards," Cati told Owen in a loud whisper. "He thinks that by going backwards he's going forwards, if you know what I mean. He does it when he gets a bit flustered." Owen didn't have a clue what she meant by this.

"I'd give you the rose," Dr Diamond said apologetically, "except it's super-frozen now, take a month or two to thaw out, and there's a danger of frostbite in the mean time." He rubbed at his nose again then turned to Owen.

"Now, young man, Chancellor sent me a note about you.

I'm supposed to have a look at you or something. Where is that note? I put it down somewhere five minutes ago. Or am I going to put it down in five minutes' time?"

"He's always trying to work out the way that time works going backwards," Cati whispered. "He says the more you think about it, the more complicated it gets."

As Dr Diamond looked for the note, Owen examined the big clock in the centre of the room. At least he thought it was a clock, although it wasn't like any clock he had ever seen. It had five faces all looking different ways, and each face had one hand on it, each hand moving at a different speed. But the hands didn't keep moving at the same speed all the time. Sometimes, one of them would speed up and go really fast, then slow down. Sometimes, they would all be moving at different speeds. Cati started to say something to him, but he hushed her. He didn't think his head would take any more complicated theories about time.

Dr Diamond found the note from Chancellor. He read it and then stood, lost in thought for a moment. Then in two quick strides he was in front of Owen, face to face, staring at the boy with his intense green eyes. Owen felt himself flinch, as if he was staring into the eyes of a fierce hawk. Dr Diamond's arms were holding Owen's upper arms. Owen remembered that Contessa had said the doctor was very intelligent, and he realised that she did not mean intelligent like somebody brainy in school, but something far more; an intelligence that was like a deep, deep well, something dark and mysterious and bottomless.

"Let me see," Dr Diamond said. "Water, yes. Afraid of it. Harsh try very hard to kill Cati. Understand that. Try very hard not to kill Owen. Mystery there, but perhaps, if…" He let go of Owen suddenly and whirled round to a desk, seizing a pencil and a piece of paper. He wrote furiously for several minutes. Owen, looking over his shoulder, saw columns of figures and theorems and equations composed of complicated mathematical symbols. Finally, Dr Diamond stopped and examined his calculations.

"I think I comprehend…" he said slowly. "Well, at least that which is open to comprehension. I think I know a little more about your friend, Cati."

"He's not Harsh, is he?" Cati said quickly.

"No…" Dr Diamond said slowly, "but not everyone will accept my word for that. And that does not mean that there isn't danger. However, Chancellor's letter simply asked me to work out if you are Harsh and that is what I have done. Now. Your turn, young Owen. Ask *me* a question for a change."

Owen thought for a minute. He didn't want to hear some complicated theory on time that would make him look stupid when he didn't understand. "What's magno?" he blurted out.

"Ah, magno," Dr Diamond said, casting a shrewd look at Owen. "Magno is the Force that Binds."

"The Force that Binds," repeated Owen, trying to sound intelligent.

"The Force that Binds, that propels, that powers, that pulls, that pushes, that casts light in the darkness, that defends..."

"Is it the same as magnetism?"

"A very astute question," Dr Diamond said, looking at Owen thoughtfully. Owen returned the look, not feeling very astute at all.

"Yes, Owen, it is very like magnetism. But I can see your head is getting sore with trying to understand things. My advice is to just try to understand one thing a day. It's easier on the brain..." Dr Diamond paused suddenly and cocked his head, as if he had heard something.

"What is it, Dr Diamond?" asked Cati.

"You don't happen to know if Johnston's been over the river to talk about a truce yet, do you?"

"I don't think so," Cati said.

"Well then, he is on his way. Let us go out and have a look."

They followed Dr Diamond out on to the balcony. He was right. As they looked across the river, they could see that the white mist had parted slightly, and through the mist the man that Owen had known as the scrapyard owner, Johnston, strode on to the riverbank. He had not changed from the day that he had set his dogs on Owen to chase him from the scrapyard, and the boy shivered at the memory.

Johnston's face was big and fleshy with small eyes, red-black hair slicked back and huge sideburns which almost met at his chin. He was tall and solid as if he had been carved out of a single block of stone. Owen was used to seeing him in blue overalls, but this time the overalls had white epaulettes on the shoulders – obviously part of a uniform. Johnston surveyed the riverbank with a calm, derisive look. He carried no weapon, but behind him, in the mist, Owen was aware that there were more men, perhaps twenty in all, each dressed like Johnston and with the same massive sideburns. Owen counted as the mist swirled around them.

"Look," Cati said. Rutgar stepped out from the trees on the other side of the river. Although they were too far away to hear what was going on, it seemed that the two men were negotiating. Rutgar turned away suddenly and disappeared into the trees. Johnston waited.

"He is looking for a parley with us," Dr Diamond said.

"What's a parley?" asked Owen.

"A talk," Cati said, "probably about us surrendering or something."

"I would imagine so," Dr Diamond said.

"*I* won't surrender to him," Cati said fiercely, clenching her fists, "not even if he has a thousand Harsh over there."

"I didn't think you would," said Dr Diamond, patting her shoulder in a kindly manner. "Nevertheless, Chancellor and the others might reckon it their duty to consider whatever offer is made. That didn't take long."

Rutgar had come back. He beckoned to Johnston. The big man sprang on to the fallen tree like a cat and ran lightly across.

"Where is he going?" asked Cati, sounding as if she couldn't believe that Rutgar had let Johnston across.

"He is going to meet our leaders at the Convoke," Dr Diamond said, "and they'll give him safe passage to do it."

"He'll see our defences!" said Cati.

"He has seen them anyway," Dr Diamond said. Then in a meaningful way, "I know that if there was some way I could get in to see what was going on at the Convoke, it would be very interesting."

Cati looked at Owen. "Somewhere to watch... come on!" she hissed. She turned to Dr Diamond. "It's been great to see you again, doctor."

"And you, Cati," he said with grave courtesy, "and to meet your new friend. I would be grateful if you would bring him back to talk about magno and other things."

"Unless... unless I've already been here in backtime," Owen said, feeling he was getting a grasp on things.

"Yes," said Dr Diamond, with a twinkle in his eye. "Yes, indeed."

"Come *on*!" said Cati.

Dr Diamond suddenly looked thoughtful. He produced a

book which looked to be full of important equations from one pocket and a battered notebook from the other. He read rapidly then started to scribble in the notebook.

"See you soon, Dr Diamond," Owen said, but the scientist and philosopher seemed to be totally wrapped up in what he was doing, and didn't answer. Cati grabbed Owen's arm and started to haul him towards the ladder. Dr Diamond did not look up. But as they were on the fourth flight down a head appeared over the rail at the top.

"Don't forget what I saw about coming back," he shouted, and Owen waved back.

It took them fifteen minutes to get to the secret hiding place looking down on the Convoke. At one stage Cati saw Samual stalking along the path and hauled Owen into the bushes to hide. Samual was muttering to himself as he walked along.

"I'm sure he's up to something," Cati said.

They waited until Samuel had passed out of sight then ran to the door of the Starry. As they passed through the sleeping forms, Owen remembered the little girl who had woken the previous day. Had the fact that he'd stumbled and touched her something to do with her waking?

They took the stairs two at a time, Cati leading, until they reached the top, and went out on to the little balcony. They looked down to see Johnston standing in the middle of the hall. Chancellor, the Sub-Commandant, Samual and Contessa stood together facing him. The head of the guard, Rutgar, stood at the door. And Pieta stood behind her chair at the fireplace. Even at this distance Owen could sense the stillness, the dangerous tension in her. If Johnston was aware of it, he showed no sign. He stood with his legs spread wide and his hands on his hips, looking about him with a lazy arrogance.

"You didn't come here to admire the hangings," Chancellor said. "State your business."

"I apologise, Chancellor," Johnston said. "It is such a long time since I have seen the old hall." The words were polite, but the tone was not and Owen knew that the man was mocking Chancellor.

"Get on with it, Johnston," Pieta growled. The man put his fingers to his lips.

"Hush, little one," he said. "Such a long sleep."

Owen didn't know what he was talking about, but he heard Cati's sharp intake of breath so he knew it was serious and he expected to see the long whip of magno snaking out towards the man. But Pieta bit her lip and turned away, burying her head in her shoulder as if to hide a terrible grief.

"Make your parley, Johnston, and go!" snapped Rutgar.

"Yes," said Johnston, "the parley. That is the reason I'm here. I am ready to offer terms."

"What terms?" asked Chancellor. There was anxiety in his voice.

"These are the terms. You abandon all defence of this place and I will return you to the long Sleep, long and dreamless, for eternity."

"And what advantage is there in that?" the Sub-Commandant asked.

"My Watcher friend," Johnston said softly, and Owen felt that there was respect, mixed with loathing in his tone. "How long have we watched each other over the centuries, not growing old, but growing weary? You alone of these people know me and know when I am speaking the truth, so listen to me now. The choice is between dying here, for we intend to annihilate you and all of your works. But if you let me put you to sleep, then at least you are alive and have – not hope, for there is no hope – but the illusion of hope, that a new day might come and you might wake again."

"It is an offer we must consider," Samual said.

"Consider nothing!"

A voice cut across the debate like a whiplash. It was Contessa's, Owen was surprised to notice. She strode across the room until she was standing eye to eye with Johnston.

"You think he would put us to sleep? Maybe he would. And the next thing would be a blade in the throat, or carried out into the everlasting cold and frozen to death. This is not a choice he is offering."

"I would certainly keep you awake a little longer than the others," Johnston said in a musing tone.

"I agree with Contessa," the Sub-Commandant said.

"I agree," Pieta said quietly.

Samual shook his head and said nothing.

"I agree also," Rutgar boomed.

Chancellor looked at the floor as if he might find wisdom there. After a long time he lifted his head and spoke. "It seems as if I too have to agree."

"You haven't seen the forces I have gathered," Johnston said, in a menacing voice. "The largest and strongest I have ever had, and if I am not mistaken, you are weaker than ever. Your little incursion across the river the other night will not have seen any of our strength. If that was the reason for it." He looked at the Sub-Commandant with a raised eyebrow, then gazed about the hall.

Although Owen and Cati knew that he could not see them, they both shrank back into the shadows, and Cati whimpered as if she could feel the cold again. Owen put out his hand to touch hers. Her skin was cold to touch, very cold, and he remembered what Contessa had said about the effects of the Harsh being permanent.

"It is time for you to leave now," the Sub-Commandant said. His voice was quiet, but there was steel in his tone.

"Fair enough," Johnston said, "but we won't be seeing each other again, Sub-Commandant. This is the last time."

There seemed to be sorrow in his voice, but his eyes were glinting under their heavy brows. Johnston turned and strode from the hall, Rutgar keeping pace close behind. Even from a height, Owen could feel the tension drain from the hall. He saw Contessa go over to Pieta and put an arm around her shoulder, whispering to her gently.

"What's wrong with Pieta?" Owen said.

"Her children sleep and do not wake," Cati said. "Every night she sits over them and calls their names and still they do not wake."

Owen said nothing. He thought about Pieta standing over a child in the Starry, calling and calling, and suddenly the fierce warrior seemed smaller and less fierce. He could see her loneliness and sorrow in the slump of her shoulders until suddenly she shrugged Contessa off, almost in anger. She got to her feet and walked swiftly from the hall. Contessa reached out a hand to touch her as she stalked past.

CHAPTER EIGHT

There was a final flurry of defence building by the river and then everything seemed to slow down. Nothing happened for two weeks, or what felt like two weeks, for Owen was increasingly uncertain about time and the way it worked. He decided to draw a rough calendar on the wall of his Den, where he marked in sunrises and sunsets, for at least that happened in the normal way.

He went up to the Nab to see Dr Diamond again. The scientist and philosopher showed him the complicated clock with five faces, each one with a single hand, and told him that it was measuring the speed at which time was going backwards.

"The five faces measure the five different kinds of time," Dr Diamond said. When he saw the look on Owen's face, he went on hastily, "But we only have to concern ourselves with the big face, which is time as we commonly know it."

Owen could see that the single hand of the clock was going backwards, opposite to the normal way. It was also moving very slowly.

"That's because time is going backwards very slowly at the moment. It doesn't always go at the same speed, you see," Dr Diamond said. "Sometimes even the Harsh have difficulty in keeping the speed up. And sometimes they manipulate the speed to their own purposes."

"What way does time move at the Workhouse?"

"That's this clock," Dr Diamond said, tapping the smallest dial. "We're on what you've heard people call an island in time. Not exactly accurate, but near enough. Most other time flows round us. Kind of sloshes backwards and forwards, in fact. There are plenty of islands in time, but most are tiny, maybe one or two people on them, being born and living and dying, and an hour is an hour and a minute is a minute the same as it always was, even when they step outside the island."

"I think I get it," Owen said slowly, "but what I still don't understand is where are all the people? I mean, the whole town, for all I know the whole country, even the whole world... where did all the other people go?"

"That is complicated," Dr Diamond said. "The Harsh long for emptiness, for cold nothingness. A time before people. Before history. That is the reason they have turned time backwards – to get back to that place. It seems that their Great Machine does away not only with time, but with the idea of human life itself."

"So they've already done away with life…?"

"It seems so. Nobody has died; they have just never been."

"So they got rid of life and now they're getting rid of time. Kind of a mopping up operation."

"I wouldn't have put it like that. But, yes, essentially you're correct." Dr Diamond knelt down in front of Owen, his eyes examining the boy's face. "I know you didn't give the right answer to Samual, when he asked you about Gobillard." He put up a hand to stop Owen from speaking. "Your instinct was, I think, correct. There is dangerous knowledge involved, however I—"

The door opened behind them. It was Samual. His face darkened at the sight of Owen.

"Time to go, Owen," Dr Diamond said swiftly, standing up.

Owen slipped by Samual without meeting his eyes. Whatever Dr Diamond had to tell him would have to wait.

The Sub-Commandant and the others were busy and preoccupied, so Owen was grateful for the company of Wesley and Cati. Much of the countryside was wooded now and there were mushrooms to be picked in the morning, and wild berries and fruit, and hazelnuts on the banks. The weather felt like Autumn, with dew in the morning and cold, crisp days. There seemed to be a mellowness in the air. Sometimes the wind would blow hard, but it never reached the strength of the storm that had trapped Owen in the warehouses. Wesley brought fish and prawns from the harbour. At night they would build a fire in front of the Den and cook fish or rabbit stew, and eat it with potatoes that grew wild in forest clearings.

Owen slept deep, dreamless sleeps, and when he woke in the morning the cold nipped at his hands and face until he had lit a fire. He had a good stock of teabags, but he knew they might be his last so he was miserly with them. Wesley and Cati tasted the tea and made faces. They drank only water or thin wine, or a warm drink that tasted of honey. Owen was surprised at how quickly the Den became a home and how much he liked to lie dozing and listening to the sound of the wind swaying the trees. He missed his home and his room, and he missed his mother, but he did not miss the miserable tension that had seemed to lurk in every corner and crevice of the house.

He realised too that he felt fitter than ever before. One day, as they raced down the forest paths, he was surprised to find himself pulling easily away from Cati. And when he looked in the mirror of the old dressing table he saw a fuller, more cheerful face looking back at him.

At night they sat round the fire after they had eaten, the flames casting shadows about them. Sometimes they sat in companionable silence and sometimes they talked quietly, Owen telling them about his life and the town, and Cati and Wesley talking about the Resisters. Owen started to understand that the Resisters had emerged many, many times to battle the Harsh, but of those battles he learned little. Cati had only a dim memory, for she had been born on the island in time and was growing up among them as any child would. However, Wesley had stumbled into the Resisters in much the same way as Owen. He had fought on several occasions, but he did not like to talk about it and would fall silent if pressed.

Sometimes, Owen saw the Sub-Commandant and Chancellor in the distance. Both men seemed strained. In the evening the Sub-Commandant would stand on the roof of the Workhouse, shading his eyes and staring across to the other side of the river as if to penetrate the white mist which grew ever more ominous.

Wesley liked to go down and look at the defences which had been thrown up along the river. "'Specting the troops," he called it. Owen went with him and was amazed at the small, stone-buttressed forts which stood every hundred metres or so. Rutgar's men had built them. Good with their hands, Wesley said with respect, although it didn't stop him from pointing out imaginary flaws in the stonework within earshot of the bearded men, who grinned and threw friendly insults at the two boys. There were no friendly insults from Samual's soldiers though. The brightly-dressed men and women patrolled in grim silence, passing Rutgar's men without a greeting or even a sideways glance.

From what Owen could see, these troops lived a hard life. When they were not patrolling they were working in the fields they had carved out for themselves on the slope behind the Workhouse. The fields were well kept and crops were already starting to appear, even though they had not been planted for long, and despite the autumnal weather. But every morning the forest had encroached on the fields during the night, and teams of men and woman had to be set to slashing and burning round the margins. There didn't seem to be much laughter among them.

In contrast, Rutgar's men had set up a row of small gardens right up against the wall of the Workhouse. They would work in them in the evenings, or sit talking, wrapped in coats against the evening chill.

One morning towards the end of the second week. Owen got up and lit the fire. He boiled water and made some tea. He took a hunk of bread that had been given to him by Contessa and smeared honey on it. He heard a movement on the path, then Cati's head appeared in the opening. Without saying anything she sat down and helped herself to some of the bread and honey. As she started to eat, they heard a noise, a faint droning.

"What's that?" asked Cati through a mouthful of bread.

They got to their feet and went out to the path. Looking up through the canopy of trees they could see, high in the sky, a single Planeman, wheeling in lazy circles above the Workhouse.

"He's out of range," Cati said. "I never saw one fly so high before." They watched the spindly craft in silence, the bread forgotten in their hands.

Later that morning, Owen looked out to see Rutgar walking down the path towards the Den. He held one of the brass tubes with the glass end that the fighters carried. His smile when he saw Owen was friendly enough, but he looked tired, Owen thought.

"I brought you something to defend yourself with," he said. "It looks as if you're going to need it, although if I judge you right then fighting will not be your main part in all of this. Don't misjudge what I'm saying," he added, seeing Owen's expression. "I know you're brave. It's just that fighting alone won't defeat the Harsh."

He thrust the brass tube into Owen's hands. It was lighter than it looked. Owen examined it. There was what appeared to be a pair of sights at one end and some kind of a trigger mechanism, shaped like a crooked finger, at the other.

"Put it to your shoulder," Rutgar said, "and aim at something."

As Owen did so, he could feel the interior of the tube warm up and the weapon began to emit a low humming noise. A

118

dangerous sound, Owen thought, like something woken from sleep that should have been left alone. He sighted along the tube and almost pulled the trigger in surprise. Instead of the bare metal sights, a square grid with a small dot in the middle had formed itself out of magno.

"Line the mark up with a rock," said Rutgar. Owen moved the weapon until the dot was centred on a rock.

"Now move it away," Rutgar said. Owen moved the weapon, but the dot stayed centred on the rock. "You have to move the whole square off the rock to change your aim."

Owen did so and the dot repositioned in the centre of the grid. He aimed the gun at a tree. The dot lined itself up again. He moved the barrel, but the dot stayed fixed on the tree. He wondered what would happen if he pulled the trigger. For the first time since he had come here, he felt powerful. He could see the spiteful face of Samual in his mind's eye, and for a moment he could hear the cold and grim summons of the Harsh. Rutgar spoke again, but Owen did not hear. His finger tightened on the trigger. The brass tube seemed to sear his cheek so that he jerked it away, and a bolt of blue light shot from the glass end of the gun and struck the tree. The tree seemed to vibrate for a moment then, with an ear-splitting crackling and popping sound, it fell in upon itself and collapsed to the ground.

Owen stared at the weapon in his hand. It was almost too

hot to touch now. Rutgar leaned over and removed it from his grasp.

"It's not a toy," he said gently, and Owen felt his face flush.

The air smelled of iron filings, and ash drifted slowly away from the felled tree, even though, as far as Owen could see, it had not burned.

Rutgar sat down beside Owen and explained the principles of the weapon, the way to aim it properly, how to make it safe when carrying it. It was powered by the same magno power as everything else. Rutgar's tone was gentle and serious, and made Owen feel even worse. He remembered the two Raggie boys and their reluctance to even touch a weapon, and the sense of duty with which they had done so.

"Used to be you would take a month to learn what I'm telling you, before you were even allowed to touch this," Rutgar said, standing up to leave. "But we don't have a month. We don't even have days, I think."

Owen and Cati watched Rutgar walk away. "What do we do now?" asked Owen.

"Let's go and see Dr Diamond," Cati suggested.

In the Skyward, Dr Diamond lay on his bed, perfectly still, his eyes closed. The sky outside seemed to darken and gust of wind threw a handful of sleet against the windows. Dr Diamond's eyes opened and he turned his head sharply towards the big clock. The clock's single hand suddenly leapt into motion, flying round the clock before coming to rest. It began to move forward again, but this time its movements were jerky and sharp. Sleet rattled against the window.

"The attack is on us," Dr Diamond said softly to himself. "Johnston rides on the Workhouse. Can the Harsh be far behind?" He sat up. "The children are coming!" he exclaimed to himself, and raced to the door.

CHAPTER NINE

Owen and Cati were halfway up the Nab when the sky darkened. They paused uncertainly. They could see little of the riverbank, but they could hear sudden shouts and muffled explosions and terrible screams.

"The fighting has begun!" Cati shouted. "We need to get down again."

As they started down the circular stairs, there was a terrible whirring sound in the air. Owen looked up startled. As he did so the long figure of Dr Diamond cannoned into him. Dr Diamond pushed Owen to one side as a barbed lance, over a metre long and made entirely of ice, glanced off the handrail beside him. With terrible force it crashed against the brass wall of the Nab, making a deep clanging sound and leaving a large dent in the handrail. The lance had broken in two pieces. Owen bent to lift one but Dr Diamond stopped him.

"It would freeze your hand," he shouted. "You'd lose your arm or worse. It is not ordinary ice and probably poisoned. Run!"

They ran, Dr Diamond coming behind them, urging them on, half-carrying Cati when she slipped. The noise of battle grew louder as they descended, and smoke started to drift up to them. They were halfway down the Nab when Owen heard an odd humming sound, followed by a warning shout from Dr Diamond. He turned to see a Planeman astride his flying craft, coming up behind them and gaining rapidly.

Close up, the craft was bigger than Owen had realised, a complicated structure of long spars and struts, with blades that stirred the air and looked too fragile to bear their great length. The craft drew alongside, the blades almost touching the Nab. The Planeman turned his head to look at them. He was crouched behind the controls wearing huge goggles, so that Owen felt that they were being looked at by a giant, hungry insect. The Planeman was wearing an oil-stained leather jacket and matted fur leggings, and Owen could see under the goggles the sideburns that all Johnston's men sported.

Abruptly, the Planeman wheeled away to the left. "He's coming in to attack!" Dr Diamond shouted. Sure enough, the craft turned in the air above them and started to descend rapidly.

"Try and keep the tower between us and him," said

Dr Diamond. They descended in a deadly game, trying to anticipate the Planeman's movements. Twice the man fired a long ice-harpoon at them, and twice it shattered harmlessly against the side of the Nab. But the ground was getting closer.

They almost made it. Owen thought that they had given the Planeman the slip. He could almost feel the earth under his feet, but the goggled man was an expert and cunning pilot. As they slid on to the last platform, the deadly craft rose from beneath it, the ice-cannon pointed straight at them. Owen could see the mouth beneath the goggles, the yellow teeth bared in an ugly grin.

"The gun!" Cati cried. Owen had forgotten he was carrying it.

"The gun, the gun!" Cati made a grab for it. She missed the barrel; her hand caught the trigger mechanism instead. A bolt of blue light shot from the barrel, cannoned off the brass side of the Nab and glanced off the edge of one of the plane's wings. The aircraft yawed wildly as the man fought with the controls.

There was a nasty noise coming from the plane now, and as Owen watched, it rose high in the air, higher and higher, the pilot fighting the controls wildly. Its ascent became faster and faster, the plane turning in tight little circles. The two children looked on in fear and pity as it grew smaller and smaller, until in the end it was a tiny speck and then nothing at all.

"The poor man," said Cati.

"He was about to kill us," Owen said.

"I know," she said, but still she watched the empty space where the plane had disappeared.

"Come on," Dr Diamond said, gently but firmly.

As they ran down the path towards the riverbank, they met wounded men going back to the Workhouse. Most of them were able to walk, although there were broken arms and ugly, blue-lipped wounds from the ice-lances. But at one point on the path they had to stand back in silence and watch as a stretcher was carried past bearing a man who did not move or open his eyes. He was one of Samual's men and the red of blood had been added to the colour of his gaudy clothes.

"I'm taking you two to the Workhouse," Dr Diamond said. When they started to protest he turned to them with a grave face. "I want your solemn promise that you will stay in the Workhouse and not go down to the riverbank," he said.

Reluctantly, they agreed. In the distance they could hear shouts and explosions and they were simultaneously afraid and drawn to the action.

"If you go upstairs in the Workhouse," Dr Diamond said, "you'll be able to see everything. And since I have your promise, I will leave you here."

They turned and ran towards the Workhouse. Dr Diamond watched them for a moment then turned back towards the Nab. He had learned a few new things that day and he had work to do.

The Workhouse building showed signs of attack when the children reached it. There were scars in its crumbling stone and shards of ice lay on the ground. They ran through the doorway just as there was a loud whistling sound, and a huge ice lance struck the wall above their heads. But it would take more than even the coldest ice to penetrate its great walls, and as Owen and Cati ran on, the sounds of attack faded. Passing the door of the Convoke hall, they saw that it had been turned into a temporary infirmary, and that there were already more than twenty soldiers on low pallets on the ground.

On and on they ran up one of the Workhouse's endless staircases until it seemed that the fighting must be over by the time they got to the top. They arrived breathlessly at an old room just under the eaves. The room was full of strange and wild stone carvings, weathered until the marks had almost faded back into the stone. Owen could make out the figures of men and women, some peaceful, some looking as if they were engaged in a terrible struggle.

Cati hardly spared them a glance. "They used to be on the roof," she said, "but everyone thought they were so mouldy that they would fall off on people's heads. Come on!"

They ran to the window. The fighting had intensified. Owen saw that Samual's troops were holding their trenches by the river as wave upon wave of Johnston's men waded across the river and attacked them. The air was full of jagged bolts of magno and ice-lances fell like rain, some flung by Johnston's men, but other, bigger ones, being flung from the white mist that covered the ground behind them, arching upwards as if thrown by machine. Of the Harsh there was no sign. That worried Owen. And above it all the Planemen wheeled and turned and sought targets among the defenders.

"Where's Rutgar?" asked Cati.

"Look!" Owen said, pointing downriver. Hidden from the Planemen by an outcrop of rock with pine trees on it, a band of men led by Rutgar had crossed the river and were making their way silently towards Johnston's lines hoping, Owen could tell, to mount a surprise, flanking attack. Using the low ground by the river, they crept forward. They were almost there when Owen saw something else. A body of men lay in a shallow depression twenty metres inland from Rutgar. There were more men than Rutgar had, and even at this distance Owen could make out Johnston's unmistakable bulk. He heard a hiss of breath from Cati.

"It's a trap!" she exclaimed. "They'll get Rutgar from behind."

The two children leapt to their feet, waving and shouting, but it was useless against the noise of the battle. They watched, horror-stricken, as Rutgar continued to creep forward, while Johnston staged the surprise attack that would wipe out Rutgar and his men.

Owen leapt to his feet and grabbed the magno gun which had lain forgotten against the wall.

"What are you doing?" cried Cati. Owen didn't reply. He lay on his stomach, the little holosights appearing in his vision as soon as he sighted along the barrel. His hands were slippery with sweat and he was finding it hard to focus. Settling himself, he sought the little floating bead and fixed its aim.

There was no more time. He felt the barrel of the weapon become warm in his hands, even before his finger closed on the trigger, as if it knew that he was going to fire. He squeezed tighter and tighter; the barrel suddenly surged with heat and he felt the searing bolt leap from the muzzle.

It missed Rutgar by centimetres. A rock in front of him splintered and he leapt backwards. He turned in shock to see who was firing on him from his own lines. Owen jumped up at the window, shouting and gesticulating towards the shallow depression where Johnston and his men lay hidden. Rutgar realised what was happening. With a warning shout he swung around. At the same moment Johnston's men sprang from cover.

With a noise that Owen could hear high above the river, the two bands came together. They were too close to use their guns and ice-lances, and they fought instead with the long bayonets from their belts. The fighting was fierce and Rutgar's men were driven backwards, but Johnston had lost his element of surprise and he could not break Rutgar's line. For a moment, Johnston and Rutgar were facing each other and the two men fought toe to toe, before a knot of fighting men drove between them.

The men fought for close to an hour. Owen could see that Rutgar's men were tiring.

"Johnston's got too many men," Cati said.

"He's getting between Rutgar and the river," said Owen.

It was true. Bit by bit, Rutgar's retreat to the river was being cut off. They could see that many of Rutgar's men were bleeding. Some of Johnston's men went down and did not get up, but Rutgar's men were also falling. They were fighting with desperation now.

"Look!" shouted Cati. One of Johnston's men had one of the Resisters on the ground. He raised a bayonet to stab when a long arc of light uncurled almost lazily towards him, wrapping itself around the man then flinging him high into the air.

"Pieta!" Owen exclaimed.

Methodically Pieta worked her way through the attackers, men falling left and right. Owen could see Johnston snarling at her, keeping well out of the range of the powerful whip. Johnston's men fell back; some of them dropped their weapons and ran rather than face Pieta. Just then the fighting seemed to pause. There was a loud, mournful hooting noise, rising and falling, and Owen knew from its cold empty tones that it was the voice of the Harsh. Cati put her hands over her ears and hung her head.

Down at the riverbank, Johnston's men had started to retreat, step by step, the defenders fighting them all the way across the river. As they did so, the white mist crept forward, enveloping the attackers for a moment only. When it retreated, Johnston's men were gone.

The bottom floor of the Workhouse was crowded when Owen and Cati got down the stairs. Men and women who had been fighting all day were eating and casualties were being attended to. They saw the Sub-Commandant looking anxiously about him, then his relief when his eyes fell on Cati. She waved at him, but then a messenger approached him and he turned away. The children pushed through the crowd of tired fighters, making their way towards the door. As they reached it, they heard a shout and turned to see Samual striding angrily towards them.

"Stop that boy!" he shouted. Several of his men at the door turned in surprise, but when he repeated his command, one of them caught Owen by the arm. Samual stopped in front of Owen and Cati.

"Do you think I didn't see what you did?" he demanded. His face was white with anger and his hand was on the hilt of his bayonet.

"He didn't do anything!" exclaimed Cati.

"I was right about you all along," the man snarled, "and I should finish you here and now!"

"What is going on?" a stern voice demanded. It was Chancellor. "What's all this about finishing?"

"I saw this boy in the high window," Samuel said. "He fired on Rutgar's flanking party. Not only did he almost hit him, but the shot told Johnston where Rutgar was. If not for Pieta, they would all be dead."

"Is this true?" Chancellor said.

"Yes, but—"

"He admits it!" cried Samual.

"He was trying to save Rutgar," Cati said angrily.

"Some of my friends were killed in that sortie," came a voice from the crowd that had gathered. Owen's tongue was stuck to the roof of his mouth. There was an angry murmur from the crowd, and it would have gone badly for Owen if Rutgar had not appeared in the doorway. There was a dirty, blood-soaked rag tied round his head.

"What's all this?" he growled.

"Samual saw Owen shoot at you," Chancellor said.

"Shoot at me?" Rutgar said softly. "Shoot *at* me?" There was a dangerous gleam in his eye. "If Owen had not fired to warn me then Johnston would have attacked us from the rear and wiped us out. Owen saved the sortie. Leave the boy alone and consider something else."

"What?" asked Samual suspiciously.

"I would like to know how Johnston found out we were going to try to flank him. Why was he waiting in that exact place? He had to know our plans. It was the same all day – everywhere we went, they were there. Every time we tried an offensive it seemed that they knew in advance. They knew *all* our plans."

"A spy?" Chancellor said.

"A spy," said Rutgar heavily. He was looking straight at Samual.

The richly-dressed man snorted contemptuously. "Your plans are too predictable. A child would know that you would try that flanking movement."

The two men glared at each other. Chancellor made an impatient movement with his hand. "Enough! We haven't seen the Harsh yet; does anybody think there's something strange about that? There's more to come. Something is afoot. I think that was only a softening-up attack. Get something to eat and go back to your posts."

Samual wheeled away. His men released Owen and Rutgar clapped the boy on the back.

"Never mind that Samual. He was born wicked. I won't forget what you did today. Now let me go and get this head cleaned up."

They watched Rutgar walk away, but Owen could tell that many people weren't satisfied with what he'd said. He was aware of people turning their backs on him as he and Cati walked towards the kitchen.

The kitchen was chaotic. Even Contessa did not look her normal calm self and she hardly spared them a glance as they helped themselves to food. When they left the kitchen, Owen saw Samual glowering at him. "Let's go back to the Den," he said.

"Right," said Cati. "I couldn't eat properly with old sourchops Samual staring at me."

They walked back along the path, meeting only a few weary men who barely glanced at them.

"I'm tired of it," Owen said.

"Tired of what?"

"People being suspicious of me. I haven't done anything to Samual or any of his lot."

"It's not you exactly that they're suspicious of," Cati said slowly.

"What is it then? My shadow?"

"It's what you are, or what you *might* be, if you follow me."

"No, I don't follow you," said Owen crossly. Cati sighed.

"Every time I say something you just get crosser and crosser. I think we'll eat this then go to Dr Diamond. And then we'd better go and see how Wesley is."

"Were the Raggies in the fighting?" Owen said, worry replacing his anger.

"I heard that the Planemen attacked them again," Cati said.

"Let's hurry then," said Owen, breaking into a trot. He did

not know that much would happen before nightfall, and that they would not be going to see any of their friends.

At the Den, Cati managed to get the fire going from a few embers and Owen put on water for one of his remaining teabags. He opened out the cloth he had been carrying. There was fresh crusty bread and cheese. Cati had snatched some pickles and preserves, and two rich slices of almond cake. They ate greedily and in silence, and when they had finished they stretched out on the soft moss floor of the Den while the fire warmed them.

Owen was just about to remind Cati that they ought to get going when they heard it – a low sound at first, but building in intensity; a hum that got louder and louder and then turned into a shriek, finally bursting forth with a racket like a hundred fire sirens. The noise drilled into their heads and drove out their thoughts till it seemed that the only thing to do was to lie down with their hands over their ears.

"What is it?" Owen roared at the top of his lungs. Cati shook her head. It was clear that she had never heard the sound before. She ran outside and Owen followed. They scrambled up the bank to the swing tree. For the first time in many days the white mist had drawn back and a great object stood on the far bank. It was like a cathedral of ice and in it, as if imprisoned, he could see the shapes of the Harsh – perhaps ten of them. Above the point of its frozen spire, lightning crackled and small but violent blizzards swept along its gleaming walls.

But even if the Harsh were frozen inside, they were still moving, their arms waving slowly and rhythmically, their mouths open in the terrible howl which the children had heard. And this howl, it seemed, had taken shape in a white beam of absolute cold, now pointing straight across the river, freezing and destroying. Every object it struck was frozen then exploded from within. Trees and boulders detonated as soon as they were touched. The beam gouged great icy trenches in the ground and in the bank where the Owen and Cati stood. The air was full of shards of frozen tree and icy slivers of rock. Far below, they could see the shapes of men and women crouched in terror and awe.

They watched for over an hour. It was clear that the beam was concentrated on the river defences, which were gradually being flattened. Owen saw Samual lead a small sortie. They crouched in the lee of the riverbank, then at a signal they rose and fired the magno guns at the ice cathedral. The bolts of magno glanced off harmlessly and then the beam swung in their direction. Owen did not like Samual, but there was no denying his courage. The red-robed man fired twice more as the beam moved swiftly towards him. Just in time he ducked under the riverbank and, bent double, ran downstream with his men as the beam fell with savage cold on the place where he had stood, leaving a hole in the ground from which icy vapour rose.

Owen heard a noise and turned. Dr Diamond was coming

across the slope towards them. He hunkered down beside them, surveying the scene.

"What is it?" Owen shouted.

"I don't know exactly," the scientist said, "but at a guess I would say that the Harsh are joining their thoughts together. They don't think the way we do. In fact, you could say that their thoughts are frozen draughts blowing about their heads. There's a lot about the Harsh that we don't understand."

"You mean they're thinking about us?" said Cati. Her face was pale and strained.

"Something like that," nodded Dr Diamond.

"What happens when it hits the Workhouse?" asked Owen.

"The Workhouse is very old and stronger than it looks," Dr Diamond said, "but if they destroy all the defences, will the Workhouse stand? I don't know."

Cati stifled a sob. Dr Diamond looked at her with concern.

"Owen," he said, "your friend is very strong, otherwise she would not be here, but their sound is hurting her. You had better take her to the harbour where she'll be out of its range."

Owen was going to object, but one look at Cati made him realise that Dr Diamond was right. With a tenderness that surprised even himself, he put his arm around her and led her gently away.

As they walked towards the harbour, the terrible noise faded and Cati brightened. "Sorry about that," she said. "I just get this frozen feeling inside when I hear them."

"They scare me too," Owen said.

"Do you think we can stop them?"

"I'd say Dr Diamond is cooking up a surprise for them right this moment," Owen said, with as much confidence as he could muster.

In fact, at that moment the scientist was clambering into the big chair surrounded by levers in the middle of the Skyward. Frowning with concentration, he started to manipulate the levers. The polished exterior of the Skyward started to move, slowly at first, then faster and faster until it became a blur, then faster again until it seemed like a flashing disc of light in the darkening sky.

Inside the Skyward, something had changed. An observer would have noted that only one of the five time clocks was now moving. A device that looked for all the world like a submarine telescope came down from the ceiling. (Indeed it *was* a submarine telescope from a U-boat that Dr Diamond had adapted.) Dr Diamond took the handles and put his face to the eyepiece. For ten minutes he turned the periscope to and fro. Then he closed the handles and the periscope rose into the ceiling again. Dr Diamond started to manipulate the levers. All five clocks started again. Outside, the revolving Skyward started to slow down. Dr Diamond pushed the last lever back into place and lay back in the chair. His face was thoughtful.

CHAPTER TEN

The warehouses had been attacked by the Planemen and there were holes in the roof and great gouges in the stonework. But Wesley had led most of the children to the basement, and the shooting skills of Uel and Mervyn had kept the Planemen at a distance. All in all, Owen thought, the Raggies had fared better than the defenders at the Workhouse.

Owen and Cati told Wesley what had happened. Wesley's face was grave. He looked towards the Workhouse. The air overhead seemed to be full of a fine sleet. "I've never heard of this. And you tell me they never fired on the Workhouse?"

"They're attacking the defences," Cati said.

"They do be looking to take the Workhouse whole," said Wesley. "Could be they want something… the Sleepers in the Starry, I would reckon."

Wesley gave them food, but they didn't want to eat. It was getting dark now. The noise made by the Harsh got louder. Cati sat as close to the fire as she could, looking miserable. As darkness fell, an eerie dome of ice hung over the Workhouse.

"They need help," Wesley murmured, "but who will help them?" They all stared mutely towards the battle then Owen stood up.

"I have an idea," he said. "I have an idea, but I can't do it on my own."

Wesley looked at Cati. She was dozing in the heat of the fire. "Looks like it'll have to be me then," he said eventually.

"Let's go," said Owen.

The two boys ran all the way. They could feel the cold on their faces as they got close to the Workhouse and there were small chunks of ice floating in the river.

"What's your idea?" Wesley gasped. But Owen was too out of breath to to tell him. They ran under the town bridge and on, the air full of ice granules. They skidded round the last corner and gazed open-mouthed on the battle scene.

Johnston's men had crossed the river and were fighting in front of the Workhouse. The Resister men and women had gathered in a hollow in front of the building where the ice-cannon could not get them and were fighting hand to hand in an icy sleet that enveloped the whole area. Owen even saw Dr Diamond in the middle of it, wearing an ancient karate suit, dealing out spidery kicks and blows.

They saw the beam from the cannon which had already devastated the landscape and now roamed restlessly, searching out targets.

"Perfect," Owen said. Wesley looked at him as if he had lost his mind. "Come on!" Owen ran off at full tilt without looking to see if Wesley was following.

They charged down the path to the Den, leaping over trees that had been cut in two and pieces of boulders strewn in their way. The Den seemed unharmed. Owen ran over to the old dressing table and gasped, "Grab the other end." Wesley's eyes widened, but he did as he was asked. Together the two boys heaved the dressing table outside.

"Up there," Owen said, pointing towards the swing tree. Together, inch by laborious inch, the two boys pushed and heaved, their task made more difficult by the trenches gouged by the beam. Once, the beam swung in their direction, making a terrible tearing, icy noise.

"Down!" Owen hissed. "We don't want them to see us yet!" Wesley ducked, clearly not liking the sound of that "yet". With a cold, malevolent roar, the beam passed them by and they resumed their struggle. Once, Wesley lost his footing and the dressing table slipped back down the hill, picking up momentum until Owen threw himself behind it and somehow managed to stop it.

"Get it under the swing tree!" Owen shouted. "Turn it round so that it's facing the river."

Owen adjusted the mirror slightly. "All right,'" he said calmly. "Ready now." To Wesley's amazement, he started to jump up and down and wave his arms in the air, shouting.

"Over here!" he yelled. "Come on, ice-cube brains!" Wesley stared at him then an inkling began to form in his mind, and he too began to jump up and down.

"Here! Bet you can't hit us with your damn beam," he shouted. "Get away on out of this place. Go on!"

Then the Harsh spotted them. The beam swung towards the boys, greedy for their warmth, and Owen felt a shiver go down his spine. Faster and faster the beam moved, roaring as it tore up the ground, thirty metres away, twenty metres, ten, and then it was on them.

"Now!" Owen shouted. The two boys threw themselves behind the dressing table. But as they tried to turn it towards the beam, Wesley slipped. Owen watched in horror as Wesley sprawled down the slope in front of them. The beam moved forward slowly as though following a trail. Frozen debris peppered Owen's face, drawing blood. Then the beam seemed to sense Wesley and started moving towards him, picking up speed. Wesley lay still on the ground and Owen saw blood on his temple. The beam would be on him in seconds.

Without thinking, Owen threw himself down the slope, trying to draw the beam to him, but it didn't deviate from its

141

path. In desperation, Owen ran right under it, so close that he could feel the material of his clothes turn hard and frozen, so close that he could feel the vibration of the terrible power projecting from it.

And then it became aware of Owen. He could almost feel its attention turn to him. Not only that, but it felt as if it knew who he was. With lightning speed, the beam turned on him so that he barely managed to leap out of its way. Again, it sought him out, and again, striking like a snake, eager for his warmth. He ran up the slope, slipping, gasping for breath, the air around him full of frozen earth and shattered timber. With his last strength he threw himself at the dressing table. The beam seemed to rear above him, and he could feel its sense of triumph at cornering its prey. It struck, and as it struck, with the strength of desperation, Owen pulled the dressing table across his body and felt the terrifying jolt as the beam hit the mirror, just above his heart.

For a moment there was nothing except the sound of the beam, then it doubled on itself, reflected back along its own path, back towards the Harsh and their ice cathedral. It struck like a thunderbolt. The Harsh's voices changed. The structure began to vibrate violently. The Harsh's movements became frenetic and their voices changed to an eerie wail. At the same time, the mirror shattered and the cathedral structure exploded with a terrifying boom.

Owen was thrown backwards. Shards of ice rained on him.

He scrambled to his feet. Down below, the attackers were looking about them uncertainly. The men and women defending the Workhouse seemed to shake themselves as though waking from a nightmare. Standing at the very front of the Resisters was Pieta. Even from a distance Owen could see the light of battle in her eyes. She raised the magno whip above her head and in one easy movement flicked it forward over the heads of the attackers, the lash extending until the tip of it covered the first three ranks. She threw her head back and laughed, and as she did so the attackers' uncertainty turned to fear. The rest of the Resisters, no longer afraid, started to laugh as well, and raising their weapons, they started forward in a wave. Johnston's men dropped their weapons, turned and ran.

Wesley was dazed but unhurt. By the time Owen got him to his feet and back to the Workhouse, the sounds of battle had faded into the distance. Johnston's men had been driven back across the river. The landscape in front of the building was unrecognisable, broken stone and trees scattered everywhere, the ground churned up into frozen ridges of earth. In the Workhouse they were tending to the wounded. Exhausted men and women sat everywhere. The Sub-Commandant and Dr Diamond stood in the entrance to the Workhouse.

"I saw what you did," the Sub-Commandant said. "It was brave and it was clever. Thank you. If you are not too tired, perhaps you would find Cati for me and bring her here."

"It wasn't just me," said Owen, "it was Wesley as well." He saw gratitude in Wesley's wary eyes. Wesley had gone along with him without ever questioning what he was doing.

"Cati's at the warehouses," Wesley said, "I'll go." The Sub-Commandant smiled and turned away.

Owen suddenly realised he was starving. But as he turned to Wesley to suggest going to the kitchen first, Dr Diamond drew him aside. "Good fight," he said enthusiastically. "That was a clever thing you did. Wouldn't have thought of it myself." Owen felt a glow of satisfaction. Perhaps people like Samual might start accepting him now.

"Come with me now, Owen," Dr Diamond said. "There will be a Convoke in the morning and hostility to you. I want you to be prepared."

Owen groaned inwardly. He thought that his trick with the mirror would have convinced them that he was on their side. Part of him had even secretly hoped that he would be carried shoulder-high into the Convoke.

"Never mind," Dr Diamond said in a kindly voice, as if he had read the boy's thoughts. "You do have friends as well."

Owen followed Dr Diamond up the Nab until they reached the gleaming Skyward. Once they were inside Dr Diamond disappeared, reappearing a few minutes later with a large plate of excellent cakes. Neither of them spoke until every crumb was gone. Dr Diamond brushed the fragments off his karate suit and looked at Owen seriously.

"I have some idea of what will happen in the morning at the Convoke and it is time for you to know some of your story, and for that you must know something of the Mortmain. And of Gobillard et Fils."

Owen remembered the cold voice of the Harsh in his head from the night he had crossed the river, the way it spoke the word Mortmain.

"I have heard of it," he said, "but I don't know what it is."

"The Mortmain has been many things to different people through the ages. It has taken many shapes as well, but usually it is an object about twice the size of a man's hand, made of brass or bronze. Quite often it is in the shape of a household object or a tool, and quite battered, until you look at it carefully."

"What does it do?"

"For the Resisters it is always the means to turn back the advances of the Harsh. Either it points the way or it fulfils some purpose. In our present case, I suspect that it is the object which can be used to turn off the Great Machine in the North and set time back on its proper course... or courses, since we know of at least five different states of time—"

"But Dr Diamond," said Owen, as much to stop another bewildering lecture on time as anything else, "if we could find it, we could stop the Harsh and I could go home. Where is it?"

"Where is it?" Dr Diamond's face was grave and he leaned

145

forward and studied Owen, his eyes suddenly dark and gleaming. "*Where is it?*"

"Is it missing?" Owen said, suddenly feeling unaccountably worried.

"*Is it missing?*" cried Dr Diamond, getting to his feet and towering over Owen. "Yes, it is missing and that is the central part of the problem, the nub, the crux, the salient point. It is missing, and the reason it is missing, Owen, is that your father took it!"

There was a long silence. Owen could hear the ticking of the five clocks and the moan of the wind against the brass walls of the Nab. How could his *father* have taken it? And yet… In a part of his memory something stirred.

"When your father was a young man, he used to come fishing in the river. He met the Sub-Commandant as the Harsh were threatening. The Sub-Commandant had just woken us for he had detected tremors in the fabric of time. We had to be cautious. Something was interfering with time, but life – your life – was going on as normal."

"What was he like?" Owen could hear the tremor in his voice.

"What was…? Did your mother not…" Owen shook his head mutely. Dr Diamond looked surprised.

"They say he… they say he killed himself," Owen said miserably.

"Suicide?" Dr Diamond stroked his chin thoughtfully.

"No, I don't think so. Not your father. He was brave, like you, and resourceful as well. He was, well, he was a happier person than you, I suppose, but that can't be helped. He fought side by side with us and we succeeded in repulsing the Harsh one more time. We were puzzled by that attack at the time, but now it seems it was part of a grander scheme, and that its purpose was for the Harsh to get their hands on the Mortmain. At which, of course, they failed."

"Where was I?"

"You were a baby. At home with your mother."

"What happened then?"

"We had a gathering in the Convoke, as we normally do before we go back to sleep. Usually, everybody is a little distracted, thinking about the long sleep to come. Nobody missed your father. One minute he was there, the next he was gone. And with him the Mortmain."

"Are you sure it was him?"

"What people say is that it must have been, otherwise why did he sneak off?"

"And what do you think?" If the question discomfited Dr Diamond, he didn't show it.

"If your father did not take the Mortmain then we have somebody very dangerous in our midst. If he *did* take it, he must have had a very good reason."

"I don't remember my father," Owen said quietly. Dr Diamond put his hand on his shoulder.

"Then you aren't in a position to judge him. Let's deal with the present and let the past – or is it the future? – look after itself."

"What about… Gobillard?"

"I almost forgot," Dr Diamond said, frowning, "and time is short. Gobillard was the first Navigator and the Keeper of the Mortmain. Much of the knowledge about him is lost, and his lore about the Mortmain."

"But the chest in my bedroom!" Owen burst out. Quickly, he told Dr Diamond about the old chest.

"Your father's?" asked Dr Diamond. "I'm afraid I do not know what it means. And remember. It is gone, lost in time along with many other things. We may never know how the chest might have helped us. But quickly. I brought you here for two things. To give you information about your father and the Mortmain, but also to see what you can discover yourself. I want you to sit in that seat."

Owen looked at the tatty old leather plane seat and when he sat in it he realised that the levers were familiar-looking.

"I adapted them from gearsticks belonging to old school buses and lorries," Dr Diamond said proudly. Owen was starting to get used to the way that Dr Diamond adapted things.

"What's it for?"

"It's for… let me think how to describe it… I can't say it's for looking back in time, because once you're out of the present, of course, there is no backwards and forwards…" Dr Diamond stopped, seeing the blank look on Owen's face.

"I'll try again." He frowned with effort then brightened. "I know – it's like turning on a television and flicking through the channels with the sound turned down so you have to guess what's going on. Except the television here is time itself."

Owen thought he knew what Dr Diamond was talking about, and the man was looking at him so eagerly that he nodded his head.

"You might see something useful and you might not," Dr Diamond said, "but it's worth a try. Now, concentrate!"

Dr Diamond began to move the levers and the Skyward started to rotate, slowly at first then at bewildering speed so that Owen could feel his own head starting to spin.

"Now!" cried Dr Diamond, hauling back on a lever so the periscope started to descend from the ceiling. As it reached Owen, he grabbed the handles on either side of it and, feeling like a submarine captain from an old film, pressed his face to the eyepiece.

At first he could see nothing. Or rather what he thought was nothing, but was in fact nothingness which was a different thing altogether. It was like he imagined outer space to be except that was cold and black and this was just… well, he thought, no temperature at all really and no colour.

"Turn the periscope," Dr Diamond said, his voice seeming to come from a great distance. At first the images were a blur but then Owen realised that he could catch them if he went very slowly. There was a vast herd of some kind of deer silently crossing a frozen tundra. He saw a building with flames coming from its windows and a flag fluttering from its highest point. He saw a boy and a girl holding hands beside a sun-dappled pond.

"You're getting it now," said Dr Diamond. "Concentrate!" Owen didn't know what he was supposed to concentrate on exactly, but he kept rotating the periscope. He realised that if he turned the left handle it acted like the focus on a camera. As he turned it, he momentarily glimpsed a house and realised that it was his own home. Then he lost the image and tried to go back to it, but he couldn't find it.

"Keep going," Dr Diamond said urgently. The next image that came up was of a man's hands, one on the steering wheel of a car, the other shifting gears urgently. After that, the images came faster and faster. Something dull and gold flying through a window and landing with a clank on metal. The swaying sensation of a car being flung round corners. Owen was aware that Dr Diamond was shouting to him, but he couldn't hear the words. In his nostrils it seemed that he could smell salt water, and then it was as if he was floating through air, and the image was of the world outside the car, spinning upside down.

The final image was the most frightening. The car was filling with dark water. There was sunlight coming through the windscreen, but it took on a greenish tinge and started to fade. The water rose higher and higher, and Owen imagined that it was rising towards his nose and mouth and he shouted out. As he did so, he saw the hands that he had seen on the wheel desperately hammering at the side window until it broke. Then he knew what was happening. That he was the person in the car and that the hands belonged to his father. The hands lifted him and thrust him through the broken window. For a moment, all was watery darkness then sunlight flooded the eyepiece of the periscope. Owen felt Dr Diamond gently removing his hands from the handles. He lay back in the chair and his chest rose and fell as he drew great shuddering breaths.

CHAPTER ELEVEN

It was almost half an hour before Owen recovered enough to tell Dr Diamond what he had seen. Dr Diamond looked troubled.

"It seems that you were in the car with your father, being pursued. In great danger, if I'm not mistaken."

Owen could almost still feel the hands thrusting him through the broken window of the car. "The hands seemed huge," he said. "Far bigger than normal."

"That is because you were a small child, Owen. A man's hands seem vast to a very small child. Somehow the car crashed into water, and your father saved you by breaking a window and pushing you through it."

"But my father was never found. He just disappeared. Would they not have...?"

"Would they not have known where to look for the car

and found his body when they found you? Is that what you are thinking? But perhaps you weren't found at that spot, or some other factor came into play. We don't know what happened."

"But I do know what happened," another voice intervened. Owen looked around, startled. The Sub-Commandant was standing right behind him. Owen had not heard him enter, but Dr Diamond seemed to know that he was there.

"Then tell us, please, Sub-Commandant."

The little man cleared away a mess of soldering irons and circuit boards and motorcycle workshop manuals and sat down.

"You know, Owen, that I am the Watcher?" Owen nodded. "When the Resisters go to sleep, I fade so that ordinary people going about their business cannot see me. I step back into the shadows of time, if you like. But there is a little time when I am in both worlds. I was down at the harbour that day. The world had woken up around me. There were cars and people everywhere; what you call normal life, Owen."

"Could people see you?" Owen asked.

"Yes, and touch if they wanted. But I tried to stay out of their way. And this is the point, Owen. I could still touch people in your time. And on my journey back I found a baby, soaking wet, but fast asleep, at the edge of the harbour. Listening to what you have just said about the car going into the water, I realise that the baby was you."

"What did you do?" Dr Diamond asked.

"There was little time," the Sub-Commandant said. "I was fading fast. I dried the child as best I could and carried him to the little shop near your house."

"Mary White's!" Owen said.

"Yes. An old woman, but she sees a lot. In fact, I think she saw me leave the child at her back door, but she made no move to talk to me. Perhaps she thought I was a ghost, for I was fading fast into the shadows of time."

"You didn't see what happened?" Dr Diamond asked anxiously.

"No, but it must have had something to do with the Mortmain," the Sub-Commandant said.

"It must have," agreed Dr Diamond. The two men fell into an anxious silence.

"Come on," the Sub-Commandant said, getting to his feet. "I'll take you home." Owen noticed for the first time that the man was limping and there was a smear of dried blood on his cheek.

Dr Diamond said goodnight and they climbed down the stairway in silence. And in silence they walked along the path towards the Den. Miraculously, the area around the path seemed to have remained untouched and Owen welcomed the familiar shadow of the trees.

The Sub-Commandant stopped at the entrance to the Den

with a further thank you for his swift thinking in thwarting the Harsh.

"Did it… did it kill them?" Owen asked.

"I don't think so. I don't think they can be killed. But I suspect you sent them fleeing north in disarray – I cannot sense their presence any more. But it is a long time since anyone did even that much. Goodnight, young Owen, and sleep free of fear."

"Wait… wait a minute, please," Owen said. "Nobody said what happened to him. My father. Did you see…?"

"I don't know," the small man said gently, "but it would seem that he did not get out of the car."

"They never found the body."

"I cannot say for certain, but if I answer truthfully then I believe that he drowned." He watched Owen carefully, but the boy only felt numb. "Do you want me to come in with you?" he asked. Owen shook his head.

He watched the Sub-Commandant walk off deep in thought. He suspected he knew what was on the man's mind. The one thing the two men had not mentioned in his story. The dull glint of metal thrown from the car. *The Mortmain*, he thought. It had to be.

As he entered the Den a shape moved in the dark. He leapt forward and tussled with it, but a swift kick to his shins sent him hopping about in agony. His lamp came on. It was Cati.

"Sorry about the shin," she said, "but I thought you were going to strangle me."

"Why didn't you put the light on?"

"I didn't want my father to find me. He would have taken me back to the Workhouse for the night and I wanted to know what had happened to you."

Tired as he was, Owen took Cati through the events of the day. She gasped at his account of the Harsh and what Owen had done with the mirror. She told him that the Planemen had come back to attack the warehouses. They had been driven off, but many children had been injured. Owen went on to tell her about the Skyward and how he had seen his father.

"Your father's a hero," Cati said indignantly. "He saved your life."

"I suppose so." Owen didn't sound convinced. He yawned.

"I have to get some sleep," he said. "You'd better stay here tonight. It's not safe to walk back on your own. There's spare blankets over there."

Owen fell on to the old sofa fully dressed and pulled up his sleeping bag. Cati made a nest out of her blankets and crawled into it. The fire had not been lit and it was cold, but Cati had enough blankets and the little Den was safe and she soon felt sleep stealing over her. For one moment, she thought she heard a stifled sob from the old sofa. She listened, but did not hear the noise again, and in a few minutes she was fast asleep.

*   *   *

They had just woken the next morning when an unwelcome visitor arrived. Owen had lit the fire and there were oatcakes cooking on an old pan, and water boiling.

"This is all very domestic," an unpleasant, drawling voice said. Owen looked up to see Samual in the doorway. Samual took in the Den, the old sofa, the broken wing mirror on the wall, the old boat propeller, and the empty space where the dressing table had been.

"What do *you* want?" said Cati.

"Just being neighbourly," said Samual. "I wanted to see how our hero was doing this morning." There was a sneer in his voice.

"We're just having breakfast," Owen said, not looking at Samual.

"Ah yes, got to keep our strength up. Particularly for the Convoke this morning." The man stepped further into the Den. Cati glared and Owen stood up. "Do you think that this is the end of the Harsh? Do you not think that Johnston is gathering his men to crush us? And do you realise that we are helpless? That without the Mortmain we cannot defeat them?" He was face to face with Owen now and the boy could see the hatred in Samual's eyes.

"It's not Owen's fault that the Mortmain is missing," snapped Cati.

"No?" the man said silkily, his eyes not leaving Owen's for

a moment. "But when the father is treacherous, does not the stench of treachery linger around the son?"

Cati, furious, grabbed a branch from the pile of firewood and drew back as if to hit Samual. But before she could swing at him, Owen grabbed the branch from behind. Samual laughed.

"Get out," Owen said in a low voice. "You aren't welcome here."

"You can say that again," said Cati, struggling to tug the branch out of Owen's grip.

"I have things to do," Samual said, "but just remember: some people may think you are a hero, but there are many who can see beneath the skin." With one final contemptuous look at Cati, he turned and was gone. Owen released the branch.

"Why didn't you let me at him?" Cati demanded.

"I nearly did, but you know, the thing is, he's right, Cati. My father did take the Mortmain. Even Dr Diamond thinks so. He was trying to say stuff about my father having had good reasons for doing it, but I knew what he meant."

"Your father saved you," said Cati angrily, "and he's not here to speak for himself. He needs you to defend him."

"I wish I could," Owen said quietly.

"I can't believe you're talking like this!" Cati's eyes were fiery and bright spots of red glowed on her cheeks. "When you needed him he was there. And now he needs you and you're coming out with all this 'I don't know if I can trust him' stuff.

Well, if you can't trust him then you can't trust me either and I can't be your friend."

Cati stormed out. Owen sat down on the sofa. He felt tears pricking his eyes. He didn't know what to think. He went back over what he had seen in the Skyward. The hands working frantically at the steering wheel. The dull golden object thrown from the speeding car that had to be the Mortmain. If only he knew where it had fallen.

Suddenly, he knew what had to be done. He stood up and scattered earth over the remains of the fire. He stuffed the oatcakes into his pocket and set out towards the Workhouse.

Preparations for the Convoke were well underway. He saw Contessa going in, and Chancellor, and Rutgar. To his satisfaction he saw Dr Diamond coming down from the Nab, taking the steps two at a time. Owen ducked as the man passed him. He seemed to be reciting mathematical formulas to himself. Owen didn't know much about mathematical formulas, but they sounded suspiciously backwards. When Dr Diamond was out of sight, Owen sprang on to the steps and ran up them.

Trying to stay low so that he wouldn't be seen, he ran up and up, on to the roof and then on to the swaying pillar of the Nab itself. He was out of breath and his legs ached, but he forced himself upwards until he had reached the walkway surrounding the polished cylinder of the Skyward. He was afraid that Dr Diamond might have locked it, but he need not have worried. When the two doors had aligned, he dived through them and fell on to the other side.

The place hadn't been left entirely unguarded. As Owen picked himself up, a hatch in the ceiling fell open on what sounded like rusty hinges. An ancient-looking polaroid camera on a broom handle dropped down, turning this way and that like an owl woken from sleep. The broom handle fell further down until the camera was in his face. The flash went off right in his eyes, blinding him. Owen made a swipe for the camera, but as he did so it shot back up into the ceiling, the hatch door banging shut after it with what sounded like an alarmed squawk.

Dr Diamond would know that he had been there, Owen thought, but it couldn't be helped. He seated himself in the leather seat and looked at the levers. He had watched carefully as Dr Diamond had manipulated them, and Owen thought he could make them work. But there might be things that he had not seen. There might be dangers that he had not heard of. Taking a deep breath, he pushed the first lever forward and then the second.

For a moment nothing happened and then, slowly at first, the Skyward began to rotate. He pushed the levers further forward and the Skyward moved faster and faster. He pushed them to their limit and the outside quickly became a blur. There were five other levers. Three went forward and one back and the last one brought the periscope down. Owen looked at them. What if he couldn't stop the machine? What if he got stranded somewhere in time? But he had to go back to the time he had seen before. He had to find out what had happened to the Mortmain. Quickly, before he had time to change his mind, he manipulated the first four levers then pressed the last one. The periscope began to descend from the ceiling. When it got to him, he folded out the handles. Gulping a little, he put his face to the eyepiece.

For a moment there was the same nothingness Owen had seen before. Then his mother's face appeared; not the sad, worn face that he had seen so often in the past few years, but a face in which a secret smile still lingered. She was looking at something that he could not see, but he was sure it was his father. Other images floated in as he turned the handles – his school, a toy car lying in the yard. His thoughts were drifting when suddenly an image of a man came into view – a man holding a knife, his face covered in blood and a look of terror on his face as he backed away from an unknown enemy. Quickly, Owen spun the handles and the man faded away. *Concentrate*, he thought. That was what Dr Diamond had said.

He tried to summon the image of the dull golden object spinning away from the car. He turned the handles slowly and a landscape of scrubby trees came into view. There were old tyres and broken windscreens and bits of engine scattered among the trees. He concentrated again, willing the picture to open out. He saw wrecked boats, piles of rusty scrap and oil cans… There was something familiar about it… then he realised. It was Johnston's yard! And just as this realisation sprang into his mind a car appeared; a silver Alfa Romeo, his father's car, the passenger door flapping open, speeding towards the yard gate, and behind it Johnston aiming a rifle and squeezing off shots. The car had almost reached the gate; it only had to turn sharply left to avoid an old truck chassis. But, as Owen's father turned the wheel, the passenger door was thrown violently open and something dull and golden slid off the seat, through the open door, and bounced off into the piles of scrap.

The Mortmain! Owen thought.

The car slowed down. A bullet struck the roof and ricocheted off. His father looked into the back, and Owen saw a small figure in a baby seat and knew that he was seeing himself. His father turned back to the wheel and the car sped out of the yard, leaving the Mortmain behind. A moment later, Johnston and several other men sped after him in a truck, passing by the spot where the Mortmain had fallen without slowing.

The Mortmain. Somehow it had been in his father's possession, but he had lost it and now it was somewhere in Johnston's yard. Owen shut his eyes and tried to fix the spot in his mind. There was a pile of broken batteries and the hulk of a steel boat in a trailer to the left of the spot. He opened his eyes and recoiled in fear. It seemed that he was staring right into Johnston's eyes which burned as they glared at him, the man's face filling the screen.

Terrified, Owen spun the handle until Johnston disappeared. He was about to stop searching, but something made him look at one more image, one that he wished he hadn't seen. Cati was standing on what seemed like an island. The wind tore at her hair. He couldn't see what she was looking at, but tears ran down her cheeks and her face was a mask of grief. Before he could focus in on her, the image started to slip away. Fearing that Johnston's face might come up again, Owen tore his gaze away from the eyepiece and pushed the handles back into place. Working quickly, but trying to remember the right sequence, he pulled the levers back into place. The periscope slid back into the ceiling and gradually the Skyward slowed and came to a halt.

Owen tried to leave things as he found them. Dr Diamond would know he had been there, of course, but perhaps not immediately. Moving quickly, he slipped outside and down the steps. He did not want to miss anything of what was happening at the Convoke.

At the bottom of the stairs he ran towards the door of the Starry. He couldn't be seen at the Convoke. He would climb to the little window that Cati had shown him, and for that he needed to go through the Starry.

He opened the door and slipped inside. The place was as he remembered it, quiet, as if the quiet had accumulated over centuries, the starlit glow of the ceiling throwing a gentle light on to those who slept on below. Owen had a strange feeling that he was not alone in the place, or at least that he was not the only person *awake* in the Starry.

He crept quietly forward until he reached the middle of the floor. At the other end he saw a woman bending over one of the beds. Creeping closer Owen saw that it was Pieta. She was standing over a boy and a girl. The boy was about ten years old and the girl was perhaps fourteen. Pieta was gently brushing the girl's hair. Both children were rosy-cheeked and peaceful, but they showed no sign of waking. It was a private moment and Owen tried to slip away, but as he did so, the magno gun which was hanging forgotten over his shoulder clanked against an empty bed. Pieta's head snapped round.

"Who is it?" she said, in a low, dangerous voice. "Who is there?"

"It's me, Owen," he said, feeling unaccountably guilty.

"What are you doing here?"

"I was on my way to…" He hesitated, but something told him that it would not be a good idea to lie to Pieta. "I was on my way up to the little balcony so that I could watch the Convoke without being seen."

"Without being seen," she said softly, and he thought he sensed a bleak smile in the darkness. "Come here." Owen walked over until he was standing beside Pieta. "Look at me."

Owen's eyes met hers. They were green and fathomless.

She held his gaze for a moment then her eyes dropped away to the two children. They had the same white skin and fine bone structure as their mother.

"You are going to spy on the Convoke?"

"I'm not a spy!" he said hotly.

"No?" she said. "I suppose you're not. You just don't want them to stare at you, not knowing whether you are bringing good or evil to them." Owen nodded dumbly.

"And sometimes it's hard to know your own heart," she continued, "and whether you are a good person or a bad person." Her voice had dropped so that it seemed as if she was talking to herself, and for a moment the fierce warrior dropped away and she just seemed like a mother gazing on her sleeping children with love in her eyes.

Without thinking, and not really understanding what he was doing, Owen reached out and placed the palm of each hand on the forehead of each child. Pieta watched him. There was a question in her eyes, but she didn't try to stop him. He took his hands away and stood up. He waited for her to say something, but those strange green eyes merely studied him.

Owen turned away from her. He felt very tired. He started to walk away, but stumbled slightly. Pieta's hand caught his elbow. He recovered his balance and continued to walk towards the stairwell leading to the little balcony. He could feel her eyes on his back all the way.

Owen took the stairs two at a time and his legs were

aching by the time he ducked through the little door and rolled out on to the balcony. He could tell straightaway that the Convoke was tense. Samual faced the others. Chancellor looked troubled, as did Contessa. The Sub-Commandant's face was harder to read.

"Look what damage they did in one attack," Samual was saying. "They nearly overran us. We can't hold out. Now is the time, when we hold a little of the upper hand, to seek terms."

"So that Johnston can put us back to sleep, and then kill us where we lie, is that what you're saying, Samual?" said Contessa softly.

"The offer of Sleep was a negotiating ploy!" Samual said. "We can force Johnston to improve his offer, give guarantees of our safety."

There was a murmur of approval from the crowd. Owen looked at them for the first time. Many of them were injured, some of them still wearing bloodstained clothing. They looked tired and frightened. He could see that the prospect of another attack filled them with dread.

"I'm not letting no Harsh put me to sleep, I do tell you that for nothing!" Wesley had been standing quietly in the crowd but now he strode forward.

"Me neither," Cati said bravely, her cheeks reddening as people turned to stare. Samual snorted.

"This is what I mean. We can't turn back an attack with a

half-dressed boy and a skinny girl." The Sub-Commandant's cool stare fell on Samual. "No matter how courageous," the richly-dressed man added swiftly.

"I'm with the youngsters," said Rutgar gruffly. "My men and women will stand as long as there is breath in them!" The words were brave, Owen thought, but Rutgar's eyes were red-rimmed and there was a bloodstained bandage on his head.

"These are issues that need to be discussed," Chancellor said. "We cannot decide them overnight. Perhaps the Mortmain can be found."

"The Mortmain should never have been lost... or stolen," said Samual slyly.

"It was never stolen!" Cati cried. "And the only reason it was lost was because he was trying to save—" She was interrupted by a loud bang followed by an alarming fizzing noise coming from the direction of Dr Diamond's leather baseball cap. Dr Diamond took the cap off. Wisps of smoke rose from it.

"Direction finder," he mumbled. "Prototype... needs work."

"I think we should end the Convoke," the Sub-Commandant said. "We all need food and rest. It will take Johnston a few days to regroup at any rate."

Chancellor nodded in agreement. Samual didn't say anything, but he looked at Cati in a very peculiar way. The malfunctioning baseball cap had stopped Cati saying too much about what Owen had seen… if indeed it *had* been a malfunction. But Samual knew now that she had information about the Mortmain. Owen rolled off the balcony and ran down the stairs. He wanted to be well clear of the Workhouse before the Convoke emerged. He was worried about what he had seen. Samual wanted them to come to terms with Johnston and at least some of the people backed him. The Mortmain *had* to be found if the Workhouse and its Resisters were not to be surrendered. There was no sign of Pieta in the Starry and he ran lightly through it, not wishing to feel sleepy, particularly now.

Outside it was dark and Owen was surprised that he had spent so much time watching the Convoke. The night air hit him and he shivered. It was much colder suddenly. He made his way back to the Den without meeting anyone. There he packed some food he had set aside, slightly stale bread and a little pie. On the bed lay a coat. Someone had been here. He picked it up. It was made out of leather, lined with some kind of silky fleece. It had a hood like a parka anorak, lined as well. It was heavy and didn't smell as good as it might have done, but he remembered the cold outside and slipped it on. Owen stood in the middle of the Den and looked around. He wondered if he would ever see it again. He put the bag containing the food over his shoulder and lifted the magno gun. He walked through the door and out on to the path, where he turned towards the river. As he did so a single snowflake touched his face. He shivered and pulled the coat closer around him.

There was a different quality to the cold, Owen thought, that told you that it was more than just a dip in temperature, that it was here to stay.

He stayed clear of the log bridge. He knew it would be guarded. But he thought there was another way across the river, a little way downstream towards the harbour. Using the debris of the attack for cover, he skirted the Resister defences, coming so close he could hear them talking quietly.

After ten minutes' walk, most of it bent double or on his hands and knees so that his back ached, he arrived at the place he had seen from the Nab. A tall pine tree had been struck by the magno cannon at ground level. The tree hadn't fallen, but it leaned over the river at an improbable angle and the very tip of it hung over the opposite bank. He didn't know how he was going to get down from it, but at least he would be on the other side. Pulling the parka tightly around him he started to climb.

The tree didn't feel at all secure. If he moved too fast, it swayed from side to side and up and down so that he felt seasick. And once, when he got to the middle, he felt the roots shift and the whole tree drop by several metres. Fear welled in his stomach as he saw the black water below. Owen clung to the tree trunk for several minutes before he was able to force himself onwards. As the tree narrowed towards the top, it became harder to climb until in the end he reached a point where he could go no further without his weight snapping the slender trunk. Yet he was still about seven metres in the air, unsure as to whether there was water beneath him or the dry land of the opposite bank.

Owen hung there quietly, trying not to look at the water and scanning the bank for signs of Johnston's men. He could see no one, nor had he seen anything from the Nab. They'd retreated right back as far as the area around the scrapyard. Owen looked down. If he let go, he might just land on the bank. But then again he might land in the water. And if he landed on the bank from the height he was at, he might break a leg or an arm and then he'd be helpless. The tree had been a bad idea all along. There was no way he could get to the opposite bank unseen. With a sigh he started to inch back until, with a terrifying creak, the roots let go.

Owen seemed to be in the air for ages, the ground rushing up towards him. Long enough for him to see that he was going to hit the ground and not the water. Long enough for him to realise, with a blinding flash, that he was scared of the water not because he was Harsh, but because he had come close to drowning as a baby. "Idiot," he muttered to himself, just as the ground rushed up and met him, the frozen, rock-hard soil of the bank. And then he was aware of nothing more.

At the moment Owen lost consciousness, something else happened. In the warm dark of the Starry there was a stirring. Slow at first, an eyelid flickering, a change in the slow breathing of one who had slept for perhaps hundreds of years. And then something more definite. A leg moving, a hand opening – a girl's hand. Then eyes opening – the same strange green eyes as those of Pieta, first one pair and then another. And then the slender girl who had been sleeping under her mother's watchful gaze that morning sat up, stretched and yawned, and turned to smile at her brother as he too stirred and yawned.

CHAPTER TWELVE

Owen opened his eyes. He was lying on his back staring up at the night sky and his first thought was that he had never seen so many stars nor seen them so clearly, each of them sharply defined so that they seemed to be raining light down on him. His head was pounding and his limbs were aching and he felt as if he was lying on a very springy bed. But he knew that he couldn't be because it was freezing cold. He turned over on to his side, moving carefully, and realised that the springy bed was in fact the branches of a pine tree – and then it came back to him, how the tree had fallen and he had fallen with it. The pine branches had cushioned his fall.

Very carefully, Owen got to his feet. His head felt like somebody had hit it with a hammer, his right arm was so bruised he could barely move it and it took a few minutes to get his legs working properly again, but he was across the river and that was the important thing. He stepped out of the tangle of branches and tried to get his bearings. Most of the fields that had been here had turned to dense forest, but he had a good idea of how to get to Johnston's yard, providing he didn't run into any of Johnston's men on the way. Owen made his way towards the edge of the trees. As he did so, he heard a soft whirring sound in the air high above his head. He threw himself face down and lay as still as he could until it had faded into the distance. He didn't know if the Planemen could see in the dark, but he didn't want to take any chances. Cautiously, he got to his feet and slipped soundlessly into the forest.

Cati didn't know what to do with herself. She had gone up to the Nab and got under Dr Diamond's feet. He had sent her to the kitchens to get some flour for him, but she knew that he was really trying to get rid of her. She hung about the kitchens until Contessa told her that the kitchens were a place for working, not mooching, and there were injured fighters who needed to be tended to if she really wanted something to do. Cati was miserable without Owen and she knew that she should go to the Den and make things better. But that would mean saying she was wrong, and Cati did not like saying she was wrong. Particularly when she knew she was right.

She was going out of the front door of the Workhouse when she met the Sub-Commandant.

"Come with me quickly," he said. "There's something I

want you to see." He walked on without waiting to see if she was following. Shaking off her mood, Cati hurried after.

The Sub-Commandant threw open the doors of the Convoke and strode in. Pieta was sitting by the fire on her own. There were several bottles on top of the fireplace and her eyes were bleary when she looked up. The Sub-Commandant walked quickly over to her. He went down on one knee and started speaking urgently into her ear. Her head straightened. She looked at him with what seemed to Cati like distrust. Her father spoke again. Taking Pieta by the hand, he made her rise to her feet and led her gently across the hall. She stumbled several times, but the night air outside seemed to revive her.

They went round the side of the Workhouse to the little door of the Starry, where the Sub-Commandant stopped. Almost hesitantly, Pieta went in ahead. Cati stood in the doorway beside her father. Almost against her will she took his hand, something she had not done since she was a small child. As her eyes got used to the gloom of the Starry, she saw a boy and a girl holding hands. They were smiling shyly. Pieta knelt in front of them, making small sounds of wonder. The two children dashed towards Pieta and flung their arms round her neck. The Sub-Commandant, smiling, drew Cati backwards, closing the door gently behind him.

"That's not for us to watch," he said gently. His hand held Cati's tightly. They walked in silence.

"Are they her children?" Cati asked.

"Yes. They fell asleep many, many years ago and did not wake, and the pain and the bitterness gnawed at Pieta."

"What will happen now?"

"Hopefully, she will be healed. And if she is healed, she may not be the great fighter that she was. But no matter. Without the Mortmain we haven't much of a chance anyway."

"But we do have a chance?" Cati said anxiously.

"There's always a chance," said the Sub-Commandant, seeing her anxiety. "We have fought the Harsh many times and each time we've held the line. Now," he went on, "what about young Owen? How is he getting on?"

"Well…" Cati began. The Sub-Commandant noticed her hesitation.

"What is it?" he said.

"We had a fight," she said, her voice low.

"Tell me about it." He didn't look at her, but Cati could tell that he wasn't pleased. She told him what had happened. How Owen had doubted his own father and how she had stuck up for the man. The Sub-Commandant sighed.

"You have to understand, Cati. So many things have let Owen down, including his sense of reality. Even time has let him down. Then people tell him that his father is a thief. Worse than a thief. A traitor. He's angry and bewildered and he blames his father. He thought that his father had killed himself. Dr Diamond thinks that he did not and I agree. But either way, Owen feels abandoned."

"I think I understand," said Cati slowly, "and I should have kept my big mouth shut."

"Exactly," the Sub-Commandant said firmly. "Now, what we have to do is to go to the Den and see Owen, and make sure that he doesn't go to sleep miserable. Do you think that's a good idea?" Her father's tone was light, but Cati knew that she wasn't really being asked a question. She nodded without speaking, and they turned away from the Workhouse and on to the path to the Den.

Her father knew straightaway that something was wrong. He paused at the entrance to the Den and Cati saw his eyes narrow. With one hand on the weapon at his waist he crept forward, Cati following. He went through the little entryway and held up his weapon, his finger on the trigger so that it emitted a low, blue light, enough to illuminate the scene of devastation. Owen's sleeping bag and sofa had been torn apart and the contents strewn over the floor, which itself was full of holes as if someone had been digging in search of something. Loose stones had been ripped from the walls, and the car radio and lorry wing mirror had been smashed to pieces.

Cati found candles in the debris and lit them. The Sub-Commandant examined the scene with great care.

"Is there anything missing?" he asked.

"Not that I can think of," Cati replied. "It's hard to tell. Have they taken Owen?"

"I don't think so. There's no sign of a struggle. Just a search."

"What were they looking for?"

"The same thing we are. The Mortmain. Which is good."

"How can this be good?" Cati said, looking at the mess around her.

"It's good because it means that the Mortmain is still lost. If the Harsh got their hands on it then the end would be near."

He took one of the candles and began to examine the walls of the Den.

"Where is it, then?" asked Cati.

"If it fell from the car at Johnston's, then the chances are that it is still there, among the scrap, unless…" His voice tailed off.

"Unless what?" said Cati impatiently.

"Unless someone picked it up by mistake," the Sub-Commandant said slowly. "Unless they mistook it for something else." He bent to pick up an object.

Cati could not see what he was looking at. She ducked round the broken sofa until she was standing beside him. The Sub-Commandant was turning the object over and over in his hands, something with a dull gleam.

"That's only an old boat propeller," Cati exclaimed. "Owen picked it up at Johnston's scrapyard…" Her voice tailed off as she realised what she was saying.

"Is it?" the Sub-Commandant said, almost under his breath,

and his eyes gleamed in the candlelight. "Is it only an old propeller? Look!" He thrust the object under her nose. There were three blades just like a propeller, but the round hole in the middle, where the driveshaft would have gone, did not look like it belonged to an ordinary propeller. It had been etched and grooved in patterns which seemed at once completely random and very precise, and when you moved the object a line would seem to disappear and reappear somewhere else, some of the lines running to the edge of the round hole and seeming to pour out of it like liquid; others were like moving shadowlines that you could only see out of the corner of your eye, then disappeared when you looked straight at them.

"It is, isn't it?" whispered Cati.

"It is the Mortmain," her father said, his eyes bright with amazement. "Owen had it here all along and did not know it."

He turned it over in his hands again and Cati gazed on it, astonished at the way it transformed itself from a piece of tarnished metal into a marvellous object, gleaming with hidden fire and meaning, then mutating back into an old propeller.

"What do we do?"

"It's not for us to decide. There will have to be a Convoke."

"What do you think?"

"I think that in this case the Mortmain is a kind of a key. I think it is the key to the Great Machine in the North. Someone will have to take it there, is my guess, and use it to stop the Machine."

"Who will take it?"

The Sub-Commandant hesitated. A cold breeze blew through the Den and Cati shivered. "It should have been Owen," he said finally. "It should have been. History dictates it. But something warns me that it will not be. That Owen is already gone."

"Gone where?"

"I saw him earlier, going towards the river. I thought he was going to see Wesley at the harbour. I should have gone after him."

"Gone *where*?" Cati insisted.

"They say that the sins of a father should not be visited on the son, but I'm afraid sometimes they are. I think Owen has crossed the river to look for the Mortmain."

Owen found it hard going in the trees. It was dense, old growth forest. The trees were gnarled and mossy, and half-rotten trunks lay across his path, hidden by undergrowth, so that he stumbled often. Ivy and creepers hung down, brushing his face like cold hands, making him jump. And there were noises as well. An owl hooting, a night jar and strange rustling noises. Once something large pushed through the undergrowth near him and he stood very still and held his breath until it had gone. He didn't know what it was, but he noted that it wasn't afraid to make noise.

It was about a mile to Johnston's house and, before time

went backwards, it would have taken Owen fifteen minutes walking through open fields. But now he had been in the forest for over an hour. The branches of the trees were bare, but little starlight filtered through them. After three quarters of an hour he had stumbled out on to a well-used path. He knew that he couldn't take it, that it was probably the route used by Johnston's men to get to the riverbank. It was too risky, so he backed into the woods again and tried to steer a course close to the path, but far enough away so that a passing patrol would not hear him crashing through the undergrowth.

As he pushed on, his face scratched by twigs and his muscles aching from the fall from the pine tree, Owen thought about Cati. He regretted quarrelling with her. He had few enough friends in the Workhouse as it was. And if he hadn't quarrelled with her, she would be with him now. Then perhaps it was a good thing they had fallen out, he thought grimly. His father had lost the Mortmain and it was up to Owen to get it back, not Cati. Still, he wished he had someone who would make a joke or talk. Anything to help lighten the gloom of the forest.

He pushed on, more and more slowly, bumping into tree trunks, briars wrapping themselves round his legs so that he had to stop and unwind them. It was almost as if the forest was alive and full of malice. An image of Dr Diamond came into Owen's head and he almost laughed out loud. He wondered how Dr Diamond would react if you asked him for the right time. The answer wouldn't be simple. A cold wind rattled the branches above and Owen wished that he was back in Dr Diamond's Skyward. Then he realised that Dr Diamond too would be angry with him for breaking into the Skyward and using the machine.

The full loneliness of his position became clear. Rutgar would be mad at him for getting through his defences and crossing the river. The Sub-Commandant would side with Cati. Samual hated him anyway. Chancellor seemed to think of him as a mere boy, and his father's son at that. *Contessa*, he thought. Perhaps Contessa would speak up for him. And Wesley, even if it was only for the sake of annoying the others. It wouldn't be enough, Owen realised. Even if he had the Mortmain, it wouldn't be enough. And if he returned without it, they would surely brand him a spy. He sighed.

After another half an hour he started to slow. The undergrowth was getting thinner and Owen took that as a sign he was reaching the edge of the forest. He didn't want to stumble into one of Johnston's patrols. After a few minutes he could see lights through the trees and then he was at the edge of the forest. He could see that the trees in front of him had been slashed and burned to create a clearing. Owen crept forward to the very edge of the trees and knew that the light he had seen was Johnston's house, far bigger than he had remembered, although it had been hidden behind trees. But there were no trees this time and the huge manor dominated the ground around it. All the windows blazed with magno light. To the left of the massive front doors were French windows, larger even than the doors. These lay open and music drifted out. The house resembled an ocean liner sailing through the night.

To his right, he could see a large encampment of tents, laid out like a small town with streets between blocks of tents, and open spaces. *For cooking*, he thought, for large fires blazed here and there. The streets were strewn with rubbish, and Owen wrinkled his nose at the smell drifting towards him. To his left, he could see the place where the scrapyard had been, but little of the scrap remained. All that was left were bits of brass, old fenders, copper water tanks. That was where he had to go.

Before Owen had a chance to move, he heard voices. He ducked back into the trees as two men walked past. They were both tough-looking, with the long sideburns that Johnston's men wore. One of them had a rose behind his ear, although where he had got a rose in Winter Owen could not tell. He waited until the two men had gone then started to edge through the trees, towards the scrap. He knew he would have to cross the open ground, but he meant to get as close as possible before he did so. The wind, which he had barely felt in the forest, was stronger now, and the treetops shuddered and shook. He felt small icy particles stinging his face. Owen moved quickly, the noise of the trees masking his passage, and within a minute he was level with the scrap. He could see a copse of small scrubby trees growing in the middle of it. Once he got there, he thought, he could get his bearings and see if he could work out where the Mortmain might have fallen when it was thrown from his father's car.

He crouched at the edge of the trees, looking up and down. He couldn't see anyone coming. The icy wind carried a burst of harsh laughter down from the tent town, and somewhere, faintly, he could still hear the music coming from the open French windows. He tried to gauge the distance, perhaps two hundred metres, exposed to anyone who might come out of the tent village, and overlooked by Johnston's manor. A great gust of wind brought a fine cloud of icy particles, and for a moment the house and village were obscured. Now, Owen realised, it had to be now. He exploded from the trees, arms and legs pumping.

It was further than he thought. Much further. And the icy blast which had helped hide him died down before he was halfway across. He felt terribly exposed and the trees seemed to get no nearer. Owen waited for the shout of a guard, heavy feet running behind him. He felt the blood pounding in his ears and his breath was coming in great shuddering gasps. Stumbling, almost weeping, he fell into the shelter of the trees. He lay still, fighting for breath, his sides aching. He couldn't remember ever having run so fast. His heart thumped madly, but gradually he was able to get his breath and sit up cautiously.

Owen had a mental picture of the way the scrapyard had looked when the Mortmain had fallen from the car. The driveway from the house still led through the scrap and the sharp corner where the door had swung open was still there, perhaps a hundred metres away. If he went on his hands and knees, he thought, or crawled on his belly, he could reach it. He moved to the edge of the trees. And as he moved he felt as if a great shadow was falling over him, and then a crushing weight, so that he was pinned to the ground. He struggled and then lay still. Rough hands turned him over. He found himself looking into the dark, fathomless eyes of the man he had seen earlier, the rose still behind his ear. Owen could smell an oily perfume, and the man's voice when he spoke was low and strangely accented.

"Now, Pretty," he said, "still yourself. Where is Pretty going? What is Pretty looking for? I think we must talk with Johnston. Johnston will know."

CHAPTER THIRTEEN

The Convoke was crowded, but there was little noise. Shadows from the fire danced round the ancient walls. The Mortmain was on a low table in front of the fire, gleaming softly. The Resister leaders stood round it. All, that is, except Pieta. She sat in her usual chair by the fire. But this time she wasn't slumped with a bottle. This time her back was straight and her eyes were bright and each hand rested on the shoulder of a child, a tall, yellow-haired girl and a solemn, yellow-haired boy, each with a look in their eyes which said that they had lived in their dreams for many, many years.

"The first thing we must say," Chancellor began, "even before we start our discussion on what must be done, is how glad we are that Pieta's children have awoken from their long sleep."

There was a murmur of agreement from the crowd. Pieta did not smile, but her eyes flashed and the children seemed to stand even more ramrod straight, proud and haughty like their mother.

"I agree," the Sub-Commandant said, "but time is short. We must decide what to do with the Mortmain."

"There is only one decision," Pieta said, "and well you know it, Sub-Commandant. The Mortmain must be taken to the Puissance, the Great Machine in the North, and a way must be found to reverse it so that time flows the way it should."

"I agree," the Sub-Commandant said.

"I agree also," said Contessa. Rutgar nodded sharply, and Dr Diamond too. Wesley looked amused at the prospect. Even Samual did not disagree.

"Well, then," Chancellor said, "we have agreed that much. The next question is, who will go?"

"Owen must go," Contessa said. "It is his duty and his right." Chancellor looked uncomfortable.

"What is it, Chancellor?" asked the Sub-Commandant.

"I fear I have bad news about Owen."

"He is gone," the Sub-Commandant said. "I knew that."

"That is not all," Chancellor said, his tone grave. "Not only has he left, but he has gone over to Johnston's side."

There was a gasp from the hall. Cati cried out, "No!" Samual looked pleased. The only person who did not react was Wesley. He kept the same sardonic smile on his face.

"How do you know this, Chancellor?" said Contessa.

"I am not at liberty to say who gave me this information," Chancellor said, his voice dense with sorrow, "but Owen was seen on the other side of the river – with Johnston. And Johnston had his arm around his shoulders. Owen was smiling."

"A spy all along," Samual said with satisfaction.

"No!" Cati shouted, jumping to her feet. "Owen was never a spy!" She burst into tears. People stared at her, but no one moved to comfort her. It was Wesley who walked over and put his arm round her, gently putting her back into her seat.

"This is grave news," Contessa said. "I find it hard to believe."

"I had difficulty believing it myself," agreed Chancellor.

"Like father, like son," Samual said. Cati leapt to her feet again, her face red, but Wesley hauled her back down in her seat and put his finger to his lips. She stared furiously at Samual, but didn't speak.

Wesley leaned over to her. "Had to of been that Samual that made up thon story about Owen and fed it to Chancellor. He's the only one crosses the river for to spy." Cati intensified her glare at Samual.

Wesley noticed that Dr Diamond was now sitting beside Pieta, talking urgently into her ear.

"I think we should not judge until we have had a chance to speak to the young man," the Sub-Commandant said firmly.

"The point is that Owen should have been the one to take the Mortmain to the Puissance. Now he cannot, so who is to take it?"

There was a long silence. The Sub-Commandant waited patiently. When an answer came, it was from an unexpected source.

"Big snows coming," Wesley said lazily. "Looks like you lot will need Boat. So that'll be me going for a start."

"I'm going too," said Cati defiantly.

"The child can't go," Samual said. "She'll get all of you into trouble if she runs into any of the Harsh."

"I'm not a child!" Cati said.

"Where I go, Cati goes," the Sub-Commandant said.

"I think I'll go along too," said Dr Diamond. Rutgar started to speak, but Contessa stopped him.

"Someone will need to stay here and defend the Workhouse, Rutgar. I think that is our job." Rutgar nodded heavily.

"I will go also," Chancellor said. "I have a responsibility in this matter."

"You done pretty well making up them minds of yours," said Wesley, getting to his feet. "I'd say we should be fit to go first thing in the morning, if youse lot can get yourselves ready by then."

"He's right," the Sub-Commandant said. "The sooner the better. The weather is closing in."

"I'll get a stock of food together," Contessa said. "You'll need plenty to get you there and back."

"There anyhow," Wesley muttered. "There mightn't be no back."

"Does anybody know how far it is?" asked Cati quietly.

"No," answered the Sub-Commandant, "nor has anyone here ever seen the Puissance."

"Owen would have been able to find it," Contessa said.

"That is open to question," the Sub-Commandant said. "Nothing has been proved."

"Owen is not here," Chancellor said, his voice harsh, "and I do not wish to hear his name spoken again. He has betrayed us. So our only option is to sail north and hope that luck leads us to it, or we find other Resisters who know where it is."

Wesley jumped to his feet. "Youse lot might have time for chatter, but us lot got Boat to get ready. I'll see youse at dawn at the harbour." He turned and slipped rapidly through the crowd, but not before he gave Cati a warm look.

Cati didn't know why Wesley had stood up for her. Or why he had stopped her speaking. She had the impression there were things going on that she didn't understand. The Convoke was breaking up and Cati allowed herself to be carried along by the crowd as they swept out of the room, talking excitedly about the voyage to come, and about how the young man had been a spy all along, falling silent when they realised that Cati could hear. She thought of unleashing a stream of bad

189

language at them, words she had picked up from Rutgar and his soldiers, but her heart wasn't in it. As the crowd passed the doorway which led to the kitchen, she stepped inside.

The kitchen was her favourite place at night, when everyone had finished. Cati liked the dim light, the gleaming pots lined up behind the stoves, the heat still retained in the giant ovens. Sometimes, she would take a leftover piece of pie from the cold room and squeeze in behind the biggest of the ovens where it was warm. When she was small she called it her house. She was too old for that now, but it was still a safe place to go when she had something on her mind. Also, since her encounter with the Harsh, she seemed to be a little cold all the time, and this was the warmest and cosiest place in the entire Workhouse. And she definitely had something on her mind.

Cati squeezed into the tiny space and leaned her cheek against the warm stone. Why had Owen been with Johnston? And if he was such great friends with Johnston then who had ransacked the Den? And if he was not with Johnston then where was he? Her father had thought that Owen had gone searching for the Mortmain. Was Owen playing some game, pretending to be friendly with Johnston?

The heat of the oven was making Cati drowsy. She felt her eyes start to close and had to shake herself awake. She didn't want to fall asleep behind the ovens. As she started to wriggle out of the space, she heard footsteps. Contessa, she thought, coming to prepare food for the journey the next day. Then she realised there were two sets of feet. The footsteps stopped close to the oven. The first voice she heard was Contessa's.

"You are sure about this course of action? It will be hard on the children."

"I have explained to them," replied the low, harsh voice of Pieta. "They understand that I have to repay my debt."

"What if Owen has gone over to the other side?"

"Do you think so? He can wake the Sleepers. It points to him being the Navigator. And if he is, he can find the Puissance. That is our only chance."

"Other people have come along who could wake the Sleeping."

"I have to try. He woke my children when no one else could. I have to find him or at least find out what happened. You will be the guardian of the children, if you will do it."

"Of course I will, Pieta," Contessa said.

"Take care of them, Contessa." There was a pleading note in Pieta's voice that Cati did not associate with the stern warrior. "They have slept for so long and are still half in the shadows."

"I will treat them as if they were my own," said Contessa.

The two women moved away, still talking, but Cati could not hear them any more. She slipped out from behind the oven and went past the sinks so that they wouldn't see her. *Supplies for tomorrow*, she thought as she ran silently up the steps. She had almost forgotten about the long journey to the North. She shivered, half from excitement, half from fear. And then there was the word that Pieta had used about Owen. She said it over and over in her head. *Navigator... Navigator...* What did it mean? And if he was the Navigator, did it mean that he had not crossed over to the enemy? And what was Pieta planning, in order to pay back her debt to Owen?

Several miles away, Owen was shivering too, but not with excitement. The man with the rose behind his ear had grabbed him by the sleeves and started walking towards Johnston's manor. He walked at an unbelievable speed and, Owen found, was incredibly strong, for when Owen tripped and fell, the man kept up the same rapid pace, dragging the boy behind him effortlessly. The man marched Owen straight to the front door of the manor which opened as he approached it. Owen half staggered, half tumbled up the steps, cracking his shins on the stone.

The door swung open on to a long corridor. There were more of Johnston's men in the corridor, lounging around on battered chairs and looking bored. Weapons were stacked everywhere: magno guns, knives, hatchets, bicycle chains, bottles containing what looked suspiciously like acid. The men watched with interest as Owen was hauled down the corridor at tremendous speed, making comments as he passed.

"Passionara caught himself a rat, so he did."

"Fine big rat."

"What you say, rat?"

"Catch yourself on, Mariacallas. Rat don't talk."

"Rat do big squeak."

"Go on, rat, do squeak." This last was accompanied by a hard kick that made Owen gasp.

"Weren't no squeak that."

"Sounds like a boy to me."

It would have been a relief when Passionara stopped in front of a large ornate door, if Owen hadn't felt twice as scared of what lay behind it. It was something important, he knew, because there was a fat, grizzled man with a white beard sitting at a battered card table. He was wearing a bandanna and a sweat-stained cummerbund. There was a ledger on the table and he opened it as Passionara and Owen came to a halt.

"Name?" he said in a harsh voice.

"You know my name, Whitwashisberd," Passionara said.

"Not your name, you damned wearer of flowers," Whitwashisberd growled. "Name of fancy rat you dangle from your honeyed fist."

"Name of fancy rat is… Pretty!" Passionara said. But the corridor had other ideas.

"Rat!" they roared. "Rat! Rat! Rat!"

"Name of boy is… Pretty Rat!" Passionara exclaimed, to a chorus of cheers from the corridor. Whitwashisberd grunted, but bent to the ledger and laboriously wrote *Pretty Rat* in the first free entry. Craning his neck, Owen could see that the ledger was crowded with names, most of them, worryingly, crossed out, with a small skull drawn in beside them. Then, with a bored expression, Whitwashisberd waved Owen and Passionara through.

Passionara opened the door, and Owen realised that this was the room that the music had been coming from. A battered old record player was playing opera music, an old scratchy recording of a man singing. The ceiling was covered with ornate plasterwork of angels and cherubs and great plaster bunches of grapes dangling in the corners. A massive cut-glass chandelier lit with magno hung from the centre of the ceiling. A log fire blazed in the fireplace. The only furniture in the room was a huge black leather reclining armchair. Johnston was sitting in the armchair, sideways on to the door. Owen had not realised quite how big Johnston was before, but now it seemed that he filled the room. Everything about him was big. The head, the sideburns, the boots, the great tufts of hair sprouting from his ears and nostrils. His eyes were closed and one massive hand moved gently as if conducting the movement. Passionara stuck his boot in Owen's backside and propelled him into the middle of the room where he landed on his hands and knees. Behind him, Owen could hear the door closing gently. Johnston held up a hand. Owen understood. He wasn't to interrupt the music.

Owen stayed on his hands and knees for what seemed like

hours, although it could only have been minutes. The music swelled and died away, swelled and died away then swelled again until it reached a crescendo, then gently and finally died away. There was a long silence broken only by the needle scratching round the old record. Finally, Johnston opened his eyes.

"Caruso," he said. Owen looked at him, not knowing what he was talking about. "At La Scala," said Johnston, as if that explained everything. He got up and moved swiftly over to Owen, towering over the boy. He reached down and grasped Owen's chin and raised him to his feet, tilting his head back until he looked directly into his eyes. Johnston's eyes were dark brown with gold flecks and full of life, like the eyes of a hunting animal. Owen felt that he was being probed for weaknesses. The man smelled of garlic and engine oil. *Like a French garage mechanic*, he thought, and fought the urge to break out in hysterical giggles. But it was Johnston who smiled. He straightened and with a flicking motion sent Owen sprawling across the room.

"The mirror was a good trick," he said, showing great tombstone teeth in a ferocious smile.

"W-What?" Owen stammered.

"The mirror. The way you turned the ice-light back on the Harsh. Never seen them so put out. Sent them scuttling back north like old maids with their skirts hitched."

"I thought you…"

"What? Worked for the Harsh? So I do. But it's contract work, son. You don't have to love them to work for them. Do you know what a Harsh lacks, son? A Harsh lacks a sense of humour. It can get a bit dull around them. They'll win in the end, though, and there won't be much laughing then."

"If they win, that's the end of you too, isn't it?" Owen said.

"Me and the boys is took care of – that's part of the deal. Them Harsh can work time the way a man works a hand of cards. Your Dr Diamond plays at it, but he's not a patch on the Harsh. Look around you. Time don't change much here, and that's what they done for me. I got myself an island in time."

Owen looked around. It was true. The manor seemed to have experienced no decay. Even Johnston's record player would have ended up as a heap of nuts and bolts if it had been outside.

"Anyway, enough chatting," said Johnston, and suddenly his voice sounded grim. "What are you doing here? And where is the Mortmain?"

"I don't know what you're talking about," Owen said, his voice sounding unconvincing to his own ears. "I came over the river to go to my own house and I got lost."

"Your own house is nothing but a few mouldy bricks on top of each other by now, son, and well you know it. No. I know why you're here. You think your father left the Mortmain here somewhere and you've come to retrieve it. Well, I've a hundred men scouring the ground outside at this very minute. Old Gobillard and his box of tricks couldn't best me, so don't think that a whippersnapper of a boy can."

Owen felt his heart sink. He had crossed the river to retrieve the Mortmain and he had ended up by handing it to Johnston on a plate. And that name again, Gobillard. The box of tricks Johnston referred to – could that be the chest in his room?

Johnston took Owen by the scruff of the neck and propelled him towards the door, which opened. Whitwashisberd looked up at Johnston with a question in his eyes. Owen saw that the pen was poised by his name, just at the place where a skull had been drawn in beside the other names. But Johnston shook his head.

"We're going north tomorrow," he said, "and we're taking this one with us. The Harsh want a cold word or two with him."

For some reason this provoked great mirth among the men in the corridor, and they started to chant. "Pretty rat! Pretty rat! Pretty rat!"

Taking a great key from his belt, Johnston opened an iron-bound door in the opposite wall of the corridor. With a sweep of his hand, he flung Owen through the door and slammed it. Owen found himself tumbling down damp stone stairs, and landing with a sickening crash in a pool of water at the bottom. He looked around him. There was only a chink of light from a high barred window, enough to show that he was in an empty stone cellar. A dungeon, he realised, without hope of escape. He had given away the location of the Mortmain and with it, the hopes of his friends. And now he was to be handed to the Harsh. Owen buried his head in his hands and felt despair wash over him.

CHAPTER FOURTEEN

The Sub-Commandant woke Cati gently before dawn. She wrapped up well and grabbed a slice of warm bread and jam from the kitchen, but still she shivered in the cold, pre-dawn air. In silence they walked down the river towards the harbour, the Sub-Commandant softly greeting the people coming the other way, Contessa's porters, who had been bringing food for the trip.

The sun was beginning to cast a chilly light by the time they got to the harbour. Boat was tied up by the quayside and the Raggies were loading it, seemingly oblivious to the biting cold. Wesley stood on the bridge with his arms folded. Dr Diamond was on the quayside with two cases of scientific instruments. He looked excited and he was trying to get the Raggies to load the instruments.

"I'd better help him," Cati said. Despite everything, she

couldn't help feeling a twinge of excitement at the voyage ahead.

"Go ahead," said the Sub-Commmandant absent-mindedly, then murmured, "Where is Chancellor?"

After much translation of Dr Diamond's backwards talk, Cati persuaded the Raggies to load the cases of instruments. Then she went on board herself. She had never been on Boat before. In fact, she had never been out on the water before, and it took her a few minutes to adjust to the slight swaying beneath her feet before she could take a proper look around.

Boat was about twenty metres long. There was an enclosed wheelhouse with an outside bridge and another wheel, for fair weather. Beneath the bridge there were cabins with diamond-pane windows facing out on to the main deck. There was a forecastle at the front with similar cabins underneath. In the middle of Boat was the engine. The cover had been taken off and Silkie was bent over it. She was wearing her ragged and oily overalls, and was working with a spanner in the middle of the huge jumble of coils and belts and flywheels which transmitted the power of the magno core to the long, seemingly spindly oars. As she worked, she was cursing steadily, emitting a stream of bad language that would have put Rutgar's troopers to shame. But when she looked up and saw Cati, her oil-covered face broke into a smile.

"Is everything all right Silkie?" Cati asked.

"Everything's *not* all right," said Silkie, scowling again. "They sail her too fast and pay never a thought to cambelts. One day a cambelt's going to snap and then where will they be? Down on power like you couldn't believe, that's where. And then they'll be looking for somebody to blame."

"Can you fix it?" Cati asked anxiously.

"Course I can fix it," said Silkie gruffly. "They shouldn't of done it, is all."

Cati realised that something had upset Silkie and she guessed what it was. "They're not going to take you with them?"

"Wesley says somebody has to look after the rest of the children when he's away," Silkie said miserably. There were tears in her eyes. She looked up and saw Wesley looking down at her, and quickly ducked her head back into the engine.

Cati sighed and walked on up the deck. There was a mast in front of the engine with an enclosed crow's nest at the top of it. Cati wondered what it would be like sitting up there, all closed in, with the wind whistling round you. She stepped round the mast and opened a door. The cabin had a low ceiling, with a small bed in the corner and a locker beside it. There was a radiator on one wall, probably using excess heat from the magno. Sunlight fell across the rough bedspread from the diamond-pane window. Cati had her things in a bag over her shoulder and she put it down on the bed, hoping that everyone would take the cabin as being hers.

Back outside, all the supplies were now on board. The two Raggies Uel and Mervyn were sitting at the stern of the boat, looking tense and alert, their magno crossbows in their hands. Dr Diamond was putting his instrument boxes in his cabin and the Sub-Commandant was pacing the deck. Cati knew that he was worried about Chancellor's lateness. She climbed the little steps up to the bow, and from that height she saw Chancellor hurrying down the path. As he did so, she felt a snowflake gently touch her cheek, and then another.

"We're in for a big snow, I'm afraid," a voice said. Cati turned to see Dr Diamond standing beside her. "By my reckoning," he said, "we are now entering the little ice age which occurred circa 1130 to circa 1310 AD."

"That's a long time," said Cati.

"Well, it won't last that long because we're going backwards so fast, but it will be a few weeks. Are you worried about Owen?" he said, suddenly changing tack.

"Yes... yes, of course I'm worried."

"Here," he said, taking a polaroid photograph from his pocket. It was starting to fade, but you could still make out Owen's face. He was in the Skyward and looking comically surprised as he faced the camera. "He sneaked back to the Skyward to take another look back through time. Whatever he saw there sent him over the river. And I'd say whatever he is after there, it isn't eternal friendship with Johnston."

"Why didn't you show this at the Convoke and tell them that?" Cati asked.

"Remember, there is still a spy in our midst," Dr Diamond said.

"S-so you don't believe that Owen is a spy?"

Dr Diamond shook his head and smiled. "No, Cati, I don't think he is a spy. I think he is an important person, with a part to play in all of this before the end. But I don't want you to discuss this with anyone else. There are undercurrents…"

Dr Diamond was interrupted by Chancellor, who jumped awkwardly from the quay on to the deck.

"My apologies for being late," he said. "I had a lot to do before we left. Is the Mortmain on board?"

The Sub-Commandant tapped the pocket of the long coat he now wore, a military-looking leather coat with a fur-lined collar and faded markings in what appeared to be Russian on the sleeves. The snow was starting to fall heavily now and visibility was dropping.

"We'll have to go," Wesley said, "or we'll never get clear of the sandbar."

"It'll be a problem setting a course though," the Sub-Commandant said. "A compass will not work with the distortion in the magno caused by the vortex, and if it snows, we will see no stars."

"I believe I have the answer to this slight problem," said

Dr Diamond airily, as though he had been waiting for this moment. "A small invention of no great consequence, a compass that works according to the timeline when time started going backwards. It remembers due north, in other words." He coughed modestly.

"It'll be no use to man or beast, your fancy compass, if we don't cast off in the next five minutes," Wesley shouted. Cati thought that Dr Diamond would be offended, but he merely grinned and set about unpacking the memory compass from its box.

The snow was falling in great soft flakes. Suddenly, things started to move very fast. Silkie, working frantically, replaced the cover on the magno motor. Seeing her pale, disappointed face, Cati ran and hugged her. Wesley shouted something and the stern rope was detached, and Uel started to haul it on board. Boat was held only by the bow cable now. With a grateful smile, Silkie broke free of Cati's hug. She stood for a moment on the deck looking up into Wesley's eyes and it seemed to Cati that even though nothing was said, a universe passed between them. Then Silkie skipped across the gunwhale and down the gangway.

The minute she did so, the gangway was withdrawn. Wesley shouted again and the bow cable was thrown into the water. Boat was free. The long oars moved slowly, barely stirring the water. Cati realised that all the Raggies were gathered on the quayside, their faces indistinct in the driving snow. She saw other faces there. Contessa, Pieta, Rutgar, all waving, their faces taut with anxiety. She felt a sudden ache in her breast, almost a physical pain, at the thought that she might not see them again. The great danger they were in had never really struck her before. She tried to call out their names, but the snow seemed to muffle her voice. She tried again, desperately this time, but their faces faded as though Boat were sailing against the flow of time and leaving them behind. Once more she called out, and again there was no reply. Feeling a strong hand grip her shoulder, she turned to see her father. Cati leaned her head against his shoulder and watched the last stretch of grey quayside fade into the snow.

And so Boat and its crew slipped away on their voyage, away from danger and into greater danger. On the quayside the Raggies strained to catch a last glimpse of their ship and its captain. Silkie wept openly. The Workhouse people watched in grim silence.

"The best of us are on that vessel," said Pieta quietly.

"No," Contessa said with a smile, "not all of the best of us."

"You had better go, if you're going," said Rutgar gruffly. "I worry about their plans for Owen. I wish you would let me go with you."

"They'd spot a big tramping goon in a minute," Pieta said, with a flash of her old sourness, but Rutgar just shrugged.

"You're right," he said mournfully. "They'd smell me before they saw me."

"We'd better get back," Contessa said, but still they stared into the snow with the Raggies who had not moved, the snow starting to settle on their hunched shoulders, gazing after the vessel which carried the hopes of the world that had been and the hopes of the world to be.

CHAPTER FIFTEEN

Owen also woke early, if he could have been said to have slept at all. The cellar was half-flooded and he had felt around in the dark until he found a low stone shelf above the water. He huddled on it miserably, half dozing, until daybreak, a thin, cold light coming through the high window. He pulled his sodden clothes round him and stood up on the narrow shelf, pacing up and down for warmth, until at last the door at the top of the stairs opened. It was Passionara.

"Get up out of the mire, Pretty Rat," he jeered. "There's rat grub for you."

His limbs barely working from cold, Owen hauled himself up the stairs, shivering uncontrollably. Passionara lost patience with him and grabbed him by the hair, lifting him off his feet and slinging him into the corridor. At the same instant, he slammed the door of the cellar shut. As the door closed, a weak beam of sunshine crept through the high window, shining across the dark cellar to the far corner, where the black water was deepest, glancing off something as white as bone. The sunlight seemed to disturb something in the dark, and after a moment, a large dark rat crossed the deep water, jumping lightly across what appeared to be smooth stepping stones. But, as the uncertain sunshine strengthened, it became apparent that they were not stepping stones, but skulls, their dead eyes staring unseeing into one more cold dawn.

There were delicious smells in the corridor. Owen was pushed into the kitchen. Mariacallas, the cook, was standing at the stove with a spatula in his hand, watching anxiously as a tray of scrambled eggs with smoked salmon, toast, Earl Grey tea and grapefruit was hoisted shoulder high and carried towards Johnston's room.

"Spill one drop I cut your liver out. I fry her for eat," Mariacallas screamed at the man carrying the tray as he left the room.

"You got feeding for Pretty Rat? Johnston says feed the rat," Passionara said.

"No time for feed rat!" Mariacallas screamed furiously.

"Is very pretty rat," Passionara said, "Johnston wants to keep it fresh for Harsh." Mariacallas scowled, but opened a cupboard and threw some hard bread and cheese on the table.

"There!" he said. "Food for rat."

Owen was ravenous. Despite the fact that the bread was stale and the cheese was hard, he wolfed it all down, drinking water from someone else's dirty cup that had been sitting on the table. He thought with longing about the teabags he had left in the Den.

As he ate, Johnston's men came and went, carrying supplies. *For the journey north*, Owen thought with a shiver. He wondered how they would be travelling, if they would be walking and how long it would take. From the quantity of supplies he knew that it was going to take some time.

As the men worked, Mariacallas screamed at them for leaving the door open or muddy footprints on his kitchen floor. One man left a trail of flour from the cooker to the door. When Mariacallas saw it, he whipped a long sharp knife from his belt. Owen did not see his hand move, but the knife whirred through the air. The man, without looking back, ducked and the blade struck the door just above his head, and stuck there, quivering.

Passionara seemed to have wandered off. Mariacallas was preoccupied with packing spices and condiments for the journey. Owen eyed the door. He thought about making a bolt for it, but each time he did, his eyes returned to the long knife which was now back in Mariacallas's belt. It was warm in the kitchen. After the sleepless night in the cellar, Owen could feel his eyes starting to close. The sounds of the kitchen grew distant. He put his head on the table and slept.

*   *   *

Passionara woke him by the simple means of grabbing him by the hair again and pulling him to his feet. Owen had been dreaming about the Workhouse, of sitting in the warm kitchen with Cati, and he looked around him bewildered before he remembered what had happened.

"You ready for big trip north?" Passionara said, grinning. "Holiday!"

"Winter holiday!" Mariacallas exclaimed, and the two men hooted with laughter.

"Hurry," Passionara said, clipping Owen on the back of the head. "Mustn't be late."

"Johnston will leave without you."

"He hopes!" Once again the two men screeched with laughter. Owen didn't think there was anything funny about their jokes at all, but he thought it best to smile politely, in case they took offence. A shove from Passionara took him to the back door, and another shove propelled him through it.

"Watch step," Passionara said. "Johnston never find no Mortmain. Not in good mood."

The world he fell into bore no resemblance to the place he had been the previous night. Snow whirled through the air so that you could barely see twenty metres away. The scrap and the tent village had all been covered, and the manor looked like something from an old painting. There was a sense of anticipation in the air as well, with men hurrying to and fro. Owen thought he could make a bolt for it now, but he wouldn't know which way to go. Besides, as soon as the thought entered his head, Passionara seized him and dragged him off towards the sheds at the back of the Manor, leading him down a bewildering warren of stone-cut buildings, containing forges, armouries, workshops of all kinds. Owen had no idea that the Johnston operation was so big. He thought about the sparsely manned defences of the Workhouse and the casualties they had taken, and wondered how long they could hold out.

At last they turned the corner into a large cobbled space. Passionara halted. "There," he said, "is how travel to north."

It took a moment for Owen to take in what he was looking at. It was the oddest vehicle he had ever seen. It had a wheel at each corner, but they weren't ordinary wheels. They were a bit like bicycle wheels, he thought; thin bicycle wheels with spokes, but the astonishing thing about them was their height. Each wheel had to be twenty metres tall, almost as high as a three-storey building. And between them, halfway between the ground and the tops of the wheels, was slung what Owen supposed you would call a pod. It looked like the body of an airplane without the tail or wings, but with the same round windows and windscreen at the front. A long, narrow ladder led from a door in the side to the ground.

"Q-car," Passionara said happily. "Skip up ladder, Pretty Rat." He swung a boot lazily in Owen's direction. Not needing to be told twice, Owen grabbed the bottom rung of the ladder and swung himself on to it. He felt Passionara get on the ladder after him and he climbed hurriedly upwards, knowing that he was liable to get a thump if he didn't move quickly enough. The ladder swayed as Owen climbed, and the snow blew down his collar and into his eyes so he was half blind by the time he got to the top of the ladder. He felt for the outlines of the door and pulled himself through, blinking the snow out of his eyes as he did so.

The interior was wider than it appeared from outside. Comfortable leather seats were grouped round tables. The interior walls were also covered in leather. There was one seat where the pilot would have sat on an aeroplane, and a set of complicated looking controls which looked more like those of a ship. There was a copper-bound wheel and a series of brass levers and pedals. At the rear of the fuselage was a small galley.

"When are we going?" he asked.

"Shut up, Pretty Rat," Passionara said, and threw himself down in one of the chairs. Owen decided that he wouldn't risk any more questions.

They waited in silence for twenty minutes, Owen feeling more and more tense, until at last he felt the whole body of the Q-car begin to dip and sway, as if somebody extremely heavy was climbing the ladder. *Probably Johnston*, Owen thought, almost with relief. At least Johnston would end the terrible silence.

But it wasn't Johnston. After several minutes Whitwashisberd's head appeared in the doorway. He was breathing heavily and he had his ledger under his arm.

"Take book!" he shouted to Passionara, who did not move. "Take book, foul flower wearer!" the man shouted again. But Passionara did not stir. It was Owen who darted forward and took the heavy ledger so that the man could climb through the doorway.

"That'll earn you no favours from the maker of records," Passionara said sourly. "If there's a skull to put beside your name then a skull it will be."

Whitwashisberd took the ledger back off Owen and went to the back of the craft. He sat down heavily and opened the ledger on the table in front of him, taking out a pen, and waited.

He didn't have long to wait. The craft lurched again and Mariacallas climbed on board, closely followed by Johnston.

"Snow gets bad," Mariacallas said.

"We'll follow the Harsh Road," said Johnston. "No need to stray off it, Passionara."

Passionara nodded and moved to sit down at the controls. Owen tried to sidle past Johnston to get a better look at what Passionara was doing, but Johnston caught him round the neck with a huge hand. Owen couldn't breathe. He struggled helplessly.

"Just because the Harsh want me to make a present of you

doesn't mean that I have to. You could get killed trying to escape."

"Accidently on purpose," Mariacallas said, and roared with laughter. Passionara joined in. Even half strangled as he was, Owen was tiring of their terrible sense of humour. Johnston's grip tightened even more. Owen's vision was blurred, but he thought he could see Whitwashisberd's hand hovering over the last page of the ledger.

"Where is the Mortmain?" Johnston bellowed into Owen's face.

"In the car," Owen gasped. "When it went into the water. My dad's car…"

"Maybe he's right," Johnston said, stroking a long sideburn thoughtfully, seeming to forget that he was strangling Owen with the other hand.

Abruptly, Johnston dropped Owen to the floor, where he lay, fighting for breath. Johnston went up to Passionara and stood over him while he performed what seemed to be last-minute equipment checks. Owen heard murmurs about "barometric relativity frequencies" and "temporal torque". Still gasping for air, he half walked, half crawled to the back of the cabin. He crept on to a chair that was as close to Whitwashisberd as he dared. There seemed to be no love lost between him and Mariacallas and Passionara, so hopefully they would keep away.

From nearby, Owen was able to study the ledger. It was

very old and enormously thick, and its pages were incredibly thin. There must have been thousands of pages in it, perhaps even tens of thousands. He wondered if his father's name was in it. He wondered if there was a skull beside it. Owen decided that, if the chance arose, he would try to get his hands on the book. Meanwhile, he had to think about escape. At that moment he glanced up and saw that Johnston was looking straight at him, a mocking smile on his lips, as though he had read Owen's mind. Fortunately, Johnston was distracted just then. There was a faint humming noise and a crackle, and Johnston whirled around.

"Did anybody stow the ladder?" he yelled. Mariacallas dived towards the open door, avoiding a fist the size of a turnip aimed at his head as he did so. Quickly, he pressed a lever. Owen peered through the door and saw the ladder folding itself into sections then rising until it was out of sight under the belly of the Q-car. Just as the last of the ladder clattered out of sight, and Mariacallas slammed the door, the pod seemed to rise and sway between the four giant wheels. Owen saw Passionara ease the lever forward and the Q-car lurched into motion. At the same time, loud music began to blare from speakers mounted under the pod.

Johnston was standing with one hand on Passionara's shoulder, and with the other he conducted the music furiously. The big wheels turned slowly, yet still they were covering a lot of ground. Owen moved to one of the round windows.

Through the snow he could see Johnston's men, hundreds of them, cheering the great machine as it moved through the camp. Owen looked to his left. Whitwashisberd was painstakingly writing: *Departure 8.34 a.m. Conditions: snow*.

The snow eddied and flurried, and momentarily Owen caught a glimpse of the Workhouse towering grim and defiant over the river, the tottering pillar of the Nab clearly visible, the Skyward glittering at the summit. Then the weather closed in again. The wind threw snow against the Q-car with renewed ferocity, obliterating not only the Nab, but the faces of the cheering men below. Owen looked out of the window, but he could see only whiteness.

On the other side of the river Pieta kissed each of her children gently on the cheek. The older child, the girl, blinked a little, as if emerging from a dream, and threw her arms round her mother's neck, but the boy only smiled a vague, secret smile. Contessa stood with a hand on each child's shoulder as Pieta walked off. As the snow began to obscure her, the girl called out. Pieta turned and spoke the child's name into the wind and snow then turned again and disappeared into the blizzard.

She reached the river and walked carefully down the bank. The snow did not seem to concern her. She examined the tree bridge then moved on. After twenty minutes she reached the pine tree where Owen had crossed. She examined the base of the tree in silence for a moment then climbed on to the trunk and moved across the river slowly, pausing every few metres to examine it. When she got to the other side, she spent ten minutes examining the place where he had fallen. She stood up. For a moment Pieta stared back across the river, pain in her eyes. Then she turned back and plunged into the forest.

CHAPTER SIXTEEN

The Q-car moved slowly but relentlessly through the driving snow all that day. As far as Owen could see, there were pine trees to either side of the vehicle, but it was moving on a clear space. The ride was incredibly smooth. After a while Johnston had retired to the back of the Q-car with Whitwashisberd. The two men pored over the ledger as if they were looking for something. Mariacallas was asleep in one of the chairs, his legs and arms sprawled out, his head thrown back and his mouth open. Owen moved slowly up to the front of the Q-car, hoping not to attract Johnston's attention.

"Come to see how her work?" asked Passionara. The man was squinting out of the window into the snow, making tiny adjustments to the wheel as he did so. Gauges and dials flickered in front of him and he referred to them constantly.

"Go damn fast, Q-car," Passionara went on. "Got to go

slow for now. When we reach proper Harsh Road she go like crazy."

"What happens if you hit a rock or a snowdrift?" Owen asked.

"No problem for big wheel. Ride right over anything you like. Rock, big snow, tree even. Look at wheel." Owen looked out of the window and saw that wheels were riding up and down, constantly bumping over obstacles, but the cabin stayed steady all the time.

"How come the cabin doesn't go up and down as well?"

"Big spring on wheel," Passionara said with a shrug. "Gyro in cabin."

Owen thought that Passionara looked relaxed driving the Q-car. He seemed happy to tell Owen anything he wanted to know about it and Owen was happy to keep him talking in case he learned something useful. In fact, Owen almost forgot who he was talking to, but there was a sickening reminder to come.

Through an eddy in the snow, Owen saw a deer standing in the middle of the road. Passionara saw it at the same time. With a whoop he pushed one of the brass levers forward and the Q-car leapt towards the deer. The deer froze momentarily then started to run. *Go on*, a voice in Owen's head said. *Go on!* But the deer had no chance against the speed of the Q-car. Passionara swerved violently off the road, ignoring the curses of Johnston from the rear. The deer made one last desperate bound and then the Q-car was on it. With a sickening jolt, first the front wheel and then the back wheel crashed over the animal. Passionara was cheering wildly now as he swerved back towards the road.

His cheering woke Mariacallas, who joined in mindlessly, even though he hadn't seen what had happened. Owen looked out of the side window. He could see the body of the deer lying in the snow. Without looking at Passionara, he turned back towards his seat. But Johnston brushed him aside. Without breaking stride, one giant fist caught Passionara on the side of the head. Passionara toppled from his seat like a felled tree and lay motionless on the floor.

Johnston handed the controls to Mariacallas. "Do a better job than this," he said, indicating the semi-conscious Passionara. Mariacallas watched Johnston walk off then turned to Passionara and delivered a vicious kick to his ribs. He giggled and did a little dance to himself then took the controls and the Q-car lumbered off into the snowy dusk.

As the Q-car disappeared from sight, a shape detached itself from the forest on the other side of the river. Pieta, running swiftly and tirelessly, seemed to glide lightly across the top of the snow. She reached the place where the Q-car had killed the deer and bent to examine the body. Then she started to run again and soon she too was lost in the gathering dusk.

The Q-car drove on through the night. Passionara woke up and made his way groggily to the back of the cabin and promptly fell asleep again. Johnston produced his record player from the pile of supplies and started to play classical music very loudly. Owen covered his ears as best he could. Whitwashisberd had fallen asleep and did not seem to be bothered by the music. Owen put up with it for almost two hours and then fell asleep himself. When he woke it was quiet. Quiet that is, except for the snoring of Whitwashisberd and Johnston and Passionara, which was enough to wake the dead. Outside, the snow was still falling and Mariacallas peered into the night, the road almost invisible despite the help of several huge spotlights which had been turned on.

Owen realised that this was his chance to get a look at the ledger. He crawled under the tables until he was at Whitwashisberd's table. The man had enormous feet and it was with great difficulty that Owen got past without touching them. His snores were deafening from this near, and Owen could feel the table vibrating and rattling. Cautiously, he put his hand up over the edge of the table and felt around. He touched something cold and flabby and realised it was Whitwashisberd's hand. He froze. The man grumbled in his sleep and Owen had to scramble out of the way as the enormous feet swung round under the table. But gradually, he settled again and the snoring fell into a steady rhythm. Owen felt about again and this time his hand touched the ledger. Slowly and painstakingly, for it was very heavy, he pulled it towards the edge of the table. Then, using both hands, he eased it down.

The cover of the book was battered and stained. There was writing in a strange language on it, but the gilt of the lettering had long since worn off and it was impossible to decipher. Owen opened the book carefully. It even *smelled* old. There seemed to be thousands, tens of thousands of entries. Hundreds of thousands perhaps. Owen started to wonder just how old Whitwashisberd actually was. He turned to the last entry. As far as he could see, names were recorded on the left-hand page and events on the opposite page. There were skulls in fresh ink drawn beside many of the names on the left-hand page, and Owen guessed that these were men who had fallen in the battle at the Workhouse. He spotted one entry which read *Frizzell Gruntion, Planeman*, and Owen remembered the Planeman who had attacked them at the Nab.

There had to be a system to the book, but Owen couldn't work out what it was. It couldn't be done by date because time was going backwards, which made a nonsense out of that system. It didn't seem to be done alphabetically. After a while, he reckoned that the names must bear some relationship to the events recorded on the right-hand page. Most of the time the events were described by pictures rather than words. For instance, there was a clock which was cracked down the middle, which Owen thought must be the day that time turned backwards. He flicked back through the pages, wondering what event would relate to the time that his father had been with the Resisters. There were so many pages and his eyes began to grow tired, squinting at the small writing in the half-light under the table.

Owen was almost ready to give up when he found it. A small drawing of a car half in, half out of the water. And when you looked closely, you could see the crudely-drawn figure of a man in the front seat and the unmistakeable round features of a baby's face in the back. Owen felt his blood run cold. With a shaking finger he traced a line across to the left-hand page. He read his father's name. There was a skull beside it. A dull pain seemed to settle across his chest. He felt tears start in his eyes. He closed the book and squeezed his eyes shut in an effort to stop the tears. When he opened them again he saw Passionara's thin features peering at him under the table.

"Now, now," he said softly, "what is Pretty Rat doing under the table?"

Owen flew at him.

Passionara tried to defend himself, but his reflexes seemed to have been slowed by the thump he had received from Johnston. Surprised, he fell backwards over one of the chairs and Owen was on top of him.

"Stop calling me Pretty Rat!" he yelled. "Stop it! Stop it!" His arms flailed at the man's face. Some of the blows were landing, but they weren't hard enough to do any damage. He could see that Passionara was grinning now, a thin, evil grin. He opened his lips and his tongue slid out. To his horror, Owen saw a small, but deadly-looking razor on the man's tongue. Quick as a snake, Passionara snatched the blade from his tongue with one hand, grabbing Owen by the hair with the other and yanking his head back so that his throat was completely exposed. Owen could see the blade clearly, its rusty edges. He could almost feel it tearing at his throat. Passionara grinned, but there was nothing funny about it. The blade arced through the air. Owen could hear his own heart beating, loud as a drum.

"What do you think you're doing, you flouncing popinjay?" Johnston roared, appearing as if from nowhere, and snatching Owen up as the blade swooped through the space where he had been. Johnston straightened, Owen swinging from one fist as though he was about to use him as a club to beat Passionara.

"Boy attack me!" Passionara wailed, with a sneaky look of dislike at Owen which didn't bode well for the future. He was circling Johnston, trying to cut at Owen with the razor blade. But Johnston kept him dangling just out of reach. *At least he called me boy, not Pretty Rat*, Owen thought. As Passionara made a lunge, his arm passed too close to Whitwashisberd. With a lazy kick, the white-bearded man knocked the blade out of Passionara's hand and it clattered on to the floor. Johnston swiftly picked it up and put it in his pocket. When he was satisfied that Passionara couldn't hurt Owen, he dropped him heavily on the floor. Dazed, Owen could hear Mariacallas giggling with excitement.

"Quiet yourself!" Johnston said. He turned to Passionara. "You hurt this, even one fingernail, I'll be giving you to the Harsh along with it, you got that?" Passionara nodded sullenly.

"Whitwashisberd," Johnston went on, "tie the creature up, bind him hand and foot and keep him there beside you." Whitwashisberd nodded grimly.

Within minutes, Owen was trussed up like a turkey, barely able to move a muscle. Whitwashisberd showed a great expertise with knots, wetting each one before he pulled it tight so that it would shrink and become even tighter when it dried. Passionara prowled just out of reach, urging Whitwashisberd to pull the ropes even tighter, and when Whitwashisberd eventually put Owen on the ground, Passionara lay watching him, his eyes alert and full of malice. Owen groaned inwardly. Now there was no chance of escape.

The first few days on board Boat were strange. It took Cati some time to find her sea legs, even though the swell was light. Snow gathered in the rigging and on the decks and had to be swept off, and all sounds were strangely muffled. Cati knew that the great empty sea was all around them for Wesley had said that he was putting far out to sea. Yet she had no sense of it, just of the small community on board. And that small community consisted of one more than had been intended. They had cleared the bar at the harbour and had been sailing for several hours when Wesley shaded his eyes and frowned and peered forward.

"How did the lassie get on board?" he said. The solemn little girl who had been woken by Owen was standing in the prow of the boat, facing out to sea.

"I don't know," the Sub-Commandant said. "I didn't see her come on board."

"Shall I ask her?" Cati said.

"No," the Sub-Commandant said thoughtfully, "leave her be."

"Nothing we can do about it anyhow," Wesley said. "I'm not putting about now to bring her back."

The little girl stayed in the prow of the boat until nightfall, despite the driving snow. When the Sub-Commandant saw that she was gone, he sent Cati to look for her with some bread and beans and cake. But Cati could not find her.

"There's a hundred places such a small lass could squeeze into and you'd never find her," Wesley said.

"Take the food and wrap it well and leave it in the bow," said the Sub-Commandant. Cati did as she was told.

Wesley and Dr Diamond had built a small case to enclose the memory compass, and were now engaged in a long and serious conversation on the nature of time. The motor beat soundlessly and slowly. "If we're going to run into something in this snow," Wesley said, "best we don't run into her too quick." Chancellor had agreed with him, then retired to his cabin.

At dusk they had dinner in the stateroom under the stern. The stateroom had big windows looking out at the wake of the boat. It was lit by candles. Dr Diamond cooked and served the meal himself on big white plates, with starched linen napkins. Cati thought it was romantic, eating under candlelight, with the ship swaying gently, snow gathering in the windowpanes. Dr Diamond and Wesley resumed their conversation about time. The Sub-Commandant ate quietly by himself and Chancellor stayed in his cabin, saying he had a headache. At the end of the meal Dr Diamond dramatically produced a replica of Boat made with spun sugar. As they were eating it, Cati felt her eyes beginning to close and she yawned.

"'Twill be the sea air," Mervyn said. "Does make you tired when you're not used to it." So when she had finished her piece of spun-sugar boat, Cati said goodnight and, yawning, crossed the deck. She checked in the bow and saw that the food was gone before she went down to the little cabin. The blankets were old and much patched, as was the sheet, but it was clean and smelled of fresh air, and she slid under the blankets with a sigh of contentment. Looking out through the little windows, she could see the snow slanting down on to the deck. She thought about Owen, wondering where he was. Cati hoped he wasn't alone in the cold night; she thought about him warm and safe, and held that thought as she drifted off to sleep, in the hope that by wishing it, it would come to pass.

The next morning the snow still fell. Cati slept late and had breakfast on her own in the stateroom. When she went out on deck, Chancellor was pacing up and down. He greeted her cheerfully enough, but he looked strained.

"Are you all right?" she asked. He sighed and ruffled her hair.

"Just hoping that our plans come to pass, Cati, and worrying that there is something more that could be done."

"It'll be fine," she said cheerfully. "We won't be beaten by a bunch of snowmen with icicles for brains."

He smiled at her and turned back to the rail, trying to see out through the blinding snow. Cati suddenly thought about the little girl and looked up into the prow. She was standing there, in her thin dress. Cati ran into her cabin. There were much-patched oilskins hanging from a hook on the wall. Cati took her own warm coat and an oilskin coat and hat. She scrambled up the ladder which led to the top of the forecastle. When she got there the little girl still had not moved, but she turned and looked at Cati as she put the coat over her shoulders, and allowed her to button the oilskins round her and put the hat on.

The girl's expression didn't change. At first Cati thought it was a blank look, but then she started to see a level of trust there, a sea of trust, which frightened her. She wanted to tell the child that you couldn't trust the world that much. It wasn't right. There was too much out there to hurt you.

But instead of speaking, Cati slid down the ladder again. She ran into the kitchen and made up a bacon sandwich and brought it out to the girl. She was looking out to sea again, but she took the sandwich and bit into it. Her eyes moved ceaselessly, although there was nothing to see except snow.

"What are you looking for?" Cati asked. The little girl did not reply and did not stop staring into the dead whiteness ahead of them.

Cati slipped away. As she walked across the deck, a large snowball exploded on the top of her head. She looked around startled, but couldn't see anyone. Then she heard a voice from high above her. Wesley in the crow's nest.

"Come on up!" he yelled. Cati didn't hesitate. She had never been afraid of heights. At top speed she flew up the ladder that was bolted to the side of the mast. Within three minutes she emerged into the crow's nest. It was surprisingly roomy, with a low roof and a glass screens that you could slide across to cut out the wind.

"For spotting fish," Wesley said, "a few of us do stay here. You do look for gannets diving and the like."

"I wish Owen was here," Cati began wistfully.

"He'd be stuck, like as not, same as the rest of us, sailing north, blind as bats," Wesley said.

"Not if he's the Navigator," said Cati defiantly. Wesley looked at her, his eyes narrowing.

"What is it you do know about the Navigator?" he demanded.

"Not much," she stammered. "I heard Contessa and Pieta talking one night... What is the Navigator anyway?"

"Don't rightly know. People do whisper. Old tales that was once told say Navigator can save us."

"Could Owen be the Navigator?"

"Might be, might not. Anyhow, Chancellor, he lets on it's all a bit of a cod, that there's no such thing as Navigators any more. Fair and sharp he was about it too."

"Then I suppose we're on our own. Looks like somebody's going to be spending a lot of time up here looking for the Puissance, whatever that looks like."

The next morning Cati woke early and realised that something had changed. The motion of the craft seemed different, and the light that flooded through the little windows was different too. Quickly, she slipped into her clothes and ran outside. The snow had stopped. All around them the sea stretched out, vast and silver-grey, flecked with white. A sharp wind whipped foam off the top of the waves and she could taste salt in her mouth. The sky was filled with leaden cloud, heavy and menacing, and a flurry of snow whipped across the deck as if to remind them that this was only a respite. To either side of Boat the oars were working faster now, and the bow rose and fell, crashing into the waves and sending spray high into the air.

"It's a bit clearer now!" Wesley shouted to her from the bridge.

"It's amazing," Cati called. "It's… it's so big!" Wesley slid down the stairs to where she was standing.

"Right enough, you never seen the sea like this before, out of sight of land."

"No. This is great!"

"Maybe it is," Wesley said, "and maybe it isn't. Take a look."

Cati followed his gaze and realised that Uel was lying on top of the bridge with his eye to the sight of his magno crossbow. He was facing astern and the bow was pointing towards the sky. When she looked to where the gun was pointing, her blood ran cold. Far off in the cold, grey sky, small, but unmistakable, were the menacing shapes of four Planemen.

"That's right," Wesley said grimly. "Somebody told on us. They knew where to find us."

CHAPTER SEVENTEEN

Cati followed Wesley back up to the bridge. The Sub-Commandant was standing with Dr Diamond.

"How long have they been there?" Cati asked Wesley.

"I'd near say they were there all the time, we just couldn't see them."

"Will they come any closer – I mean, attack?"

"I think we're safe enough," the Sub-Commandant answered, "for the time being at any rate. The wind is blowing in their faces and they're having trouble making headway against it."

Dr Diamond produced a pair of binoculars which had a suspiciously home-made look about them. "I think you're right," he said.

"Can I look?" Dr Diamond handed over the binoculars. Cati scanned the sky until she could see the Planemen and took an involuntary step backwards, so close did they seem. They had been in the air a long time, she could see. Their clothes and beards were matted with ice, their lips chapped and cracked. Behind the rimed glass of their goggles she could see their bloodshot eyes. The machines bucked and twisted as they fought the wind for control, but there was a grim determination about the way the Planemen hunched over the controls that told her they would never give up.

"We're all right as long as the wind holds," Dr Diamond said cheerfully, taking the binoculars back.

"As long as it holds," said Wesley, "but the minute it drops…" He drew his finger across his throat in a cutting gesture.

"Don't listen to him," said Dr Diamond. "Even if the wind does drop, they'll not come near us as long as Uel and Mervyn are here."

"But a watch will need to be kept," the Sub-Commandant said.

"I can do that," said Cati. "In the crow's nest."

"Good. You can cover the rest of the day. Tomorrow we can do it in watches."

"All right," nodded Cati, feeling glad to have something to do, although wishing that it could be something less threatening.

"Where's Chancellor?" Wesley asked.

"In his cabin," replied Dr Diamond. "He started to feel seasick when we picked up speed."

"We'll have to manage without him then," the Sub-Commandant said. "We'll have to take Uel and Mervyn off normal duties. We need one of them ready to shoot and one of them resting at all times."

All that day the Planemen hung in the sky, not gaining any ground, but not losing any either. Chancellor remained in his cabin. Dr Diamond stayed in his. The Sub-Commandant sent Cati to bring food to him. When she went in he was almost invisible behind a large, ancient-looking book, and he barely glanced up when she put the plate down beside him.

Outside, an occasional flurry of snow hid the planes, but they were always there when the snow died away again. Between steering and watching, Cati had to eat a quick meal standing up. The sea had got rougher and, apart from the Raggie boys who were busy, no one else was comfortable with the idea of the crow's nest as it swayed sickeningly from side to side. Bringing her food out on to deck, Cati could see the sun setting in the west, a great glowing orb, tinting the dark clouds round it a foreboding orange. Looking up, she saw that Wesley was strangely agitated. He walked to the rail on both sides and looked at the oars then returned to the helm, still obviously unhappy. As she watched him, Cati felt a tug on her sleeve. She looked down to see the little girl standing there.

The girl tugged again then turned and walked away. Cati followed her.

The girl went through the open door in the rear bulkhead. Just beyond the door, steps led down to the hold. It was dark and Cati had to hold on as she went, although the girl seemed able to keep her balance easily. They got to the bottom and walked along a short companionway. The girl stopped. She pointed at the floor. At first Cati didn't know what she was doing then she saw there was a brass ring set into the floor. Cati grasped the ring and a hatch swung open. As it did so there was a loud gurgling noise. Peering into the dark Cati could see a stopcock set into the hull, a kind of tap going through to the outside. That was the source of the gurgling, Cati realised. Someone had opened the tap and water was flowing in from outside! Peering into the darkness beyond she could see that bilges were already full of dirty, oily water.

Cati desperately tried to close the tap, but she wasn't strong enough. She turned and ran up the gangway calling for Wesley. Seeing the look on her face as she burst on to the deck, Wesley vaulted over the bridge rail and landed lightly on the deck. He ran down the companionway, followed by Cati. When she reached him he was already on his knees, wrestling with the brass valve of the stopcock. The flow of water diminished to a trickle and then stopped. But the damage was done.

"Will it sink?" Cati asked anxiously.

"Sinking's not the problem," said Wesley, his voice tight and angry. "She'll float with the hold full of water. It slows us down though, slows us down something desperate till we get the water out. I knew I could feel something on the wheel."

Cati heard footsteps behind her, and turned to see her father. The small man looked into the bilge without expression.

"This was done deliberate," Wesley said and his eyes flashed with fury. "This isn't no accident. Thon stopcock never opened itself."

"We need to form a human chain," siad the Sub-Commandant, "to get rid of the water as fast as we can."

Wesley stirred himself. He ran back up on deck and called to Uel and Mervyn. Then he ran up to the bridge. Dr Diamond came out of his cabin. Even Chancellor came out, looking pale and ill. Emerging into the daylight, Cati could feel that the vessel had slowed and was wallowing slightly, taking longer to recover from the waves.

"Come up here, Cati!" Wesley called out. When she got to the bridge, he told her to take the wheel.

"I've never…" she started.

"You have to," he interrupted. "You're the lightest of all of us, so you'll be the least use slinging buckets."

Cati felt her face grow red and she clenched her fists, but held her tongue. She knew that he was right. She put her hands on the wheel and it twitched and turned so that it felt like a live

236

thing. A live thing carrying a great burden, for she could feel the dead weight that had pulled Boat lower down in the sea. Instinctively, she turned to look behind. She could make out the Planemen in greater detail now. They were definitely closer.

The other six crewmen formed a chain as best they could, Wesley scooping out the water from the bilge with a bucket then passing it up the line to the next man. Cati could see that there weren't enough of them and that Chancellor was weak and slow. It was going to take a long time. She turned to look at the Planemen again. Although they were hard to see in the fast-closing dusk, they were closer still. The wind in her face freshened and she could see Dr Diamond looking up hopefully.

"What are you looking for?" asked Cati.

"Smith had a daughter," the doctor murmured, almost to himself.

Smith? The man who had abandoned the Raggies? Cati was familiar with the story, but she didn't see what it had to do with what was happening now.

Darkness fell. Cati peered out into the night. Below her the men worked tirelessly. Looking towards the bow, she could see the little girl standing there. After an hour she saw Chancellor sway and almost fall. Dr Diamond sent him to his cabin and the others redoubled their efforts. Cati had an itchy feeling at the back of her neck and every five minutes she turned to stare, but the night was starless and she could see nothing. It seemed to her that the wind stayed fresh and she hoped against hope that it was enough to stop the Planemen.

As the night went on the temperature dipped. Cati couldn't feel her nose or her hands any more. Then she realised that she could go into the wheelhouse and take the wheel in there. She strapped up the outside wheel and stepped inside. The wheelhouse was warm compared to outside, and she felt guilty looking down at the others working in the cold and dark. As the night stretched on, the wheel became lighter in her hands as the water level in the bilge fell. The buckets went up and down from the hold in a slow, weary rhythm. Her eyes felt grainy and sore.

Close to dawn, Cati could sense a definite change in the way the craft handled. It was dancing over the waves instead of ploughing through them. At the top of a wave she could see a cold glimmer of light in the east. Down below, the rest of the crew worked on, grey and exhausted. Cati looked over her shoulder. It was still too dark to see the Planemen, but she was sure now that they were travelling at their old speed. She heard Wesley call out that they could stop bailing. *None too soon*, Cati thought as a fresh flurry of snow, blowing horizontally in the stiff breeze, blocked her view of the deck. The last thing she saw was Dr Diamond slumping on to the deck, Uel and Mervyn leaning wearily against the mast.

That was when they came, the Planemen, screaming in

238

under cover of the snow. Blue flame blazed across the deck. Cati was dimly aware of Mervyn and Uel scrambling over the bridge, weariness forgotten. The Planemen wheeled about the masthead like spindly, evil birds and then dived to attack again. The water alongside the craft boiled, and she felt a hard jolt through the wheel. Desperately, Cati spun the wheel away from them. She felt strong hands grab the wheel away from her, and was aware of Wesley, white-faced, alongside her. In his hands Boat came about, faster and more agile than she would have believed possible, but still the Planemen came.

Another flash seared the deck and through the snow she saw Dr Diamond thrown heavily against the base of the mast. She turned to the left. The snow cleared momentarily and she saw one of the Planemen skimming the wavetops, heading directly for the wheelhouse. Closer and closer he came so that she could see the gaunt features, the rime-crusted beard, the cracked and frozen leather jerkin, the grim, staring, red eyes, and the great hands grasping the controls and moving, she knew, to trigger the terrible power of the magno cannon.

Cati stood fixed to the spot and she knew that she could no more have moved than she could have snatched the Planeman from the sky. Suddenly, a burst of blue flame shot from the roof of the wheelhouse above her. The Planeman veered wildly to the side to avoid it, but the bolt of magno seared the side of the plane and struck his shoulder a glancing blow. As he dipped dangerously close to the waves, Cati could see a jagged rip in the shoulder of his leather jacket and smoke rising from it. Grimacing with pain, he eased the craft into the air, turned and flew away from Boat.

Another Planeman came skimming across the waves astern of the boat, firing as he came. Cati saw flame streaking towards the windows of the dining cabin and heard a great crash of crockery falling to the deck, but both Mervyn and Uel were firing now and the Planemen were having to use all of their skills to avoid their fire. One of the Planemen raised his hand in a signal and they all wheeled about and flew swiftly away. The snow began to ease. Boat rose on a wave and Cati heard another crash as more of crockery fell to the deck.

Dr Diamond! she thought. She had seen him hit! Shaking herself out of her stupor, Cati ran out of the wheelhouse and down on to the deck. Dr Diamond raised himself gingerly on to one elbow. There was a deep gash on his temple, and he was deathly pale.

"Are you all right?" she asked anxiously.

"Am I think I," the scientist said, looking groggy. He swayed and Cati reached out to support him. "Hap... What happened?" he asked, making an effort to correct his speech.

"The Planemen attacked. They must have got ahead of us during the night."

"Now I remember," he said. As Boat crested a wave, Dr Diamond swayed again and Cati had to grab the mast to stop them both falling over.

"I think I'd better lie down," said Dr Diamond. Cati helped him across the deck to his cabin, trying to avoid the great scorched furrows left in the deck by the Planemen's guns. He lay down on the bed and Cati wet a cloth and bathed the gash on his head until she was sure that it was clean.

"Thank you, Cati," he said softly. "I think I'll stay here for a while." Turning at the door she saw that the man was almost asleep already.

She went back to the wheelhouse. Wesley was still at the wheel. He was talking in low tones to the Sub-Commandant. Both of them looked grey with exhaustion.

"They must have known we were leaving," he was saying, his voice angry. "They couldn't have guessed it."

"Possibly," the Sub-Commandant said, "but perhaps they picked up our trail by accident."

"What about the stopcock?" Wesley demanded angrily. "How did it get open?"

"Strange," the small man said, "I admit that it is strange…"

"It's a whole lot more than strange," said Wesley. "There's someone aboard this here—"

"Cati," the Sub-Commandant interrupted. "How is Dr Diamond?"

"I think hes all right. He's doing a bit of backwards talking, but I think that's just the bang on the head. He's lying down."

"That's one good thing," Wesley said. "We're going to

241

need all the help we can get, not that it'll make any difference anyhow."

"Why's that?" asked Cati. "They didn't put a hole in us, did they?"

"Might as well've," Wesley said. "Take a look at thon." He pointed towards the oars on the left-hand side. A deep scorch mark ran across the top of them and two of them were splintered, not yet broken, but bending out of shape each time they touched the water and threatening to snap. Cati remembered the hard tug on the steering she had felt when the Planeman attacked down that side and she realised that was what she had felt.

"If that goes," Wesley said, "it's the end of us."

Boat limped on through the day. The Sub-Commandant insisted that they keep up the same pace.

"Fair dos," Wesley said, "but if the weather gets up a bit, she'll snap."

"Does that mean we have to stop?" asked Cati. The Sub-Commandant explained that they could still keep going, but they would have to disengage the two damaged oars and the two oars on the other side, opposite the damaged ones, otherwise they'd end up going round in circles.

"Them Planemen would catch us in a second," Wesley said. Behind them, a line of Planemen hung in the frozen sky, a kind of terrible patience to the way they were flying now.

Cati noticed that one of them was flying slightly lower than the others and seemed to have difficulty keeping his place in the line.

Dinner that night was subdued. The sleepless night had taken its toll. Dr Diamond had stayed in bed for most of the day and was now managing, with difficulty, to get his sentences the right way round. Uel and Mervyn looked tense and tired. Chancellor could barely lift his head to eat. Only Wesley and Cati's father seemed alert; the Sub-Commandant calm, eating methodically, Wesley's eyes darting suspiciously round the table, scrutinising each face in turn.

"Stop that," Cati whispered to him.

"What?"

"Looking at me like that. I didn't open your precious stopcock."

"Somebody did."

"Well, it wasn't me. You probably left it open yourself."

"Whatever the two of you are squabbling about, please don't," the Sub-Commandant interrupted. "We're all tired. We'll take four-hour watches tonight, in twos. Wesley, you can take the first one with me."

Wesley looked at him with approval. If two people were working together then there was no chance of anyone interfering with stopcocks or anything else without being seen.

The night passed without incident. The Sub-Commandant took two watches, with Wesley and with Chancellor. Uel and

Mervyn took the four hours in the middle of the night. Cati took the dawn watch with Dr Diamond. She shivered when she walked out on to the deck, not with cold, although there was a deathly chill in the air, but with awe. The night sky had cleared and every star shone as brightly as they must have done at the beginning of the world, the great constellations stretching off into infinity. Slowly, she clambered up to the wheelhouse, reluctant to step into the shelter for the movement of the boat made the stars seem to spin and wheel in the dark sky.

"Fascinating," Dr Diamond said when she entered the wheelhouse. "Do you see anything different, Cati?"

"Just that the stars are so bright."

"Yes, they are bright, but they are also different. The constellations are not where you would expect. The Milky Way should be over there. The Plough should not be visible in that quarter."

"Why's that?" Cati asked.

"Well, if you interfere with time then you also interfere with space. Things are dragged out of place in unexpected ways."

The night passed without incident. Cati found herself holding the wheel, almost dozing, while Dr Diamond made measurements from the stars with a series of sextants and protractors and other oddly shaped instruments he had brought from his cabin.

When the dawn came, the air itself seemed to glint and sparkle with cold. The sky was cloudless and the sea was a deep, cold green flecked with white. When Cati went out on to the bridge ice particles stung her face.

"The wind carries the foam off the top of the waves," Dr Diamond said, "and it freezes in the air."

They looked back along the wake of Boat. The Planemen hung in the air at the same distance as before. Except that this time there were only three of them.

CHAPTER EIGHTEEN

There is one good thing about being under Whitwashisberd's table, Owen thought, *and one bad thing.* The good thing was that he had been thrown almost on top of a small inspection window so that he could see out. The bad thing was the proximity to Whitwashisberd's feet from which emanated an almost indescribable stink.

Despite the tightness of his bonds, Owen managed to get his face up against the window. The snow had stopped. He could see pine trees stretching out silently to either side of the Q-car. The huge wheels enabled the craft to move through the trees, but it swayed and bumped as it went. Earlier, he had heard Johnston tell Whitwashisberd that they would be reaching the true Harsh Road soon, and that they would pick up speed then. Owen wasn't sure if he liked the idea of that. He was tired and he pressed his face against the cold glass to wake himself up. As he did so, he thought he saw a black shape moving through the trees behind the Q-car. He looked again. There was definitely something there, running lightly and tirelessly in the snowy spaces between the pines. *Someone*, he thought, *who is following the car*.

Owen felt his heart leap. The figure was carrying something in a coil at its waist. A long whip. It was Pieta! She was keeping pace effortlessly, but what would happen when they reached the Harsh Road?

There was a sudden stir in the cabin. "Harsh Road coming up!" Passionara sang out. "Get us some speed. Get the boy quick to freezebones Harsh." This provoked gales of mirth from Mariacallas. Owen thought that he would like to strangle both of them.

The ground was more open now. The trees had given way to scrub and then to clear, featureless snow. As it did so, the Q-car started to pick up speed. He saw Pieta clear the edge of the trees and accelerate as she realised what was happening.

Then Owen saw something odd. The edge of what seemed to be some kind of crash barrier protruding from the snow. He saw what was unmistakeably a motorway sign, bent and aged, but still recognisable. Ahead, a long, snow-covered space led off into the distance. *It* is *a motorway*, he thought. The Harsh had taken a motorway and turned the whole thing into an island in time.

Things started to happen quickly then. The Q-car leapt forward as it hit the road. Owen could see that Pieta was running at full tilt now, but it wasn't fast enough. Just as she started to fall back into the darkness, he saw her reach to her belt. The Q-car bounced on to the motorway, the jolt of it throwing him backwards. By the time he had got back into position at the window, Pieta was gone. No one could help him now. He was being delivered to the Harsh who could turn time backwards, and make an entire motorway an island in time. Owen closed his eyes and let despair wash over him.

On and on through the night the Q-car sped, moving so fast that the landscape through which they passed was reduced to a blur. Owen was exhausted, but he couldn't sleep. His legs were tight with cramp and the cords binding his arms were so tight he could no longer feel them. Passionara was driving. Johnston and Mariacallas sat at the rear of the cabin, drinking gin and playing whist. Whitwashisberd drank gin as well then fell asleep so that the floor on which Owen lay vibrated with his snores, adding to Owen's misery. With the first glimmer of dawn he fell into a disturbed sleep, punctuated by the drunken yells of Johnston and Mariacallas.

Owen's fitful sleep was finally broken by loud shouting. It was Passionara.

"Hey, wakey wakey, gents! You want me drive all night to hell?"

There was no answer from the others. They were all drunk and snoring. Passionara let the Q-car coast to a halt. He got out of his seat and walked back down the cabin. Owen quickly shut his eyes and pretended to be asleep. After a moment he could feel the man leaning over him. He could feel actual breath on his face.

Owen remembered the look of hatred on Passionara's face after Whitwashisberd had kicked the razor blade out of his hand. He had never felt more helpless in his life. The man stayed there for a minute and Owen squeezed his eyes shut even tighter as if he could block him out. In the end, Passionara merely muttered something under his breath and Owen sensed him move away. Cautiously, Owen opened one eye. Passionara was examining the sleeping men. He bent over Johnston and fiddled at his neck. Johnston grunted, but did not wake. Passionara straightened, holding a key on a chain, and did a silent jig to himself. He went to a small cupboard under the rear bulkhead and opened it. It was the gin store. Passionara picked out a bottle and put it in his pocket. Then, moving cautiously, he replaced the key round Johnston's neck and started back up the cabin. Owen squeezed his eyes shut once more.

Owen did not open his eyes again until the Q-car

lurched into life. Passionara was at the controls, but this time he was swigging from a bottle of gin as he drove. Owen stared out of the window. The sun shone brightly and the whiteness of the snow outside was almost unbearable. The wind blew fine powdery snow against hidden objects, creating strange shapes so that the world outside looked like no country he had ever seen. As the morning wore on, Passionara started to sing. He shouted back to Owen.

"Hey, Pretty Rat, you like songs from time of shows? You like that damn fine Vera Lynn? Tell me. I sing for you. I cut throat after."

In fact, Passionara had a good voice and his singing took Owen's mind off the danger he was in. Passionara introduced songs from Sandy Shaw and the Sandpipers, and lots of other people Owen had never heard of, but then things started to go wrong. Passionara started to repeat verses. Then he began to forget the words. Finally, he went completely out of tune and was reduced to humming loudly off-key. The gin bottle rolled past Owen's nose. It was completely empty.

In the end there was no more singing. Gradually, Owen realised that another snore had been added to the chorus in the cabin. Craning his neck around as far as it would go, he saw that Passionara was fast asleep, slumped over the controls. They were careering down the Harsh Road at terrifying speed with no one in control.

The end wasn't long in coming. The Q-car started to veer off-line. For several minutes it travelled down the snow-covered motorway on what would have been the hard shoulder. Then it struck a road sign buried under the snow. With a ringing sound the sign snapped and flew high into the air. The Q-car turned sharply sideways and ran at high speed right off the road and into the countryside, snapping trees like twigs, crashing over hidden obstacles. Johnston stirred in his sleep, but it was too late. Owen saw a huge wall rearing up in front of them. Before he had time to brace himself, the Q-car struck with a massive crash. The force of the collision propelled Owen the length of the floor. With a sickening impact he hit the bulkhead beside the sleeping Passionara. Mariacallas hurtled down the floor after him, and struck Owen with an impact which drove the breath from his body.

For several moments there was chaos. Swearing and sweating, Johnston plucked the drunk Passionara out of the driver's seat and simply flung him the length of the cabin. Mariacallas seemed a bit dazed and was dancing around the cabin with a long, thin knife in his hand looking for imaginary foes. Whitwashisberd was awake with his book open in front of him and by the way he was looking at the still-sleeping Passionara, it was open at the page featuring the drunk man's name, Owen thought.

It turned out that the wall they had struck was made of soft snow piled up by the wind, and there was little actual damage done, although the Q-car was almost buried in it. Johnston took the controls and drove the Q-car forward and back until he had got it clear. He lay back in his seat looking terrible. His great sideburns were matted, and his eyes were red and veined.

All at once, he sat up and looked through the side window of the cabin then leapt to his feet. He suddenly seemed to become aware of Owen and with half a kick and half a push he propelled the boy back down the cabin until he fetched up under Whitwashisberd's chair again. Then he threw open the hatch and unfolded the long, spindly ladder. Johnston clambered down followed by Mariacallas, and Owen could not see them for a few moments. When they reappeared in his window, they were trudging across the snow towards a large flat area. Reaching it, Johnston took something out of his pocket and threw it. There was a blinding blue flash and a large noise. When the fine haze of ice that hung in the air after the explosion had cleared, Owen saw that there was a small lake underneath the ice, the water black and cold against the snow. Johnston and Mariacallas threw off their clothes and, with whoops and wild curses, they plunged into the freezing water.

Whitwashisberd saw what they were doing. With what sounded like a grunt of enthusiasm he clambered to his feet and lumbered towards the hatch. Owen could feel the whole Q-car shaking as he went down the ladder then he reappeared in the window, almost running across the snow, shedding his clothes as he went. Owen looked away. He felt bad enough without being put through the ordeal of seeing a naked Whitwashisberd.

On the outside of the cabin, a piece of ice stirred; a piece of ice which seemed to have eyes that glittered with determination every bit as cold and adamant as the frozen earth over which the Q-car had travelled. When Pieta had seen the Q-car reach the edge of the Harsh Road she realised that she would not be able to keep up. With one swift movement she had reached for the magno whip at her waist. She lashed it backwards and forwards over her head until she had woven a rope of burning blue flame. Then one immensely powerful flick had sent it speeding towards the back of the Q-car. With a hiss, the end of the knotted cord of light wrapped itself around the jutting tailpiece of the Q-car. Still running at full tilt, Pieta had flicked the whip again. A great shiver ran along its length and she was lifted off her feet as the light cord contracted at great speed, hurling her through the air as if she was flying until she landed, feet first, on the rear of the speeding vehicle.

There she stayed through the night, using her belt to bind her to the riveted bulkhead of the Q-car so that she would not be thrown off. So frozen were her clothes that you would have thought she was a statue, were it not for those green eyes, stern and unblinking even in the icy gale which buffeted her.

Owen heard a noise at the hatch. He turned to see a head coming through, but a head unlike any he had ever seen. It seemed sculpted from snow, with long, stiff hair of ice. The ice person moved quickly into the cabin and Owen shrank back as it approached. Then he saw the eyes. The same eyes he had seen, bold and fierce, in the battle with Johnston's men; the same eyes he had seen narrow with sarcastic humour at the Convoke; the same eyes he had seen soften with love at the sight of her children. Pieta.

She unwrapped the cloth round her face.

"Pieta, I—" he started to say.

"Can you walk?" she interrupted him brusquely.

"I don't know. I can't really feel my legs."

Pieta took out a small knife and began to cut through the ropes. At first Owen couldn't feel anything, but moments later the blood began to flow back and he had to bite his lip to stop from gasping out at the pain. With a quick glance at the unconscious Passionara, she hauled Owen to his feet and slashed the cords on his arms. Her clothes crackled with frost as she bundled him quickly towards the hatch. His legs were numb and weak and she had to support him. Pieta looked quickly through the hatch. The three men were still in the water.

"I can't climb," Owen said.

"You won't have to," said Pieta, giving him a shove between the shoulderblades. Unbalanced, and with his arms too weak and numb to catch the sides of the hatch, Owen tumbled through. Looking up as he fell, he saw Pieta jumping after him. He landed in a deep snowdrift. Pieta landed beside him. She urged him to his feet. He got up, feeling his still-numb legs almost useless in the deep snow. Pieta put her arm round his shoulders and half dragged, half carried him away from the Q-car.

Owen felt terribly exposed as they moved slowly across the snow. Pieta was making for a low ridge several hundred metres away. He glanced over his shoulder. The three men were still in the water. He could hear Mariacallas's high-pitched laughter. At least he wouldn't have to put up with that terrible sense of humour again, he thought to himself.

As they approached the ridge, feeling gradually returned painfully to Owen's legs and he was able to carry more of his own weight up the slope.

"Keep low," Pieta said as they reached the top of the ridge, but no matter how low they kept they were silhouetted against the skyline. Owen waited for an angry shout, but none came. Almost on their hands and knees they crossed the ridge and fell on to the other side.

"Rest for a moment," said Pieta, "but then we have to move."

"They'll see our tracks," Owen suddenly realised. "They'll find us straight away!"

"I'm not so sure," Pieta said quietly. "Look." She pointed

north. Owen could see great yellow snow clouds massed on the horizon.

In the Q-car Passionara woke up. He shook his head and spat out a tooth with an expression of disgust. He looked around. He was on his own. He went to the window. In one direction he could see footprints leading away across the snow. He went to the other window. He saw Johnston, Mariacallas and Whitwashisberd still in the black water. He looked under the seats in the car. He went back to the window and counted the figures in the water. He went to the other window and looked thoughtfully at the footprints. He went to the driver's seat and started the engine. The car trundled across the snow towards the lake. Johnston looked up in surprise.

Owen found the going easier after his brief rest and Pieta only had to stretch out an arm now and then when he stumbled. It helped that they were on the windward side of the ridge so that the snow was not as deep. Ahead of them they could see the dark mass of the treeline.

"If we can get under the trees, we'll be able to hide," Pieta said.

"Is everybody all right?" asked Owen. "Cati and the rest?"

"They have gone north," Pieta said. "They have the Mortmain with them. They are looking for the Puissance."

"But that's no good. Even if they reach it, they won't be

able to find the right place; they won't know what to do." Pieta looked at him strangely. Owen felt his face burning. Why had he said that? What did he know about the Puissance and how to make time go back the right way?

Two things happened then that stopped Pieta questioning him further. A fat snowflake drifted down and landed on Owen's cheek. And behind them, the Q-car crested the ridge. Johnston had opened a hatch at the top and was scanning the ground in front of him with one hand shielding his eyes. He pointed and they heard a distant shout.

"Run!" Pieta said. "Run like you've never run before!" Owen ran, stumbling and falling and picking himself up again, a great lung-bursting, nightmarish run where, it seemed, the trees did not get any nearer and the Q-car gained on them every second. *The snow will save us*, he thought desperately. *The snow will hide us*. And yet the snow drifted down in large downy flakes, not thick enough to conceal them or their tracks.

And then they were nearly at the tree line, but the Q-car was almost on them. Pieta turned and lashed the magno whip across the surface of the snow. A huge curtain of white rose from the ground, a spiralling blizzard, and the Q-car disappeared behind it. Owen could hear Johnston's bellow of rage and then they were in among the trees.

Safe! thought Owen. Safe, that is, until he realised that they had not reached the forest as they had thought. The place they had reached was not that of the deep forest, but a line of trees only five or six deep. Owen stopped and teetered and would have fallen if Pieta had not caught him by the arm.

They stood on the brink of a sheer gorge and, far below, at the bottom of a cliff, was the green-blue water of a fast-rushing river. They were trapped. Following Pieta, Owen started to run along the top of the gorge, keeping in the shadow of the trees. Behind them he could hear the Q-car crashing through the trees like some large and angry beast. They reached a stand of tall Scots pines beside the river. Pieta uncoiled the whip. The blue flame lashed out with the speed of a snake striking. There was a crack, a sizzling sound and then, with a mighty crash, the tallest of the trees fell right across the gorge, forming a long, smooth bridge.

"We have to cross at a run," Pieta said. The Q-car was very close now. Owen looked down at the coil of green water below them and felt the familiar sick fear rise in his throat.

"I can't," he said. "I can't."

Pieta didn't hesitate. With a flick of her wrist she drew the whip across the back of Owen's legs. He yelped at the searing pain and she flicked her wrist again. The pain and shock were indescribable. Owem saw her flex her wrist again and he recoiled on to the fallen tree. She swung at him again. And so he crossed the bridge at a run, driven like a beast, tears of pain and humiliation in his eyes.

Halfway across, he heard a roar of triumph. He could not help stopping and turning to see, half expecting the lash again.

But Pieta had done what she had set out to do. The Q-car emerged from the trees; Johnston, face and sideburns coated with snow, yelled again. Passionara was driving. He turned the vehicle to cut them off, setting a diagonal course. Too late he saw the gorge, and they heard Johnston's enraged cry. The Q-car stopped on the very edge of the gorge, teetered and righted itself, teetered once more, and once more righted itself. Owen could see Whitwashisberd sitting in his usual place. The ledger was open in front of him.

The Q-car teetered again, but through the windscreen Owen saw that Mariacallas had come to the front of the vehicle. In vain, Passionara tried to push him back. The extra weight was enough to turn the teeter into a slide, and the slide into an uncontrollable descent. Owen stopped his ears against Johnston's roar of terrible anger. But as the Q-car slid past them, Owen could see Whitwashisberd, writing something in the book with an air of calm satisfaction, and Owen knew he was drawing a tiny skull next to his own name. There was a bang and the rumble of rocks falling into the gorge. And then the Q-car was gone.

CHAPTER NINETEEN

On and on Boat sailed and still the damaged oars held. Wesley kept looking back at the three Planemen following them. If they stopped for two hours, he could have put a splint on the oars, he said, but everyone knew that they couldn't halt and risk another attack from the Planes. Cati spent most of her time in the crow's nest. When she was on deck, she kept looking into people's faces and wondering which one of them had opened the stopcock. She even wondered about Dr Diamond then felt ashamed for doing so.

Besides, she liked being in the crow's nest. She brought up some blankets to keep her warm and sat all day huddled in them, watching for danger and for the Great Machine in the North, although she had no idea what it might look like. And then there were the strange things she saw. A great iceberg, dirty white on top and a deep sea-green where it met the water, which sailed past them like a stately palace of ice. There were plenty of ice floes as well – growlers Wesley called them – and once she saw one float past with a great white bear standing on it, looking as through it was the most normal thing in the world to be floating on a big piece of ice in the freezing, inhospitable ocean. Then there were the whales. Small ones which swam alongside Boat, and then the huge ones she saw in the distance, their backs looking like blue-black mountains as they surfaced.

On the fourth day since the attack Cati climbed the mast as usual. She could see Wesley at the wheel and the little girl standing in place at the bow. Far below her, tendrils of smoke curled out from under Dr Diamond's door and were snatched away by the icy wind. Mervyn was crouched behind the wheelhouse, watching the Planemen. Cati couldn't see Chancellor or her father. She hauled herself into the crow's nest, the skin of her face stinging from the ice particles carried by the wind, particles which had scoured every exposed surface on Boat until they shone as if they had been polished daily.

Cati scanned the sea around the ship, but it was empty. Then she looked towards the horizon. For a moment, she thought she saw something – a tiny black tendril right on the limit of her vision which seemed to curl upwards. She rubbed her eyes, but it had disappeared. She was about to call down to Wesley when she realised why she couldn't see the horizon any more. It was obscured by black cloud, cloud which, even as she watched, grew larger, seeming to race towards them. As it did so, the register of the wind seemed to alter, going from a steady roar to a vicious whistling sound. By the troubled look on Wesley's face, Cati knew that he had already seen the cloud.

All afternoon the black cloud built on the horizon and Wesley stayed in the wheelhouse, in worried debate with the others. When Cati came down to eat, she asked Dr Diamond if anything had been decided.

"There are a few choices, none of them good," he said, scanning the horizon. He looked peculiar as he was wearing a pair of heated ice-goggles of his own invention. "We can keep going as we are and hope that the storm blows the Planemen off course. Or we can turn back and ride in front of the storm, and hopefully keep the oars intact. The problem with that is that we have to go under the Planemen."

The seas continued to build. The bow of Boat rose and plunged, sending sheets of icy spray high into the air. Wesley slowed the craft a little, and bit by bit, the Planemen got closer, although you could see that they were having difficulty controlling the Planes in the high wind. Mervyn and Uel were both crouched in the sheltered spot behind the wheelhouse now, the magno crossbows following every movement of the planes.

"They can't hold them off for ever," Chancellor said.

"True enough," replied Wesley.

Night fell. But it wasn't night the way Cati knew it. As they went further north, it seemed that the sun didn't set properly, so it was never completely dark. Dr Diamond said it was always like that in the far north, but Cati preferred it when night was dark and day was light. When the storm finally struck, no one could see anything anyway. One minute they were cresting the waves, the next the sky seemed to be blotted out and Cati had to close her ears against the terrifying shriek of the wind as the sea seemed to rise up around them, mountainous and boiling.

Cati ran to the wheelhouse. Uel and Mervyn ran in behind her, for to stay on the deck was to be swept overboard.

"Where's the little girl?" Cati asked, having to shout to make herself heard above the noise of the storm.

"It's all right," Uel shouted back. "I saw her go below."

Cati had to hold on to the doorframe to stop herself being thrown to the floor. Down below she couldn't see the deck for boiling, seething water. Wesley's face was taut with concentration as he fought to control the wheel. Through the window Cati could see rank upon rank of vast, white-crested waves advancing on them. Boat took an age to climb each one before plunging down the other side with dizzying speed. Dr Diamond stayed on the left hand side of the wheelhouse where the damaged oars were, peering anxiously though the spray and angry foam in an attempt to see how the oars were faring.

"Don't fret, doctor," Wesley said with a tight grin. "I'll know about it if them oars snap."

On through the dark, tempestuous night Boat sailed, and still the oars held. And each time, when they thought that the storm could get no worse, the wind blew stronger, and the waves grew bigger, and the wind shrieked still louder.

The Sub-Commandant took Dr Diamond aside. "The oars can't possibly hold," Cati heard him say.

"If they go then there will be three oars working on one side and five on the other," Dr Diamond said. "Wesley won't be able to steer straight."

"We have to take the oars off the other side so that there are three on each…" the Sub-Commandant said, but before they could act, they were interrupted by a gasp from Cati and a curse from Wesley. In the distance, and bearing down on them with the speed of an express train, was the biggest wave any of them had ever seen. Cati thought it was like a mountain of water, vast and threatening with icy spume like lightning flying in great sheets from its leading edge. In a moment it was on them and the oars beat frantically as Boat began to climb what seemed to be a sheer cliff of water. Up and up they went, Boat tipping further and further backwards until it seemed to Cati that they would tumble down and be lost in the boiling water. And still they climbed. Then, they were at the very top, teetering on the crest of the wave for what seemed like eternity.

They almost made it, but just at the very moment that Boat tilted forward for the race down the other side of the wave, there was a loud crack, followed closely by another. The damaged oars had snapped. Boat's bow dropped and it slewed around so that it was racing in a diagonal line across the back of the wave. The side with the broken oars rose higher and higher into the air as the craft tilted on to its side. Cati was thrown against the wheelhouse door. A locker full of maps and charts fell open and the contents rolled about the floor. As the tilt got worse, the chart table snapped its moorings and followed the charts, striking Cati a heavy blow on the leg. Just when it seemed that Boat could not tip over any further without capsizing, Wesley gained control again and Boat straightened – just in time to face the next wave.

"I can't hold it like this for long," he gasped. The wheel shuddered with every stroke of the oars and his shoulders were knotted with effort.

"Someone will have to disconnect the other oars," the Sub-Commandant said.

"It would be suicide to go out on deck," said Chancellor. "You'd never reach the engine hatch."

"True enough," Wesley said.

"What about under the deck?" asked Dr Diamond.

"No good. You wouldn't fit in the space." Another wave hit the bow of Boat and Wesley wrestled with the wheel, beads of sweat breaking out on his forehead. He managed to correct

Boat's course and turned back to the others.

"You wouldn't fit," he added, "but she would." He inclined his head towards Cati. "It's fair and tight, but she'd get in there all right."

"I don't like it," the Sub-Commandant said. "The linkages are powerful. If Cati gets caught in one…"

"We've no choice," said Dr Diamond gently.

"The girl wouldn't be strong enough," Chancellor said.

"She'll have to be," said Wesley said. "I can't hold Boat much longer."

"The magno motor is powerful, but perhaps we can cut it for a moment or two from the wheelhouse," suggested Dr Diamond.

"Dangerous—" the Sub-Commandant began.

"Stop it!" snapped Cati. "Stop talking as if I'm not here. If the job has to be done, and I'm the only one that will fit, then tell me what to do and I'll do it."

Dr Diamond gave her a long, considering look. The Sub-Commandant shook his head, but said nothing.

"Right," said Cati, "how do I get to the motor?" Wesley tapped the floor behind him with his foot.

"Uel and Mervyn," he said, "lift them boards." The two boys sprang forward and started to pull up the floorboards.

"I have a plan," Dr Diamond said. "It will take you about five minutes to get to the motor. The two forward blades are attached by a hook. We'll turn the engine off for exactly two minutes so that you can unhook them."

"How will I know the time?" Cati asked. Dr Diamond produced two identical hourglasses from his pocket.

"The Harsh haven't been able to make sand run backwards yet," he said. "When the motor stops, turn this on its end."

"You damn well better hurry," Wesley said, and she could hear the strain in his voice. "Crawl straight and crawl quick."

The Sub-Commandant helped Cati down into the dank hole revealed by the lifted planks. When the time came to release her hands, he did not let go and she had to gently break his grip. With a quick smile, she ducked into the dark space.

There was only just enough room. The underside of the deck grazed her head and she couldn't straighten up enough to crawl so she had to wriggle. Filthy, cold bilge water swirled around and within a minute her clothes were soaked. As Cati began to crawl under the exposed deck, she could feel the wood above her head thrumming with the power of the storm. And each time a wave struck she was thrown sideways against the unforgiving beams which supported the deck. The only thing that made it bearable was the faint glow of magno from the engine compartment ahead.

Dr Diamond had said five minutes, but it felt like half a lifetime before she reached the motor and was able to stand up. Cati could see the magno core of the motor, contained in a kind of brass case, open on top. To each side there were five levers. On the left side the levers were attached to five oars, and they moved smoothly, like a rower's arms and elbows, but to the other side only three of the oars worked properly. The other two had splintered stubs of oar attached to them. Just as Cati registered this, the engine stopped. She froze. They should have given her more time. Wesley must not be able to hold it any more. The motion of Boat changed immediately, the rising and falling movement being replaced by wild corkscrewing.

Cati knew she was wasting time. She took the hourglass from her pocket and placed it upside down beside the motor. She saw straightaway that the link between the oar and the lever was a giant hook and eye arrangement. She grasped the hook on the front left oar and heaved on it. It didn't budge. She tried again. *The sand is running through the glass far too quickly!* she thought. She also realised that if the motor started with her arm in it, the arm would be crushed. Desperately, Cati pulled at the hook. The sand was half gone and she hadn't even got one oar off. She shifted her grip to the lever and pulled. Still nothing. She moved the lever around a bit and then realised that if she pushed it down, it seemed to go without resistance. She pushed down and down, and then there was a creak of protest and the oar came loose.

There was still time for the other one. Cati grasped the lever with confidence this time, but it wouldn't move! Scrambling to her feet she looked down at it. The metal below the lever seemed to have corroded and jammed it.

Frantically, she looked around. There was a monkey wrench hanging from a peg above the motor. She grabbed it and hammered with all her might at the lever. It shifted, but the sand was almost gone, the last few grains trickling into the bottom of the hourglass. She grabbed the lever and it moved downwards, not smoothly, but moving. It was almost free, but as it moved the last centimetre, the motor started again. Instinctively, Cati thrust the wrench into the motor. The lever, which was descending like an axe, stopped. She pushed and it came free. She snatched her hand back, and just as she did so, the strong brass wrench snapped like a twig and the lever plunged through the space where her hand had been seconds earlier.

Cati lay back against the ribs of the little vessel. She could feel it start to rise and fall again. Her heart was pounding. Owen would be impressed with her, she thought, then felt the return of a dull ache. Owen would never know.

The journey back to the wheelhouse seemed longer. When she reached the other end, filthy and exhausted, the Sub-Commandant lifted her out of the hole and held her for a moment.

"You did very well," Dr Diamond beamed.

"Sorry about that," Wesley said. "I couldn't hold her any more. We had to start the motor again."

"That's all right," Cati said with a weak grin, remembering the sound that the wrench had made when it snapped.

The Sub-Commandant said nothing, but rested his hand on her shoulder.

It still took all of Wesley's skill to keep Boat on course since it was now short four of its ten oars, but at least, he said, he didn't have to fight Boat as well as the sea. However, his face was pinched with fatigue by the time dawn came. If it could be called a dawn. For despite the fact that the sun didn't really set this far north, the sky was completely hidden by heavy black cloud, and the waves were so high that, even if there had been a horizon, you wouldn't have been able to see it. In the end, the Sub-Commandant persuaded Wesley to step down and let Mervyn take the wheel. The Sub-Commandant had insisted that they all stay in the wheelhouse, so Wesley lay down on the floor and wrapped himself in a blanket. Cati was able to do no more than doze on the hard floor.

"At least there's no sign of the planes," said Dr Diamond.

"The wind will have blown them miles away," the Sub-Commandant said. Suddenly, there was a shout from the corner. The Sub-Commandant whirled round. Chancellor, who had been sleeping, was sitting bolt upright, his eyes staring.

"The Mortmain!" he shouted. "Where is the Mortmain?" The Sub-Commandant was beside him in an instant, placing a gentle arm on his shoulder.

"It's all right," he said. "It's all right. The Mortmain is safe."

"The Planemen will have it!" Chancellor shouted. "The Planemen must have it or send it to the bottom of the sea!"

"The Planemen are gone," the Sub-Commandant said gently but insistently.

Chancellor blinked, then slumped back against the wall. "I was dreaming," he said weakly. "I thought the Planemen had taken the Mortmain."

"The Mortmain is safe and the Planemen are gone. The wind took them in the night."

"Maybe not," Dr Diamond said quietly. They followed his pointing finger. Just a few hundred metres off the bow, the three Planemen rose into the air from behind a wave. Their leather jerkins were so coated in ice that it seemed as if they were wearing frozen armour. There were signs of damage to the planes – a bent vane, a ragged tailpiece and long icicles hung from their undercarriage – but they were intact. And Dr Diamond could see that they were hunting now.

CHAPTER TWENTY

Pieta urged Owen across the tree bridge, but her urging was gentle this time. He was numb and exhausted, and the back of his legs felt on fire. She made him sit on a large rock, giving him some flat cakes which she took from a small bag slung over her shoulder. He realised that he couldn't remember the last time he had eaten. As he ate, she knelt beside him and rubbed snow into the burning welts on the back of his legs.

"There was no time," she said, looking up into Owen's face. He knew she was right. While he was hesitating, paralysed by his fear of falling in the water, the Q-car would have been on them. Pieta finished tending to his legs. Her touch was gentle. She took a cloth from her bag, tore it in strips and wrapped it round his legs. The snow was still falling sparsely, but Pieta looked around her, seeming to smell the air, and she looked worried.

"There is a lot more snow coming," she said. "We should move, try to find trees we can shelter under. We can't use the Harsh Road. They will wonder what happened to Johnston. Maybe they will come looking for him."

They set off, Pieta leading the way, Owen walking as best he could in her footsteps. They walked all morning and into the afternoon, but there was no sign of trees. Pieta stole worried looks at Owen. The boy had taken far too much physical and mental punishment, and now he stumbled along as though in a dream. As she began to recognise the sort of place they were in, her worry grew. There were icy pools everywhere, small clumps of scrubby birch and elder. The ground beneath their feet was frozen and Pieta believed they had found themselves in the middle of a bogland – a great icy fen where there would be little proper shelter.

As the afternoon wore on, the snowflakes become smaller, turning hard and sleety so that they stung Owen's face. At the same time, the wind from the north became stronger, stirring up the surface of the snow and flinging it in their faces. They pressed on, not because they had any aim or destination, simply because Pieta knew that if Owen stopped and lay down, he might never find the will to get up again.

They had been walking on smooth ground for some time, smooth ground without shelter it was true, but at least it was easier to walk on. Then, as it began to get dark, Pieta suddenly realised why the ground was so smooth and shelterless. Kneeling quickly and scooping away the snow, she revealed hard, black ice. They were walking on the surface of a lake, frozen and bleak. Behind her Owen swayed and almost fell. She put her arm round him. He mumbled something and leaned against her shoulder. Night was coming and the temperature was plummeting. There was one last desperate hope. Something Pieta had once learned about another level of Resisters. Something proud and bitter and dark of thought. And these marshes and fens and boggy lakes were the stronghold of this resistance.

Stumbling now with tiredness, for she had run day and night after the Q-Car, Pieta pushed Owen forward into the storm and the growing night. On and on they went, beyond any limit she had ever known, and when Owen fell, she picked him up and put him over her shoulders and carried him. Until at last a small mound of earth reared up in front of them, ringed in ancient whitethorn bushes. Pieta pushed through them, the sharp thorns tearing at her clothes and skin, and fell exhausted. With one last effort, she took the whip from her pocket and sent a searing flame up the trunk of one of the trees.

She waited, but nothing happened. She realised that the falling snow had covered Owen and brushed it away from his face. "The debt of my children is repaid now," she said. "There is nothing else I can do."

The boy's eyes were closed and he did not answer. Pieta

staggered to her feet. Her hands and legs were frozen and useless. She made to move forward, but her legs gave way and she fell on to her knees. As she did so something hard and merciless wrapped itself round her neck, choking off her breath. Frantically, she tried to twist and throw off her attacker, but it was no use. As she struggled, she was aware of a ghostly shape, bent over her.

Suddenly, the pressure eased slightly. Then Pieta heard a female voice, harsh and gravelly and full of dark authority.

"You said to the boy the debt of your children you have repaid. You burned my tree. Now you have to start paying him for your own life, for you would surely be dead now if he was not here."

The pressure round Pieta's neck grew again and she felt her sight grow dim, her limbs grow weak, and she pitched forward into the snow and knew no more.

CHAPTER TWENTY-ONE

All day they tried to hold off the planes, but without the extra speed it was useless. The Planemen had realised that they could hold their craft steady for long enough to fire on Boat, whereas Uel and Mervyn had only the wildly pitching deck from which to fire. The planes swooped and dipped around the boat, firing carefully and steadily. They were too far away for any one shot to do massive damage, but at the same time, each shot did a little harm. Bits of the railing were carried away. The deck was scorched and cracked in places. The hull had been hit several times. In the mid afternoon, one of the bolts of magno plunged through the wheelhouse glass, exploding shards around the crew and burning a half-metre hole in the back wall. Wesley risked an expedition across the deck and down into the bilge. He reported that they must have sprung a plank for there was water in the hold.

Uel and Mervyn did their best, but too often their shots arced wildly off into the dark sky. Then another shot from the Planemen hit the deck beside Uel. He rolled on to his side, white-faced, with a jagged wound in his right hand. Cati bandaged it as best she could, but he couldn't operate the crossbow any more. The Planemen grew in confidence, sweeping in at wave height and firing across the deck, and this time their fire was doing real damage. On one sweep the forecastle was set alight, and Dr Diamond and the Sub-Commandant had to brave the open deck again and again with buckets before they had it under control.

The water was still pouring into the bilges, and Cati could feel that the weight of it was slowing Boat again, and still they were tossed around by the huge waves. Cati marvelled at the ability of the little craft to take so much punishment, but she knew that it could not go on. She remembered what Chancellor had said about the Mortmain being sent to the bottom of the sea. Why had he said that? The scene in the wheelhouse was chaotic now. Dr Diamond and the Sub-Commandant ran from place to place putting out fires, but still the woodsmoke stung her eyes. Sleety spray came through the broken window every time they crested a wave. The injured Uel crouched miserably in a corner, clutching his hand. The Planemen were like angry birds as they swooped over Boat.

"We'll try to make it to night-time," Wesley said through gritted teeth. "They might let up then."

But what will happen after that? Cati thought. *They'll simply come back at dawn.* Just then, she looked to her left and saw that the little girl was standing there, staring out across the waves, seeming completely unperturbed by what was going on around her.

Cati followed her gaze. She thought she could see something, a shape perhaps, something that seemed to blend with the grey and stormy sea. *Probably something belonging to the Harsh coming to finish us off*, she thought miserably. Maybe it was the little girl who had undone the stopcock. Cati looked at her again, but she kept her calm gaze fixed on the sea.

The Planemen withdrew and took up position behind Boat. They seemed to be talking among themselves, taking a rest before a final attack, Cati thought. Wesley's attention was taken up with Boat now, but suddenly he straightened and peered out into the storm.

"What is it?" the Sub-Commandant asked.

"Damned if I know," said Wesley, "but I'd say it's with them lot of Planemen behind us."

As it got closer, they saw that it was a ship of some kind. Cati could see that the Planemen were aware of it too. After a while one of them rose in the air and flew off towards it.

The ship was much closer now, moving at t

speed. It was big; so big that it barely rose and fell on the waves, and even when it was still a mile away, the great prow reared above them.

"A freighter of some kind," Dr Diamond said. But as it neared, they could see that there was something strange about it. For a start, it was red with rust, and hadn't seen paint for many years. Whole sections of its huge metal plates were missing. The giant mast lay broken across the deck. There seemed to be tangles of broken equipment and overturned oil drums lying everywhere. So much of the huge ship's superstructure was missing that you could see right through it in places. Great gouts of oily black smoke billowed from its funnel as it bore down upon them at speed.

"What is it?" asked Cati.

"I think I know," Wesley said, and there was a strange expression in his face. "I think I know."

"It is the Grim Captain," the Sub-Commandant said quietly.

"The Grim Captain is just a story," said Chancellor shortly, but Cati thought that if there was such a thing as a Grim Captain then this was the grim kind of ship he would command.

The Planeman who had gone to investigate rejoined the others. He spoke to them quickly and then without warning they swooped on Boat, this time in a furious attack, no longer caring for their own safety. Mervyn landed hits on them, and one of the planes trailed fire, but their own bolts of magno were landing everywhere on Boat. They felt the deck vibrate beneath their feet.

"We can't stay afloat much longer!" Wesley shouted. A great wave crashed over the deck and extinguished the flames that licked at it, but as it did so half a dozen other fires sprang up. Mervyn fired desperately and the damaged plane was hit again. It shot across the bow of Boat and landed in the sea with a great hiss. One of the remaining planes slewed in the air to avoid the stricken plane and struck the mast with a clang. It hung there, tangled with the mast, its pilot struggling to free himself. The remaining plane swooped in and the trapped Planeman grabbed its undercarriage. As he was hoisted aloft, Mervyn's last shots seared the air around them. But it was too late. The overloaded plane climbed high into the air, hovered for a moment, and then turned slowly back the way they had come.

Their work was done. The deck was full of holes and flames were starting to lick up through them. Boat was listing badly to one side and barely moving. And the ship was almost on them. The massive bow bore down on their frail craft. Cati was sure that it must plough over them until, with its engines shrieking in protest, water boiling at its stern, the ship shuddered to a halt alongside.

In the lee of the ship the storm seemed almost to have disappeared. A wall of rusty and scarred steel reared up above them, and the Boat banged gently against its side. As Cati stared, a rope ladder suddenly tumbled down from the freighter. The ladder had been mended and knotted all over; some of the rungs seemed rotted and others had snapped.

"It could be a trap," cautioned Chancellor.

"I'm not climbing that," Cati said.

"You don't have a choice," said Wesley, and his voice was serious. They looked down. Water was oozing through the deck at their feet and the motor had stopped completely. But still they looked doubtfully at the rotted hulk beside them and the dangerous-looking rope ladder dangling beside the bridge. Until, without a word, the little girl walked to the end of the rope ladder, grasped it and started to climb confidently.

"That's it then," the Sub-Commandant said. "You next, Cati."

One by one they took hold of the ladder and climbed. Wesley paused before he climbed, taking a long look around the ruined Boat that had sailed proudly out of the harbour. Rubbing the handrail and muttering something under his breath, he began to climb without looking back. Not even when the Sub-Commandant, supporting the injured Uel, got on to the ladder and the burning Boat turned on her side then slipped beneath the waves with a gentle hiss.

It was a long climb up the side of the ship. The rope ladder swayed against the rusty and jagged metal plates so that Cati's knees and elbows were cut and grazed. Every so often a plate would be missing and she would find herself staring into the dark void that was the booming, cavernous interior of the ship. She didn't know what was down there, but she found herself scampering up the ladder away from it.

When finally she fell over the rail on to the deck, Cati lay there for a moment, exhausted, then lifted her head cautiously to reveal a scene of terrible squalor. Empty barrels and paint tins littered the deck, which was splintered and broken in places. There were deep rents and missing hatch covers. There were tangles of rusting cable and broken winches. Broken chains dangled from splintered masts. Cati turned towards the bridge. It was, if anything, in worse shape than the rest of the ship. It was a towering structure, as high as a ten-storey building, with many windows, all of which were broken. There were large holes everywhere, and part of the roof seemed to be missing. But the worst thing was that the entire structure was bent to one side, leaning out over the water as if it had been nudged by a giant elbow. The wheelhouse itself seemed to have suffered the worst devastation. All its windows and their frames were gone and the interior was full of tangled metal, and every piece of buckled metal bore the scars of a thousand storms.

And then in the middle of it Cati saw him – the Grim Captain – the wheel of the ship gripped in his icy hands, as it had been gripped for countless years and countless icy seas.

The man was tall and heavy-set and motionless, as though carved from a block of stone. His face was hidden by a massive white beard streaked with brown and black. And above the beard his eyes burned with a fierce light and Cati felt her knees go weak, and felt her heart hammering in her breast, with fear, yes, but also with a terrible pity, as if all the loneliness in the world had been given to one man and he had carried it as a burden for time out of mind.

She sensed Wesley standing beside her and knew that he felt the whole thing.

"The Grim Captain," he breathed, seemingly unaware that he had spoken. Just then the Sub-Commandant and Uel tumbled over the rail. The Grim Captain raised one hand and grasped a lanyard above his head and pulled it. The ship's siren rang out and Cati had to cover her ears. He rang it again and again, three times in all they heard the note of the ghostly horn, long and sad. Then, accompanied by loud moans and clangs deep in the bowels of the ship, they started to move again, slowly at first, then picking up speed, the whole ship shuddering and creaking as it crashed through the waves.

"There's somebody knows where they're going," Wesley said. They followed his gaze. The little girl was once more standing in the bow, looking out across the storm-tossed ocean. Chancellor leaned wearily on the rail, until Mervyn pointed out that the stanchion holding it was almost completely rotted through. The injured Uel was shivering uncontrollably.

"He needs to be out of the wind," Dr Diamond said. There was a doorway in the front of the wheelhouse, its metal door sagging on the one hinge that was left, but none of them felt any eagerness to enter the dank space beyond.

"I must ask the Captain if we may take shelter," the Sub-Commandant said. Wesley looked at him as if he was mad.

"Are you sure?" Dr Diamond said.

"I have to speak to him," the Sub-Commandant said. "We have work to do and I need to know if he will help us."

"He'll freeze your blood," said Chancellor.

"I don't know," Cati said slowly. "I don't think so." *Unless*, she thought, *terrible sorrow can freeze your blood*.

They watched as the Sub-Commandant stepped through the doorway and into the darkness beyond.

Several minutes later they saw the Grim Captain turn from his station at the wheel, but Cati could not see the Captain's face. It seemed that they talked for a long time. Cati was getting worried about Uel, who was sitting on the deck, pale-faced. With five minutes' swift work, Dr Diamond had converted his ice goggles into a makeshift heater which he put under Uel's jacket, but it didn't seem to help.

At last, the Sub-Commandant came back. He seemed stooped with fatigue, and his expression was that of someone who had been given terrible tidings.

"He will give us passage," the Sub-Commandant said wearily. "He will take us to the Great Machine in the North."

"Did he ask a price?" Chancellor demanded. "Is there a tariff?" The Sub-Commandant shook his head wearily.

"There is something he wants," he said, "but he won't say what it is. It is something which must be given freely, without being asked for." Dr Diamond said nothing, but he shook his head as if the Sub-Commandant's words had confirmed something he already suspected.

The Sub-Commandant turned and beckoned to them to follow him through the door. Cati shivered as she stepped through. But it wasn't as bad as she expected, if you didn't count the water slopping about, and the discarded tools and junk that littered the corridor from one end to the other, and the groans and bangs and coughing sounds echoing up and down.

After a minute the Sub-Commandant led them down a twisted metal staircase. Then a most peculiar thing happened. Cati was at the bottom of the staircase one minute, and then there was a kind of a flicker and she was back at the top again. She looked round alarmed.

"Don't worry, Cati," Dr Diamond said, "it's nothing to do with the ship. It's a sign that we're getting close to the Great Machine in the North. When you interfere with the fabric of time, you get distortions – little slippages like the one you just noticed. It will happen more and more as we get nearer."

They stopped in front of a set of doors which had once been carved and varnished, but were now dilapidated. The Sub-Commandant pushed them open. Inside were the remains of what had once been a beautiful stateroom. The walls had once been panelled with leather, although only strips of it remained now. A chandelier sagged drunkenly from the ceiling, many of its glass pendants either shattered or missing. Expensive furniture in various states of disrepair lay on the floor. To Cati's surprise, she saw a stained marble fireplace on one wall. Dr Diamond walked through the room, examing the furniture and various broken objects, muttering things like, "Louis Quatorze, very fine," and "early art deco… impressive…"

Wesley, meanwhile, started to pile broken pieces of furniture into the fireplace to make a fire. Dr Diamond looked as if he was going to object.

"It's all broken anyway," Cati whispered to him, and he nodded and smiled a little wistfully. Soon Wesley had a blazing fire going and Uel seemed to have revived a little.

"Who is he?" she whispered to Dr Diamond. "I mean the Grim Captain."

"We all thought that he was a legend. But that's the problem with being adrift in time. Legends have a habit of turning up. The story is that he did a great wrong, but in the process threw away the one thing he valued above all else. And now he cannot rest."

"Like the Flying Dutchman?"

"Just like the Flying Dutchman, except in the Grim Captain's case it is his own mind that drives him; the memory of what he did will not let him rest."

"Can he not do something to make up for it?"

"I don't know. There are some crimes for which there are no amends. Perhaps his is one of them."

They made themselves as comfortable as they could in the ruined stateroom. They were exhausted, since they had not really slept the previous night. One by one they all slipped off to sleep – except for Chancellor, who sat by the fire and stared into it. And the Sub-Commandant, who watched him from the shadows, his eyes stern and unblinking.

CHAPTER TWENTY-TWO

Owen woke up in what seemed like a smothering dark. He sat bolt upright and realised that he was in a bed with dark drapes pulled round it. Vaguely, he could see the flicker of a fire. Something told him that he was underground. There was a certain smell, but he couldn't put his finger on it – earth and roots and buried things perhaps.

Cautiously, he moved one of the drapes aside. He could see a fire flickering in a large stone fireplace. Pieta was curled up beside it on the floor, sleeping like a cat. He stuck his head out cautiously. He was in what seemed to be a very large room, its ceiling lost in the shadows. At first he thought that the room was covered in vast drapes, sweeping down gracefully from a height, but then he realised that they were not in fact drapes, but cobwebs, accumulated over hundreds of years. But Owen also knew that the shapes could not be natural, that some hand had created them, woven them even. The light was eerie too. There was no magno here. The walls seemed to emanate light, a greenish phosphorescence. He moved to get a better view and suddenly his arm was seized in a claw like grip and with ferocious speed he was plucked from the bed.

Owen found himself standing in front of the tallest woman he had ever seen. She was wearing what appeared to be a ball gown. When she moved, gorgeous flower patterns showed, but it was so faded with age that the designs seemed to come and go. Her face was long and haughty and brown as oak, and her eyes were a golden colour. *Like an eagle's*, Owen thought. Her feet were bare and her black hair was piled on top of her head. When she turned her head slowly, he gasped. One side of her face was riven with a scar that ran like a fissure from the temple to the edge of her jaw, a scar that reminded him of the old tree on the riverbank that had been struck by lightning.

"I am Long Woman," she said, her speech rapid and accented, her voice harsh. "You are Navigator."

"My name is Owen," he stammered.

"You are Navigator," she repeated in a tone which told him not to contradict her again.

"Where am... Where are we?"

"You in my place. I find when they bury me in bog."

"Bury you? Are you... I mean, alive, or..."

"Alive? They bury me, no?" She tossed her hair back and

laughed, a harsh sound like a rook cawing. "Now come eat," she said. "You not have much time."

"What about Pieta, my friend?"

"She sleep, not wake; she lead you freeze in storm." The Long Woman made a gesture of contempt.

"It wasn't like that. She rescued me from Johnston. It wasn't her fault."

"Right, right, you say. Maybe I wake her later." The Long Woman didn't sound all that interested one way or another. She led Owen through a doorway into another room.

If the first room with its cobweb drapes had been strange then this one was more eerie still. The walls were moist and boggy, with mosses and lichens growing on them. In the middle of the room was a table set with the strangest feast that Owen had ever seen. Each place setting had a plate, a knife and an oddly shaped fork with two prongs. The centrepiece of the table was a large bowl filled with eels. As Owen watched, one of them lifted its head and then slithered over the others so that they all writhed.

There were bowls piled high with mistletoe berries. Inside a tall glass bowl, snails moved slowly over the glass, leaving a trail of slime behind them. Other plates had mounds of evil-coloured fungus, carefully sliced. There were sickly puffballs and plates of jelly-like aspic which quivered as though there was something living inside. There were pale and lacy toadstools that seemed to be pickled in bluish liquor. Each place had a large silver drinking vessel, and as Owen looked, something seemed to dive from the rim of the nearest one, landing in whatever liquid filled them with a distinct plop.

"I not make you eat," the Long Woman said with her harsh laugh. "This food for other guests, come later."

All Owen could think was, whoever they were, he didn't want to meet them. The Long Woman led him through the room into a pantry. This time, he saw with relief, there was nothing that crawled or oozed on offer. Instead, there were boxes of wrinkle-skinned sweet apples, hazelnuts, hard-skinned cheese. He ate hungrily and, at the Long Woman's order, filled his pockets.

"Can I ask you something?" he said.

"Ask question," said the Long Woman.

"Why did you call me Navigator?"

"Because you are Navigator. Only one to bring all back to right time, unless Harsh kill you stone dead."

Owen shivered at the thought of the Harsh. He couldn't believe that he had almost forgotten about them. "How do I do it?" he asked. "How do I bring everyone back to the right time?"

"Use Mortmain. You have it?"

"No. I went to look for it, but I couldn't find it."

"What hell," she said with an elaborate shrug. "Maybe it find you."

"They were taking me to the Harsh, to the Great Machine

291

in the North. Johnston was going to give me to the Harsh," Owen said.

"They take you to Puissance; that where you must go. Only place to use Mortmain."

"I don't understand. What do I do? Where is the, the... Puissance."

"You not know?" she said disbelievingly. "You not know!" And her mocking laughter filled the whole room.

"How *should* I know?" he said angrily.

"Do not be cross with me, my dear friend," the Long Woman said, suddenly stooping to him and taking his face between her thin, strong fingers, her face hovering over his so that she looked like a snake ready to strike. "Do not shout at me or I snap your neck like small twig. You pay attention?"

"Yes, yes... I'm sorry," Owen did not doubt for one moment that she meant what she said. She scrutinised his face, as if to make sure that he really was sorry.

"Better," she said. "Your father not tell you where Puissance was?"

"My father is dead."

"I see now. Father should tell son these things. I tell you. You are on frozen lake now. River not freeze, go too fast. Lake freeze. Frozen lake goes all the way to coast. There is Puissance. Many mile."

"How are we going to get there?" Owen said, his heart sinking.

"I look after how. You know what to do, you get there?" He shook his head. "Who help you? Your friend, she good for fight, not for think."

"Can you help me?"

"Not like that. I cannot leave lake. Is forbid. But I can show you a little." She knelt on the floor and took a long pin from her hair. Using the tip of it, she traced out a map. First of all a jagged coastline, then an inlet, which showed a lake narrowing to a thin neck, then open sea. Opposite the mouth of the inlet she drew an island.

"Island is like mountain outside, like castle inside. Stone underneath, very deep. Great Machine is down in rock, very deep." She drew another wide line in the sand going from the coast to the ice island. "Is ice bridge for Harsh to get to island. They no like water. Like ice."

Maybe I could cross the ice bridge as well, Owen thought, shivering at the idea of the sea.

"Come with me," the Long Woman said, standing up swiftly. "We have to get you quick to coast." They walked up a long passageway and she opened the door at the top. They stepped out into a blizzard, snow driving at them horizontally across the lake.

We'll never get to the coast, Owen thought as he tried to shield his face against the icy blast. But the Long Woman led him on until they reached an enclosure of living willow. She opened a gate and motioned Owen inside. He stepped in and she closed the gate carefully behind him.

It was calmer in the enclosure. The willows broke the force of the wind, although their straight trunks looked suspiciously like bars. The Long Woman looked upwards and whistled softly. Owen was surprised to see several dogs sprawling across the branches of a large tree growing in the middle of the enclosure. The dogs were like massive greyhounds with long hair and handsome, aristocratic faces. They were different colours, but one was coal black, and this was the one that the Long Woman summoned.

"Arcana," she called softly. The black dog stood up and stretched in an almost catlike way, and turned his head towards them. Owen took an involuntary step backwards. The dog's eyes burned red like hot coals. "Arcana, there are guests for journey."

Arcana stretched again and gave a single sharp bark. Suddenly the snow that lay deep on the floor of the enclosure started to stir. Other dogs were sleeping under it, and one by one they stood up and shook off the snow. Owen realised that the Long Woman had kept one hand on the bar of the gate. The dogs were all facing towards them, and from one of them came a low growl.

"Not to be trusted," the Long Woman said softly. "No, not to be trusted. Arcana!"

The black dog uncoiled and slid to the ground in one easy movement. It stood with its back to Owen and the Long

Woman. One by one the other dogs backed away and sat down. Except for one brindled dog who stared past Arcana at Owen, her eyes burning. Arcana took several paces forward. Without warning the brindled dog lunged at the black dog. But her teeth clicked shut on air, and suddenly Arcana was on her back, his teeth buried in her neck, driving her down until her growls turned to whimpers and a trickle of blood ran from the spot where Arcana's teeth were fixed. When he was satisfied that she was subdued, Arcana released her and, with her tail between her legs, she slunk off to join the others, although not without a sullen and dangerous look over her shoulder at Owen.

The Long Woman then opened the gate and led them all out into the snow. Suddenly, Owen understood what she was doing. Standing in the lee of the enclosure was a sleigh, incredibly long and thin, consisting of a carriage mounted on two long, narrow blades which curved up at each end.

"Is ice runner," the Long Woman said. She took down a long harness which was hanging from the willows and started to put it on the dogs, each of which stood patiently in its place. Arcana took up position at the front. "Dogs will run all day all night. You start now. Get to Great Machine Puissance in time."

"What about my friend?"

"You want take her? Maybe she no go. Maybe she stay for dinner." The Long Woman smiled, showing sharp little teeth and Owen shuddered as he remembered the strange feast he had seen laid out.

"No, no… I'll take her with me… if that's all right."

When they got back to where Pieta lay sleeping in front of the fire, the Long Woman leaned over and whispered something in her ear. There was a pause then Pieta leapt to her feet, looking around her mistrustfully.

"It's all right, Pieta. This is the Long Woman. She is helping us."

"I know who the Long Woman is," Pieta said. "I called her to help us."

"Good thing I hear," said the Long Woman, "else Navigator die in snow, all lost for ever."

Owen saw the startled look in Pieta's eyes, although she tried to hide it. The Long Woman saw it too. "You not know boy Navigator?"

"Some of us thought he might—"

"Who else could boy be?"

"Some… some people didn't want to believe it," Pieta said.

"They said my father stole the Mortmain." Owen felt anger wash over him.

"Navigator cannot steal Mortmain. Navigator is Keeper of Mortmain. Cannot steal what you own."

Owen was more confused than ever, but Pieta was nodding thoughtfully.

"Is time to go," the Long Woman declared. "Dogs get tired waiting; they eat each other for entertain."

"I'm not going anywhere until you tell me what the Navigator is," Owen said.

"Not time," the Long Woman said in a cool, dangerous voice, but Pieta held up her hand. "Quick then, quick, quick."

"The Navigator is the person who forms a link between the temporal world, your world, Owen, and the islands in time. The Navigator has the power of waking the Resisters from sleep..."

"...The Navigator is Keeper of Mortmain. The Navigator is for ever bound to the Resistance. The Navigator is the faithful. The Navigator is the betrayer."

"Betrayer?" Owen said, bewildered. "I've never betrayed anybody."

"The Navigator has betrayed the Resisters in the past," Pieta said gently. "That's why Samual was so hostile when he suspected that you were the Navigator."

"And my father? They thought he betrayed them as well."

"Yes, but I did not believe it then and I do not believe it now."

Pieta and Owen followed the Long Woman out into the snow. The dogs were whining and snarling, eager to be off. Pieta looked at them suspiciously.

"Get in," the Long Woman said. For a moment Owen

thought that Pieta was going to refuse. Quickly he got in, hoping she would follow him. It was surprisingly warm in the sled. A hooped leather cover kept the snow off, and underneath the cover were warm, soft skins which you could pull up to your throat.

"Come on," Owen urged. Reluctantly, Pieta clambered in. The Long Woman handed a set of reins to Owen.

"You will not need them," she said. "Arcana knows what he has to do. Take this." She handed Owen a crude iron knife. "Cold iron. Harsh don't like it. Stick it in door, they can't open it." Owen put the knife inside his coat.

"Also this." The Long Woman took a pin from her hair, a small one this time. She bent to the ground and dug in the snow with her long hand. Owen looked down. She had uncovered a tiny white flower. She plucked it and pinned it to his coat.

"What is it?" he asked.

"Fleur-de-lis," she told him.

The dogs were getting anxious now. One of them started to howl and suddenly they all lifted their heads and howled, the hair on their backbones standing on end so that Owen thought he could see the static crackling in their coats. The Long Woman suddenly seemed even taller. Her long shadow fell over them, so black and hard that Owen could almost feel it. Over the howling of the dogs she spoke out in a terrible and ancient language. The dogs howled even louder and pulled at their traces until she raised her hand and brought it down in a slicing motion. First Arcana and then the rest of the dogs leapt forward.

The Long Woman leaned over Owen as the sledge shot past her and it seemed that he could smell her perfume, heavy and cloying, with something of the earth about it, something of the grave. A look of terrible regret was on her face, a look of anguish endured over years, and Owen drew back from her, and even Pieta drew her breath in sharply, and then they were gone. The snow around them flew up into the air and there was a sound like a great sigh. For a moment they were blinded and when the snow fell to the ground again and Owen looked back, he could see nothing but a little wooded island breaking the vast flatness of the lake. An island which dwindled even as he looked, the only sound the runners of the sleigh as they hissed across the ice.

Three miles south, a river ran parallel to the lake, going towards the sea. It was a fast river, tumbling through gorges, and its speed and savagery meant that it would not freeze. A careful watcher might make out a dark shape being carried downstream by the furious current. It was a raft. At the front of the raft sat Johnston. Mariacallas was steering the boat with a crude oar. Passionara sat in the middle of the boat, maintaining a stream of venomous cursing. Johnston was grim-faced and there was a bandage about his head. He carried Whitwashisberd's ledger under his arm.

CHAPTER TWENTY-THREE

Try as she might, Cati could not get used to the little fluctuations in the flow of time, which increased as they went north. One minute she would have just got into the bed she had made for herself, ready to go to sleep, and the next she would be back standing on the freezing floor. Or when time would flicker the other way, forward, when she was about to take a bite out of an apple and would find herself standing there with an apple core in her hand. It got so that she couldn't remember what she had done and when she had done it, even if she had done it at all. Wesley looked bewildered every time it happened to him.

Only Dr Diamond didn't seem to mind. He spent all his time at the rail with his binoculars, studying the twisting shape on the horizon.

"What is it?" Cati asked him.

"I think it is what we are looking for." he said quietly, "although I still don't know what we're going to do when we get there." He weighed the Mortmain thoughtfully in his hand.

"And the Harsh will be waiting for us," the Sub-Commandant reminded them.

On and on they sped. The Grim Captain never seemed to leave the wheel. His eyes were fixed on the horizon. Cati saw the three Raggie boys gather often just beneath the bridge, talking intensely among themselves. She asked Dr Diamond what they were talking about, but he just smiled, sadly she thought, and said that if the Raggies wanted to tell her, then that was their business.

The weather had settled into bitter cold, with little wind, and at night the stars shone brilliantly, although Cati noticed that sometimes they seemed a bit elongated, stretched out of shape. As though they were painted on some flexible material and somebody had pulled it. And still the shape on the horizon grew, so that it was now a funnel, narrow at the bottom and wide at the top. Except that this tunnel twisted and writhed and seemed to go on without end into the sky.

After two days on the ship, Cati overheard Dr Diamond and the Sub-Commandant talking together anxiously.

"I haven't seen him since last night," Dr Diamond said.

"He hasn't been himself lately," said the Sub-Commandant. "Have you searched?"

"Yes, but it's a big ship. If you don't want to be found, you

302

could hide for days. But he is somewhere on board. I can feel it."

Cati knew that they must be talking about Chancellor and she realised that she hadn't seen him since the first night they came on board.

"It's very worrying," Dr Diamond said gloomily.

"I know where to find him," said a voice beside Cati, making her jump. It was Wesley. "I know where he is, and I reckon it was him tried to sink my Boat. Come on!"

"Shouldn't we tell the others?"

"I want to have a word with him about Boat first. Are you coming or not?"

Cati turned and followed Wesley. He led her through the door in the bridge and past the stateroom. They went down one stairwell after another, each one colder and more gloomy than the last.

"Where are we going?"

"Engine room," said Wesley grimly, "and be careful."

The condition of the ship down here was even worse. There were great jagged holes in the gangways, and broken metal stairways spiralled off into nothingness. And all the time Cati could feel the booming and clanging of the engine getting nearer and nearer. Finally, they reached a massive steel door. Wesley threw his weight against it, and with a rusty protest it swung open. They stepped out on to a gangway above the engines. The engine room was a vast cavern of dangling cables and open sumps and broken dials. Pipes leaked great gouts of steam or oozed oil. Massive piston rods rose and fell, making the ground shake, tappets clattered, and in the middle of the engine room, two great boilers roared and hissed and flared.

"Come on!" Wesley shouted. Cati followed him. They went down a metal stairway until they reached the floor of the engine room. The heat was intense. Wesley walked purposefully towards the giant boilers. Huge fires blazed at the foot of the boilers. Even at this distance Cati could feel a sheen of sweat on her face, but Wesley kept going forward and she followed.

As they clambered on to the final catwalk, Cati could see the boilers glowing a dull orange, burning who knew what kind of fuel.

"Look," Wesley said. At the foot of the biggest boiler and dwarfed by its bulk, a figure crouched. Chancellor. He did not see them as they approached. They were three metres away from him and the heat was like a wall. They stopped. Even above the noise of the engine room they could hear his voice, thin and piercing.

"Cold," he moaned, "so cold, so cold."

"Chancellor!" Wesley called out. The man spun around and as he did so he put his hand on the railing beside him. Cati was also holding the rail, but she snatched her hand away as sudden cold seared it. She looked down. Despite the heat, the rail was covered with frost. She looked up. Chancellor's face was whiter than anything she had ever seen.

"What do you want, Raggie?" Chancellor demanded. "Can a man not get a little heat in a cold world?"

"It was you tried to sink Boat, weren't it?" Wesley said. Chancellor did not reply. "And no one ever seen Owen with Johnston." Wesley went on evenly.

"We thought it was Samual!" exclaimed Cati.

"All damn lies," Wesley said, his fists bunched now.

"There *was* a spy all along," Cati said. "It was you!"

"Johnston got told every move the Resisters did make," Wesley said.

"I don't understand," Cati said. "Why are you working with the Harsh? After everything… all they want to do is freeze us for ever!"

"No," Chancellor said, "they aren't like that. You don't understand. They wanted to make an island in time for us. I went to see them, to save us."

"They wouldn't save us," Wesley said. "And even if they did, what about everybody else?"

"All the people who lived all through time," Cati said, horrified. "What about *them*?"

"That is true," Chancellor said, and this time his voice was full of sorrow. "All those people." Great tears welled in his eyes, which froze as he bowed his head. Wesley and Cati watched as the tears formed into long icicles.

"We would have taken care of the future," Chancellor said. "There would have been someone left alive. There would have been hope. A small hope, but still a hope."

Cati thought of the loneliness of the man, as he tried to take terrible decisions for the good of everyone. Chancellor raised a hand to his face as though to wipe away the long icicles which had formed on his eyes. Then, in one sudden movement, he snapped off an icicle, and with a vicious flick of his wrist, his eyes filled with hatred, he sent the icicle speeding through the air, a stiletto of ice, with its long blade aimed precisely at Cati's heart. There was nothing she could do. It seemed she could hear the whistle of the ice blade as it cleaved the air, and she closed her eyes and waited for it to strike her.

Time flickered.

Cati opened her eyes. Once again she saw Chancellor reach up as if to wipe the ice tears away, but this time she knew what was going to happen. And so did Wesley.

"No!" he shouted and lunged towards Chancellor just as the man started to flick the tear towards Cati. Wesley's shoulder hit Chancellor on the hip, throwing him off balance, and the deadly tear, instead of hitting Cati, struck the pipe at her shoulder with an icy clang.

Chancellor staggered backwards, his arms flailing as he sought to regain his balance. He reached out for a pipe to stop himself, but the ice that formed on the pipe the second he touched it formed a glaze so that his fingers slipped off. Cati and Wesley could only watch in horror as he staggered backwards towards the fiery mouth of the ship's furnace.

"No! No!" he cried out. Cati hid her eyes, wishing that time would flicker again and bring them back to before all of this happened. There was a roar, a huge hissing sound, and the heat of the furnace dimmed. Cati opened her eyes. The furnace was almost black now, and it seemed as if the cold in Chancellor's bones had almost extinguished it. Then suddenly the flames leapt up again and a huge cloud of boiling steam billowed out at them.

"Come on!" Wesley yelled. "Let's get out of here." He pushed Cati in front of him as they dashed towards the exit, just ahead of the scalding steam. They stumbled through the door and Wesley threw his shoulder against it. With a protesting creak, it swung shut. Wesley slumped to the floor.

"Is he… is he gone?" Cati asked. Wesley nodded.

"Like ice thrown on a fire. Good thing the way time flickered when he threw the tear at you. Or else…"

"He must have been working for the Harsh all along," she said.

"Aye. Remember the fight by the river? The way they always knew what we were going to do next."

"He always took the other side against Owen too, acting like he was just being reasonable."

"He done the stopcock as well. They turned him good. You

got to watch them Harsh. There's more to them than ice… What's that?"

The ship was slowing, the great engines juddering to a halt, the hull creaking and groaning with a sound of rivets popping. They ran quickly up the gangways towards the open air, trying not to slip on the oily deck, or fall into one of the gaping holes. Eventually, they burst into the open air. Cati gasped in astonishment. Even Wesley swore quietly to himself and took a step backwards. Somehow they had reached the Great Machine in the North, and the object they had seen on the horizon towered above them, bigger than anything Cati had ever seen, a great whirling, twisting mass that grew bigger as it went up and up, rising from a point on an island. As it disappeared into the sky, massive storms raged, sheets of lightning crackling about it. And as it spiralled upwards, a roaring filled the air. On and on it went, its vastness humbling and terrifying. If it had been night, Cati thought, then even the very stars would be sucked into it.

"Goes on for ever," Wesley breathed.

"Yes, it does," the Sub-Commandant said. "It goes on to eternity. In a way, it *is* eternity."

"It's like a giant waterspout or something," Cati said.

"That's a good comparison," Dr Diamond replied, "except it's not made of water, it's made of time." The scientist's face was pale with excitement. "Look closely."

Cati stared at it as it writhed over them. It seemed that she

308

could see vast oceans appearing and fading, stars being born, planets dying. There were continents covered in trees which seemed to wither in an instant. A great city which went from shining citadel to ruins in the blink of an eye.

Dr Diamond's notebook was in his hand and he was scribbling furiously. Cati saw that her father was looking at her.

"What is it, Cati?" he said quietly. "What's wrong?"

"It's Chancellor," Wesley said. Quickly he told the Sub-Commandant and Dr Diamond what had happened. The Sub-Commandant turned away and bowed his head. Dr Diamond opened his mouth to say something then he too turned away. They stood in silence for several minutes. The ship drifted on the cold, black ocean and chunks of ice struck its hull with low thuds.

"He betrayed us all," the Sub-Commandant said bitterly.

"He went to the Harsh to parley and was corrupted," Dr Diamond said. "Don't be too hard on him."

"I should have seen it." The Sub-Commandant's fists were clenched. "I should have read it in his eyes. It was there you know. His treachery were there to be seen for those who looked."

"He was a proud and subtle man," Dr Diamond said. "He knew how to hide his duplicity from us."

They might have stood there for ever had the sound of the great spout of time not changed, adding an ominous and ever-increasing shriek to its tumultuous roaring.

"We have to hurry!" Dr Diamond exclaimed. "Or the Puissance will reach a pitch that we can't stop."

"We have to get to the Machine itself," the Sub-Commandant said.

"Where's that?" asked Wesley.

"The part at the bottom is the Great Machine," Dr Diamond said. "It generates the Puissance, which is the vortex; what Cati called the waterspout..." He hesitated. "Chancellor was a traitor in the end, but I think the Harsh exploited his desire to do good, to save something from the ruins."

Dr Diamond took out a small pocketbook. Between the pages was a pressed and faded cornflower. "You were a friend and comrade once," he said. "This is how we remember you."

And he cast the cornflower into the sea. For a moment it floated on the frozen ocean, a symbol of Spring and hope, and then it disappeared beneath the black water.

Owen had lost all sense of time passing as the sleigh sped silently across the ice. The cover was stiff with ice, but it was pleasantly warm beneath the skins and he dozed on and off, waking once in the night and looking up to see a clear sky and thousands of stars. The dogs ran tirelessly, their breath streaming out behind them like pennants in the cold air. The next time he woke it could not have been more different. It was grey dawn and it was snowing hard. Pieta had pulled down the cover behind them so that it acted as a roof, leaving a thin slit through which they could see. They shared the food that the Long Woman had given him. It was warm in the sleigh and Owen started to wish that the ride would last for ever.

Pieta had thawed a lot from the ferocious warrior he had first met, and he felt brave enough to question her about the Long Woman. She told him that there were many islands in time, some small, some large. Some were dedicated to resisting the Harsh and their allies, and some were devoted to other, unknown purposes, like that of the Long Woman. "But if the Workhouse ever falls," she said, "all of them will fall."

After a while Owen slept again. His body had taken a lot of punishment and he hadn't slept much since he had been captured by Johnston. But when he woke it was night again and he was confused.

"I didn't sleep all day, did I?" he asked.

"No," Pieta said, with a frown. "Time is changing fast and both day and night are short now. I hope we aren't too late."

That dawn the snow cleared and they could see a great writhing column on the horizon. Arcana slowed the dogs to a halt. He sniffed the air cautiously then lifted his muzzle and howled long and loud. The other dogs joined him and their cries split the air. Then the ice runner leapt forward again, twice as fast, so that a spray of ice crystals from the runners hung in the air long after they had passed.

CHAPTER TWENTY-FOUR

The ship moved slowly forwards as Dr Diamond studied the Puissance with his telescope. He had spotted the ice bridge which led from the mainland to the island.

"They'll be guarding that," the Sub-Commandant muttered. "We'll have to land on the island somehow." He seemed preoccupied and sad since the death of Chancellor.

Overhearing this, Wesley went hunting for a boat to take them ashore. The ship had once had lifeboats but now the shattered remnants hung from davits fused with rust. But on the foredeck Wesley found a small boat which had probably been used for painting the hull, for it seemed that gallons of multicoloured paint had been spilled on it. Fortunately, the spilled paint had preserved the woodwork, so Uel and Mervyn started to repair a few sprung planks and fashion oars from old bits of timber they found around the place. The little girl stood in the bow and did not turn around. The Grim Captain stood similarly unmoved at the wheel.

Slowly, they inched nearer to the island. Cati could see the mainland clearly. It seemed bleak and treeless. There seemed to be an opening into an estuary, or a lake, and a fast-flowing river emptied into the sea not far from it. As she watched, an object emerged from the mouth of the river. There were people sitting on it.

"Look!" she said to Dr Diamond, but he was engaged in a complicated calculation and did not turn around. "Wesley!" she called. Wesley came over and followed Cati's pointing finger. He looked then deftly plucked the doctor's binoculars from his coat pocket.

"'Scuse me, doc," he said, although Dr Diamond didn't hear. Wesley looked through the binoculars then whistled softly.

"Here," he said to Cati, "take a look for yourself." She put the binoculars to her eye.

"That's Johnston, isn't it?"

"And two of his men. Looks like trouble for somebody."

Cati swung the binoculars around. At the mouth of the lake inlet she saw more movement then suddenly a sleigh came into view, a sleigh travelling at breakneck speed and pulled by a team of the biggest dogs she had ever seen. Cati focused on the back of the sleigh. There were two people in it. Suddenly, she felt her heart jump. She could barely speak.

"Wesley... W-Wesley..." she stammered, "it's Owen and Pieta!" Wesley grabbed the binoculars.

"You're right, girl," he said, "and they're headed straight towards Johnston."

It was true. Even without the binoculars Cati could see that Johnston's raft had beached itself on the icy margin where the lake met the sea, and that the sleigh was heading straight towards it.

"Owen!" she shouted. "Owen, look out!" Wesley joined her in jumping and waving, then Dr Diamond and the Sub-Commandant, but it was to no avail. Their voices were shrill and tiny against the monumental howl of the Puissance.

"Quick, boys," Wesley said. "Let's get that boat into the water." He ran over to Uel and Mervyn, who were struggling with a rusted davit as they tried to lower the little boat.

"They're nearly past. They'll escape!" Cati shouted. She could tell that Johnston hadn't seen the sleigh yet.

Then time flickered again. And this time it was not helpful. Johnston turned in time to see the sleigh, and it was obvious that Pieta and Owen had not seen him yet. Johnston grabbed a magno gun from the raft and levelled it at the sleigh, ready to blast its occupants as it swept past. Cati watched, not able to tear her eyes away. Then suddenly, three long, loud siren blasts split the skies. Cati looked up. The Grim Captain had sounded his siren in warning. Pieta and Owen heard it, or at least the dogs did, for the sleigh skidded to one side and came to a halt, just out of range of the deadly gun.

Behind, Cati heard the light splash of the boat slipping into the water.

All that day Owen and Pieta had seen the whirling column of the Puissance get larger and larger, until now it seemed to fill the sky. Owen could not take his eyes off it, could not look anywhere else, the howling mass of it riven with bolts of lightning. And, like Cati, he caught sight of moments in time, half-glimpsed images of shining seas that emptied and turned into desert in an instant, planets flaring up and shrinking to dull, cold ashes. Pieta spoke to him several times, but he ignored her, mesmerised by the sight of time being undone.

And so they came to the edge of land, the dogs wild-eyed with exertion, but still leaping onwards, driven on by the great red-eyed Arcana. The sleigh reached the sea and turned smoothly without dropping speed to follow the line of the shore. Breakers crashed on the shingle beach and huge chunks of ice crashed and growled. Owen could see to his right the ice bridge that the Long Woman had talked about, a sinister-looking structure, although elegant, one single curve of ice, solid to the sea floor, for otherwise the Harsh could not cross the open water. It was his only way in as well, for he knew that he could not force himself to cross the angry sea. And yet the Harsh guarded the bridge. And even if he crossed, he did not have the Mortmain. And even if he did have it, he didn't know what to do with it.

They swept around the shore. Ahead of them Owen could see the mouth of a fast-flowing river rounding a point so that a natural harbour was formed in its crook. Owen found that he had picked up the reins, which had lain unused for the entire journey, so sure was Arcana of his leadership. But now the black dog seemed to hesitate and check his stride.

"Something's wrong," said Owen. As he spoke, he heard three siren blasts, long and loud and sorrowful. Arcana came to an abrupt halt and stood staring ahead, lips curled back. Owen followed the dog's eyes and saw Johnston.

If they had gone another thirty metres, they would have been sitting targets, Owen realised. Then Pieta was out of the sleigh, her magno whip in her hand. There was a flicker and to his astonishment Pieta was back in the sleigh, climbing out again. He heard Johnston laugh a heavy, sneering laugh.

"You see what the Harsh have done to time, lad?" Johnston said. "Another while and it'll all be sucked in."

"Pretty Rat come to put time right," said Passionara, and Mariacallas cackled with laughter. Arcana growled and took a step forward. The two men jumped back, almost tripping over each other in their haste.

"Good doggy, good doggy," Mariacallas said nervously. Arcana's red eyes bored into him. But Johnston did not seem concerned by the dogs. He kept his eyes on the whip in Pieta's hand.

"Let us past!" Pieta said. Owen looked over Johnston's shoulder and saw the source of the siren blasts.

A massive ship stood off the coast. A ship with holes in it and a bridge that tilted to one side. A ship that he would have thought derelict, except for several small figures on her deck. And then, rising and falling on the waves, Owen saw a small boat coming towards them.

Just then, one of the people it carried stood up and waved. *Cati?* he thought. It couldn't be Cati. She was many miles away, but something in his heart told Owen that it *was* Cati. He could see that the boat was headed for the pier, and knew that was where they needed to be.

He looked up again. Johnston had taken another step forward. Both weapons were still at the limit of their range, but Johnston was edging forward, and Owen knew that the magno gun would come into range before the whip. Johnston knew it too. He moved forward in a stalking motion, keeping low to the ground. Passionara and Mariacallas followed. Pieta tightened her grip on the whip. Owen felt a cold, clear anger flood over him. All he wanted to do, he thought, was see a friendly face again. He was fed up with being thrown around the place and tied up by Johnston. Even Pieta's grim companionship was too much sometimes. He stood up in the sleigh and brought the reins down hard on the dog's backs.

"Arcana, go!" he shouted. The dogs exploded forward. Owen was thrown backwards and landed on his back. Pieta, caught by surprise, just about managed to grab on to the sleigh and was dragged behind it as it flew, straight towards Johnston. There was nothing the man could do except dive out of the way. Arcana, in passing, made a lunge for Mariacallas. With a frightened yelp the man leapt head first into a snowdrift. And as Pieta was dragged behind the sleigh she managed to free one hand and catch Passionara around the legs with the whip. Passionara tumbled, head over heels, high into the sky, until he too landed head first in the snowdrift, right beside Mariacallas.

Owen could see that the boat had docked. Wesley and Mervyn stood on the dock, beckoning to him, and as he watched, Cati joined them. He could see the Sub-Commandant holding the boat against the quay. For a moment he thought that the dog team were going to charge straight over the edge of the quay, then, at the last moment, they swerved sideways and came to a dead halt. Owen jumped out and ran over to Cati and Wesley.

"I can't believe it, I—"

"No time for sentimental stuff," said Wesley gruffly. "Get your backside into that boat or Johnston will have us." The big man had recovered and was charging in their direction.

"I can't," Owen said, "I can't." His mouth felt dry. His stomach lurched as he stared at the seething water below him.

"Come on!" Wesley shouted, but Owen could not move. All seemed lost until the little girl, who had been sitting unobserved in the bow of the boat, stepped ashore. She took Owen by the hand and led him to the edge of the dock and together they stepped into the boat. The Sub-Commandant and Dr Diamond exchanged a glance.

As they rowed back to the ship, Owen quickly tried to tell them what had happened. Johnston's yard, the Q-car, Pieta, the Long Woman. There was too much. And then Wesley shoved an oar in Owen's hand and told him to stop gabbing and start fending off the ice growlers that were starting to threaten the little boat. But as they approached the ship, Cati whispered to Owen, "Are you still mad at me?"

He shook his head. "No. You still mad at me?"

She looked at him for a moment. "Don't know," she said. "I'll have to think about it." And she turned away, but not before Owen saw the smile on her face.

Owen stood up and looked back at the land. He could see the ice runner speeding up the hill behind the pier. When it reached the top it stopped and he heard a distant howling. He raised an arm in salute. The howling intensified briefly then the dogs leapt forward and the sleigh disappeared over the crest of the hill.

Then they were up beside the ship and all hands were needed. The Grim Captain had turned his ship to give them shelter, but the ice clanged against the hull and threatened the boat again and again. It took a long time to get everyone on board and hoist the boat. But as soon as they did, the ship started to move, painfully at first, then building up speed. Owen looked down at the water as though seeing it for the first time.

"How did I do that?"

"You had some help," Cati said.

"That little girl…?" They looked around, but could not see her.

Time was flickering more and more now. Added to that, day and night were passing with bewildering speed. Owen felt he was in an old black and white film that flickered and jumped as you watched it. The ship went faster and faster, crashing through the waves, heading straight for the island. There was so much juddering and banging that Cati was sure that bits of the ship would fall off. And then she realised that they *were* falling off. First a bit of plate, then a piece of handrail, then one whole chunk of the leaning bridge fell into the water. But still they sped.

"Listen to me," Dr Diamond said urgently. "I calculate from the angles of diminution and the various defined, though highly mobile, interstices of the Puissance vortex, that the source of it is approximately 293.44 metres below sea level."

"What's he saying?" Wesley asked impatiently.

"It means that we have to get down to the source of the vortex, right down in the middle of the island," said Cati.

"Not *we*," Owen said, surprising even himself, "*me*. I am the one who has to reach the source. I am the Navigator."

They all turned to look at him. Nobody said anything for a moment. Then the Sub-Commandant took the Mortmain carefully from his coat and handed it to Owen.

"This is yours then, and your father's before you," he said, meeting Owen's eye for a moment then stepping back.

"Land ahoy!" shouted Mervyn. They were in the lee of the island. The ship slowed and all eyes were drawn upwards to the towering Puissance, the vortex spinning with almost diabolic speed now. The Sub-Commandant was the first to tear his eyes away. He saw that the island was a crag growing out of the ocean, the top of an underground mountain perhaps with a crater at the summit, like a volcano. It was into this crater that the Puissance disappeared. At the foot of the island was a little stone jetty and stone steps led upwards.

"That's where we need to be," the Sub-Commandant said.

"Let's get the leaky tub into the water then!" shouted Wesley over the roar of the Puissance.

As they struggled with the rusted davits again, no one noticed Johnston's raft halfway between the island and the shore, Passionara and Mariacallas rowing furiously. By the time they were in their own boat and rowing for shore, Johnston had almost reached the island.

The water was still choppy and the currents were strong,

and they had battled for several minutes in silence before Cati looked around worriedly.

"Where's the little girl?" she said. "We've left her behind."

"I think she'll be all right," Dr Diamond said. "Look!"

They turned and saw her. She was standing on the bridge beside the Grim Captain and his hand rested on her shoulder.

"That was the thing that he wanted," the Sub-Commandant said, "the thing he wouldn't ask for."

"A bit of company," Wesley said, and sniffed.

"Or forgiveness," Dr Diamond said quietly. "Do you not see it, Wesley? He was not always known as the Grim Captain. In the mists of time his name was Smith."

"What?" Wesley gasped. "The man who did abandon the Raggies? And me on his boat. I should've..."

"Perhaps, Wesley," Dr Diamond said gently, "but when he put the children into an open boat and abandoned them all those years ago, he lost the only thing he truly loved."

"His daughter," the Sub-Commandant said. "For she sneaked on to the boat when he wasn't looking and was lost along with all the other children. For centuries he has wandered the seas seeking her, and now she is found."

As they watched, the Grim Captain caught the little girl under the arms and lifted her. She reached up for the siren and pulled it three times. The Grim Captain set her down. He looked down on the little boat, raised one hand and touched the peak of his cap. Then the ship turned and started to steam away, picking up speed as it went, so that by the time they had reached the pier and scrambled on to dry land it was almost lost in the night.

CHAPTER TWENTY-FIVE

"If I'm not mistaken," Dr Diamond said, "then the objects that resemble stone beehives at the top of the steps are in fact entrances."

"Entrances to what?" growled Wesley.

"To the home of the Harsh. But also to the source of the Puissance."

"I'm damn well worried about something," Wesley said. "We haven't seen any of them Harsh yet."

"They'll be waiting," the Sub-Commandant said grimly. Pieta loosened the magno whip at her belt.

"Best get going then," Wesley said. Owen checked that he still had the Mortmain in his pocket. Wesley told Uel and Mervyn to stay with the boat, for what he described as the unlikely event of them returning.

"One thing to remember," Dr Diamond said. "On no

account must you touch the vortex. Remember that." Owen turned to Cati. She was shivering.

"Are you all right?" he asked.

"The Harsh," she said. "I can feel them. Nearby." Owen touched her forehead. It was icy cold.

They set out on the long climb to the top. The path was old and crumbling, and howling winds generated by the Puissance threatened to sweep them off it. But that was not the worst part. The time flickers increased to such a rate that Owen barely knew where he was, or whether he was about to say something or had just said it. Everything was confused, nightmarish, and the sound of the vortex above them became more and more threatening. At one point he slipped and fell. Then got up and slipped and fell again, and once more, the flickering of time making him repeat the motion painfully. At the last, he thought he wouldn't get up. He would just lie there. Then he felt his arm being squeezed and looked up and saw Cati smiling a small brave smile at him, and he felt ashamed. He climbed to his feet and went on.

After what might have been a very long time or might not, there was no way of telling any more, they reached the top and found themselves right beside the Puissance itself, majestic and terrifying beyond all knowing. Owen felt his mouth go dry and his knees go weak. Dr Diamond took out a notebook, but did not write. All of them stared at the black, writhing surface through which they could see, like a film moving at incredible speed, flashes of history, yes, but more and more darkness punctuated by the light of a few stars as though all of the world's history had already been sucked into the hole, and now they were seeing what went before, the events which were close to the void.

"Time much... we haven't much time!" Dr Diamond shouted.

"Get to one of the entrances!" the Sub-Commandant commanded. Then, without warning, they were under attack. Passionara leapt on to the Sub-Commandant's back and Owen whirled to find himself face to face with Mariacallas.

"Hello, Pretty Rat," he hissed, and Owen realised that he was being pickpocketed, the man's hands searching his clothes at incredible speed.

"Is this what you're looking for?" Owen heard Dr Diamond say. The scientist was holding up his heated ice goggles. Of course, Owen realised, they were looking for the Mortmain but they didn't know what it looked like! Greedily, Mariacallas swung round towards Dr Diamond. To his right, Owen could see the Sub-Commandant struggling with Passionara, who had steely fingers round his throat. Pieta had her whip in her hand, but she could not get a clear shot.

Mariacallas darted towards Dr Diamond, but Dr Diamond backed away again, to the very edge, holding the goggles as high as he could. Mariacallas made one last lunge. Swift as lightning, Dr Diamond threw the goggles off the edge. Mariacallas threw himself after them and disappeared with a despairing cry.

The Sub-Commandant struggled desperately with Passionara. He was too small to shake off the steely-fingered man, but suddenly another small figure flew towards them – and Cati landed on Passionara's back.

"Leave him alone! Leave him alone!" she screamed, pulling at his fingers, and when that did not work, sinking her teeth into his wrist. Passionara cried out and his grip loosened. With one final desperate effort the Sub-Commandant wrenched free. Passionara stumbled backwards, still with Cati wrapped around his neck. Dr Diamond shouted a warning and Owen saw what was happening. Passionara was overbalanced and falling towards the vortex. The Sub-Commandant reacted fastest. With lightning speed he reached for Cati and tore her from Passionara's back. With a wail, Passionara toppled into the vortex and was snatched away. But as he did so, his hand reached from the vortex and grabbed the Sub-Commandant's sleeve. With horror, Owen watched as the man's hand was drawn towards the whirling mass, his fingertips just touching it before he pulled away.

There seemed to be silence then, although the flickering and howling did not stop. Cati looked at her father in disbelief. Owen thought that there was something transparent about him.

"What... what will..." she began, her voice trembling.

"Be still, my child," the Sub-Commandant said in a gentle, sad voice. "It is time for me to go now."

"Go where... Not..."

"No, not death as such, but I have been touched by the Puissance, and I belong to time now. I have to go, otherwise I will die here, in the next few minutes."

"You can't go..."

"You must let him go, Cati," said Dr Diamond.

The Sub-Commandant put his arms around his daughter and held her. "You will be the Watcher now. Watch well!" he said.

Owen now realised why Cati was treated as special by the others – *she* was a Watcher as well.

"Owen," the small man said urgently, "I have to tell you something. It was me who gave your father the Mortmain. He didn't steal it. I suspected he was a Navigator, so it was his to guard. I also thought we had a traitor and I wanted to protect it. I never thought it could be Chancellor."

Owen said nothing. Cati started to weep. The Sub-Commandant touched her face. "Just as you will watch the world from the shadows of time and look out for danger, I will be watching you too, from the deepest shadows of all, the shadows at the beginning of all things."

The Sub-Commandant turned, and with one last warm smile to Cati, a smile from which it seemed all the care had gone, he stepped into the vortex and was gone.

They stood there for a long time, or what seemed like a long time. Dr Diamond held Cati tight. Owen felt numb. He had not realised how close he had become to the small, serious man. "Somebody a body could respect, somebody a body could respect," Wesley was muttering over and over again, and Owen knew how he felt. Pieta made a choking noise and turned away. Then there was an ominous crackling sound and Owen looked at the Puissance. It was now running all black.

"Better hurry," said Wesley, "or there'll be nothing for Cati to watch over."

"Quickly!" Dr Diamond exclaimed, leading them to one of the beehive huts. "Just step inside."

Owen watched as Dr Diamond, Pieta and Cati ducked through the little door, Cati turning a tear-stained face to him as she did so.

"Notice something?" Wesley said as he ducked inside. "I seen the monkeys, but I never seen the organ-grinder."

It was true, Owen realised. They had not seen Johnston. Then he stepped inside and found himself falling through blackness.

*   *   *

They were in a kind of chute, Owen thought, a steep chute, black at first but turning lighter as they fell, lighter and colder. Ice, he realised. He was aware of the others in the chute with him at first, but just as the chute started to level, he came to a fork. As he slid towards the right hand fork, he caught a glimpse of Cati's foot in the other fork. Desperately he made a grab for the rim of the chute, but it was too late. His fingers clasped the smooth ice momentarily, then lost grip and his momentum carried him on. He was on his own. The descent went on for another minute or so. With relief Owen noted that time had stopped flickering. And then, with a heavy thud, he was out of the chute.

He leapt to his feet, fists clenched. But there was no one to be seen. He was in a room filled with extraordinary-looking objects. There were delicate mechanisms shaped like hourglasses, tiny trembling gauges capable of measuring the finest variation. A long metronome consisting of metal so fine it seemed like filigree. The walls were covered with brittle cog mechanisms, all moving. On a fine glass screen, numbers appeared and disappeared as if someone had breathed them on to the glass on a cold day.

Owen stepped forward. The room looked out on something, protected by a glass screen. He crossed the room to the screen and peered through. It was the Puissance, he realised, spiralling down through a tunnel, black as jet now.

And around it a staircase led down and down. *I have to reach that*, he thought.

There was a plain wooden door in the wall. Owen opened it and stepped out on to a corridor. But this was not like any corridor he had ever seen. It was all white. *Like ice*, he thought, *but not ice*. Beautiful objects were set into alcoves along the walls: a delicate ice flower; a milky-coloured vase with intricate and ancient carvings; rare and beautiful lamps; exquisite porcelains. *Like a castle inside*, the Long Woman had said.

Owen walked carefully along the corridor. He had never been anywhere so *still*. *Frozen*, he thought, *although not frozen in the cold sense*. Still he walked on and still there was no turning, and then at the end of the corridor he reached a doorway. He put his hand on the doorknob, a wooden doorknob, cool but not cold to the touch. He hesitated, but time was running out. He had no choice. He turned the knob and opened the door, and knew immediately that this was where the Harsh waited for him.

Cati heard Owen call out and realised that he had gone the other way. She was numb with grief and almost paralysed by the nearness of the Harsh, and she opened her mouth to tell the others, but no sound came. At that moment she was as near to despair as she had ever come. Then she saw in her mind's eye the smile that her father had given her when he stepped into the vortex, a smile no longer weary but full of youth, and it seemed to flood her bones with vigour and she knew that this was his last gift to her. *I won't give up*, she told herself. *They won't freeze me*. And then she landed with a bump on something soft.

"Get off me bloody legs," said Wesley. The four of them were standing in a room of ice. There was a slamming sound from over their heads. Cati looked up to see that a lid had closed above them.

"Owen went the other way," she said.

"I know," Dr Diamond replied. "It was a trap."

He walked over to the walls and started to examine them closely. Pieta took one look at the ice and lifted her whip. She lashed it against the wall. The ice melted a little then froze again. She lashed again and again, but each time the ice refroze.

"It's not ordinary ice, is it?" Cati asked.

"No, it's not," Dr Diamond said, "and as a trap, it's pretty ingenious. Look." They looked and saw a film forming over the surface of the ice and disappearing. It happened again.

"What is it?" asked Cati.

"It's our breath," Dr Diamond said. "Each time we breathe out, the moisture from our breath freezes on the ice. Each layer of ice that is added, our cell gets a little smaller. Until eventually, as long as we have breath…"

"It'll squeeze the rullocks out of us," Wesley added.

"If it is a trap then they have Owen," Pieta said. "We have to find him."

"Any ideas, doc?" asked Wesley.

Dr Diamond was fishing around in his pockets. He pulled out what looked like a small gyroscope. "I call this an infinite sonometer," he said proudly.

"Does it work?"

"I don't know actually. In fact, I've never tried it."

Wesley sighed heavily and theatrically. Dr Diamond placed the device on the floor and started it spinning. It gave off a low hum at first. The sound built and built, until first Cati and then the others had to cover their ears. Then the sound stopped.

"Ultrasonic now, you see." Dr Diamond explained.

"Better work pretty quick, doc," Wesley said. "We're breathing a fair bit of moisture by the look of them walls."

Owen thought about turning and running, but his legs wouldn't carry him. He was trapped. The Harsh had waited for him, confident that he would come to them. There were eight of them, white shapes sitting in a semi-circle. White shapes he thought, until he looked again and stifled a gasp of shock. The white shape was merely a kind of white dust – ice perhaps – which floated in the air around them. The Harsh were *people,* he realised, and not only that, they were young people, or seemed to be anyway. A little bit older than him, sixteen or seventeen, perhaps. They had brown eyes and high cheekbones and blond hair. And very, very white skin. They looked… bored was the word that sprang to mind. One of the girls, curled up on a chair, yawned and examined her fingernails. Each one of them was beautifully dressed, in pale, cold colours. Then they started to speak.

"That's him. That's the boy who broke our beam." It was a boy's voice, low and modulated and might have been pleasant if it hadn't been for the sneer in it.

"It was a *very nice* beam," a spoiled, petulant-sounding girl's voice said.

"It *was* a nice beam," the boy agreed, "but he broke it with his mirror." Owen realised they were talking about the ice beam he had bounced back at them at the Workhouse.

"You were trying to kill us!" Owen said. And immediately regretted it. The Harsh might look like spoiled, rich children, but they had great power.

"He singed my hair and my shoes were absolutely ruined!" the smallest girl said. She gave Owen a peevish look and some of the white dust around her billowed towards him. He felt a terrible pain in his chest, as though an icy hand had grasped his heart, and he fell to his knees. The girl tossed her head and returned to examining the ends of her hair. Owen felt the grip relax.

"Now he's going to try to break our Puissance machine," the oldest of the boys said.

"And we worked so hard."

"*Soooo* hard."

"Well, not all that hard actually," the little girl said and they all started to giggle, and for all that they had pleasant voices, there was something grating about the sound.

As they giggled, Owen started to think. They were obviously incredibly powerful and clever. But they were so… *immature* was the word that came to mind. Then he heard a voice that was deep and hard and anything but immature.

"So the little Navigator navigated his way here after all."

It was Johnston. The man had entered the room behind Owen and stood there now, regarding him with cold amusement.

"You shouldn't have let him come in here, Johnston," one of the girls said.

"No," agreed another. "You shouldn't have. What do we do now?"

"Freeze him, I suppose," Johnston said. His voice was casual, but Owen sensed a tension in it. "Freeze him, and then I'll take him away and interrogate him, make him tell me where the Mortmain is."

This time Owen could hear the anxiety in Johnston's voice. Owen realised what was happening. Johnston wanted Owen alive because he wanted the Mortmain for himself! Johnston gave the appearance of working for the Harsh, but really he was trying to double-cross them.

"Yes, I suppose we should do that," one of the drawling voices said.

Suddenly, Owen didn't care any more. He was sick of the Harsh and their cold childish voices, and their toying with time and people's lives as if they were playing a cruel game.

"You can freeze me if you like," Owen said furiously, "but that still makes you just nasty little children."

"I'd be careful what you say to them," Johnston said in a warning voice.

"I don't care! They can turn time back if they like, but they'll still be just as empty. It doesn't make any difference to them what kind of world they live in, whether they live in our world or in their own empty one. They'll still be cold and miserable."

Owen saw that the vapour surrounding the Harsh had started to change, swirling as if they were agitated. Their cold, pinched faces seemed twisted as though with pain.

"They're jealous of us, they're jealous of the heat and the warmth and the light!" Owen yelled. The Harsh seemed to be writhing inside their vapour clouds now, the vapour becoming more dense and hard to see through. But as Owen looked, they seemed to age, so that the childish faces became old and sagging, and the room filled with a cold whispering of loss and despair and emptiness. And anger, Owen realised; an anger that was directed at him.

The icy vapour around the Harsh cleared and he could see

their real selves clearly now. They were haggard and ancient, with long, wrinkled faces and sparse hair and empty, corrupt eyes. They were time lords, Owen realised, old beyond all imagining, subtle and corrupt. They waved their long, bony fingers as though to ward off his words and the sound of their voices was a long, evil complaint.

One of the women turned towards Owen and he could feel her gaze like a cold weight on him. She pursed her thin, proud lips, sucked in her breath and blew. A great freezing maw of icy air blew towards him. Desperately, he flung himself to the ground and felt the blast of foul, chilled air pass over his head. Owen's eye was drawn to the open door behind Johnston. He thought he could see part of the shaft containing the Puissance through the door. If only he could get through it.

The knife! he thought. *The Long Woman's knife!* If he could just get to the door...

Suddenly, there was a loud crackling and an enormous crash. Johnston and the Harsh were momentarily distracted. Owen seized his opportunity and ducked under Johnston's arm. He reached the door. He slammed it shut, grabbed the knife from his jacket and jammed it into the wooden door surround. The Long Woman had said it would hold. That they would not be able to open it. It held. Just. He could feel the strain in the wood, ice creeping across it, as the Harsh bent their will on to it. The door remained closed, but for how long? Owen turned and raced down the corridor. The shaft was right in front of him, as was the staircase, and as he looked, Dr Diamond, Cati, Pieta and Wesley came racing out of a side corridor.

"The bang…" Owen gasped.

"That was us," Cati said. The little gyroscope had worked. It had spun and spun, emitting higher and higher sound waves, until it reached a frequency that even the hard ice could not bear. With a great rending crack, the ice walls had flown apart. They had not known where to go then, but Cati had felt the Harsh nearby and had led them, her face a mask of cold pain.

"Look!" Pieta exclaimed. The door with the iron knife in it trembled. Great bulbs of ice had formed in the apertures and in the lock.

"It can't hold for ever," Wesley said.

"Quick, run!" Dr Diamond spoke urgently. "We'll hold them for as long as we can."

"I can't leave you; they'll kill you," said Owen.

"You have to go, Owen." Cati spoke quietly and there was a new authority in her voice. He turned to her, surprised. She seemed to have matured in the past hour.

"Would you go on," Wesley said, "till I get a good go at these Harsh." He spat on his hands and rubbed them together. Dr Diamond took up a karate stance. Pieta cracked the magno whip by her side.

"Go," Cati whispered. "You are the Navigator. Everything depends on you, don't you see?" Then she gave him a quick peck on the cheek and turned to face the door.

"Run, Owen!" Dr Diamond said. "Run!"

Owen turned away from his friends and ran to the stairway. He put his foot on the first step and looked at them one last time. If he failed, he would never see them again. And if he succeeded, he realised, he would not see them again.

But I will succeed, thought Owen grimly. *I will succeed.*

Down he fled, down the staircase which spiralled around the Puissance, all its power concentrated in a writhing coil now, a coil of deep, black nothingness. Down he fled, his heart racing, his legs buckling with fatigue. And from above him came the sounds of battle. He slowed as if something was dragging at him. He knew that his duty was to stop the Puissance, but he had left his friends in mortal danger.

A long, cold, triumphant howl echoed in the stairwell and the sounds of battle stopped. Half running, half falling, Owen cleared the final steps. In front of him was a doorway. A doorway that seemed somehow familiar. He threw himself through it and slammed it, turning the key in the lock, and let his head rest against the shut door, sobbing for breath. Then he straightened and turned around.

Owen rubbed his eyes. He did not believe what he was seeing. It was all as it had been, but it should not have been here, not at the bottom of a long shaft in an island in a frozen sea. But it *was* here. In every detail. It was his own bedroom. It seemed as if he could see everything more clearly than he had ever seen anything before. Every faded flower on his bedspread. Every dust mote. The old chest. The guitar. The dartboard. The replica fighter hanging on fishing line from the ceiling.

Owen moved forward in wonderment, letting his fingers trail over the familiar surfaces. He put his hand into his jacket and took out the Mortmain. But what was he supposed to do with it? He looked around, but could see nothing new. Desperately, he paced the room. *A clue*, he thought, *a clue*. Then something came back to him. What was it the Long Woman had said? Look for the fleur-de-lis. The fleur-de-lis was a flower with three leaves, he remembered, and he had seen one before in this room. He went quickly over to the chest and looked at the lettering – J M Gobillard et Fils. What had Johnston said – *Gobillard's box of tricks*? This had to be it. It had been there all the time. His father had entrusted it to him. He stared at it. Just above the broken lock Owen saw it.

A fleur-de-lis.

He knelt down and looked at it. He realised that there was a tiny opening in the centre of the fleur-de-lis. And above it some kind of disturbance in the air. The air was moving round and round, and as he followed it from its tiny beginning to a small hole in the ceiling that he had never noticed before, it got a little bigger, a minature vortex, and he knew that if he followed it up and up, it would eventually become the raging Puissance that towered over the island. All of time was being sucked into the tiny aperture in the fleur-de-lis. Gobillard had somehow managed to contain whatever enormous power was needed to turn time backwards in this chest. But what now? He looked at the Mortmain, and it dawned on him. It wasn't in the shape of a propeller. It was in the shape of a fleur-de-lis. And the hole where the lock had been torn out was in the same shape!

Quickly, he placed the Mortmain in the hole where the lock had been. It fitted! It fitted, and as he watched, it began to turn slowly, then more quickly, then faster than the eye could follow, a blur of terrible speed. Above his head the roof seemed to dissolve until he was looking right up through the centre of the vortex, black lightning crackling from one side of it to the other. Owen put his hand on the chest to steady himself and suddenly he could see scenes of his own past appearing and disappearing in the walls of the Puissance, the Sub-Commandant disappearing into the Puissance, the Long Woman, Johnston, the battle for the Workhouse.

He looked further up, realising that he could see back in time. The scenes were indistinct, becoming more so, but he could make out his father's car as it veered into the harbour – and was that a figure swimming away? It was too hard to tell. Then it seemed that he heard his voice called. Right beside him in the vortex Owen could see what had happened several minutes ago. And he did not like what he saw, for it was the pitiful remnants of his friends who had fought so that he could get to the chest with the Mortmain. Wesley and Pieta limped in front, leaving a trail of blood on the ground. But behind them came a grim-faced Dr Diamond, carrying what appeared to be a lifeless Cati.

"Cati!" Owen called out, reaching out to his friend, but as he did so the image faded, the Mortmain tightened inexorably around the vortex, and it became fainter and fainter until in the end he could not see it all.

It was gone. It was over. The Great Machine in the North had been stopped.

The bedroom door flew off its hinges and crashed against the wall. There was a howl of outrage, a freezing blast. But Owen rested his head against the old chest and heard, and felt, no more.

CHAPTER TWENTY-SIX

It was the sunlight which woke him, streaming in through the high window. He was lying on his bed, fully dressed. He sat up and shook his head. The Harsh, the Mortmain. And then he remembered Cati being carried by Dr Diamond. If he had dreamed all of it then why did sadness sweep over him the way it did? He looked around. The room looked as it always had. He jumped to his feet and ran to the door and snatched it open, and saw the corridor, as it had always been, a little dusty, in need of a fresh coat of paint.

Owen jumped up on to the chest and looked out of the window. He could see the rooftops of the town, and beyond it the harbour and the masts of the fishing boats. The empty windows of the Workhouse loomed over the river. And Johnston's scrapyard, half-hidden by trees, did not look any bigger. He jumped down. *Of course*, he thought, *the chest!*

Owen hunkered down and examined the lock. There it was. A lock in the shape of a fleur-de-lis. And yet it looked as if it had always been there, battered and scratched like the rest of the chest. Perhaps it *had* always been there.

Owen felt as if his head was going to burst. Quickly, he grabbed some clothes from the pile of dirty washing on the floor. *That hasn't changed*, he thought. He couldn't find his trainers, so he pulled on an old pair of boots and ran downstairs.

As he reached the bottom of the stairs Owen glanced into the living room. His mother was kneeling on the floor, looking at something. She turned towards him. "Come here," she said in a calm, worn voice he had not heard for a long time. "Look!" She was holding a photograph of Owen as a baby with his parents. The lost photograph.

The photo had faded, but all three were still smiling, and his mother was smiling now too. She took Owen's hand, squeezed it and looked into his eyes, and as she did so a weight lifted from him. The mother he had known was back. Things were going to be different now. Then she straightened up and looked around as though seeing the house for the first time.

"Look at the state of this place," she said. "Go on. Get out from under my feet until I get this place into shape." He squeezed past her and slipped out of the front door.

Everything was as it had been. The neat housing estates in the distance. The two fields leading to the river. As fast as he could, he ran across the fields to the river. He straddled the tree which lay across the river and waited for the familiar tug of fear of the dark water below. But it did not come. Had he dreamed that as well? Owen crossed the river and ran to the Workhouse. Its damp stone walls were the same as ever. He went inside, but there was nothing but fallen timbers and grass and young trees growing through the ruins. He went round to the side of the Workhouse, pushing through undergrowth, looking for the door to the Starry, but he could not find it. Neither was there any sign of the fortifications along the river.

Owen searched all morning and then he followed the river down to the harbour, walking under the town bridge and listening to the sounds of the traffic overhead. He went down towards the warehouses, but somebody had put chain link fencing across the entrance and he could not go any further. He put his face against the fence and remembered Boat and the Planemen attacking it as the Raggies fished. Or *did* he remember it?

Owen sat on the harbour wall all afternoon, trying to work out what had happened, if he had dreamed everything. He couldn't have, he decided. There was too much, too much detail. And yet...

He walked home through the town. As he turned towards the river, he saw a scrap lorry labouring up the hill in a cloud of black smoke. From behind he could see an elbow leaning on the driver's door. Owen was sure it was Johnston. But then it wasn't unusual to see Johnston driving a load of scrap through the town.

He went up to the swing tree and looked out over the river, half thinking he might see the Sub-Commandant crouched below him. But there was nothing except the river and the mountains in the distance. He sighed. Disheartened, he walked down the hill towards the Den. It was getting dark. Owen lifted aside the bushes that hid the entrance and went in.

It was a moment before his eyes adjusted to the dark. *The propeller*, he thought, *the Mortmain*. He went to the wall. There was a lighter space on the wall where it had hung. He turned then to look at the table and his heart leapt. There, in the middle of the table, was a blue, faded cornflower – the cornflower that the Resisters used as a sign of remembering. And beside it, a tiny glowing piece of magno! And there was more. As he bent to the table he saw something written in the dust. It read:

Do not forget. From the shadows, Navigator.

And underneath it in the dust, her name,

Cati.

She had survived. Carefully, Owen wrapped the magno in a piece of paper and put it in his pocket. The cornflower he pinned on the wall. They were all asleep in the Starry now, until they were called again, he thought. Except for Cati. She was the Watcher. What was it her father had said? Stepping back into the shadows of time. She could see Owen perhaps, but he could not see her. He went outside. It was almost dark.

"See you again, Watcher!" he shouted. But there was no answer from the darkened river valley.

"See you again soon, Cati," Owen said again, almost to himself this time. And the wind sighed across the valley and the grasses rustled, and the trees whispered as though in reply.

Coming soon...

A second story about
Owen and Cati

CITY OF NIGHT

EOIN McNAMEE

HarperCollins *Children's Books*